THE
EARTH AND
THE SKY

Also by Debbie Lee Wesselmann

Trutor & the Balloonist

THE
EARTH AND
THE SKY

STORIES BY
Debbie Lee Wesselmann

SOUTHERN METHODIST UNIVERSITY PRESS
Dallas

Requests for permission to reproduce material from this work should be sent to:
Rights and Permissions
Southern Methodist University Press
PO Box 750415
Dallas, TX 75275-0415

Some of the stories in this collection appeared first in the following publications: "The Earth and the Sky" in *Gulf Stream Magazine* and *Kinesis*; "Stone Daughter" in *The Literary Review*; "Ingrid, Face Down" in *Folio*; "Snow Angels" in *North Atlantic Review*; "Life as a Dragon" in *Kelsey Review*; "Down Under Silver Lake" in *Alaska Quarterly Review*; "Core Puncher" in *Beloit Fiction Journal*; "At the Lesser House of Pablo Neruda" in *Ascent*; "The Nearly Invisible People" in *The Crescent Review*; and "Shinkansen" in *Florida Review*.

Grateful acknowledgment is made for permission to quote from "Cat," from *Selected Poems of Pablo Neruda*, translated by Ben Belitt. English translation © 1961 by Ben Belitt. Used by permission of Grove/Atlantic, Inc.

Library of Congress Cataloging-in Publication Data

Wesselmann, Debbie Lee, 1959–
    The earth and the sky : stories / by Debbie Lee Wesselmann.
      p.   cm.
    ISBN 0-87074-420-8 (cloth). — ISBN 0-87074-421-6 (paper)
    I. Title.
PS3573.E81495E28   1998
813'.54—dc21   97-22679

Cover art by Barbara Whitehead
Design by Tom Dawson Graphic Design
Printed in the United States of America on acid-free paper
10 9 8 7 6 5 4 3 2 1

For my parents, Glenn and Gen

Thank you for raising me to appreciate diversity
and for never wavering in your love and encouragement.

I would like to thank the following for their close readings of stories in this collection: Robbie Clipper Sethi, Janet Peery, Allen Wier, Jiangying Zhou, Nancy Parello, Mimi Schwartz, Joyce Lott, and Machiko Matsui. I am indebted to Kathryn Lang for her commitment to the publication of my work and for her literary guidance.

Above all, I'm deeply grateful to Daniel Lopresti, my husband, traveling companion, and strongest supporter.

Contents

The Earth and the Sky

The Americans did not understand anything Claudia was trying to tell them. We stood outside the villa in two confrontational lines: Claudia and I facing the four Americans, adults in the middle, a blond girl at either end. At first, Claudia didn't seem to notice that they spoke little, if any, Italian—she whizzed through our family's list of rules, putting up one finger for each item: garbage in the public dump down the street; no loud radios; no borrowing our family's telephone except in the case of emergency; no blocking the overgrown road leading up the hill because our tractor needed a clear path; no loud parties; and after ten at night use this key to unlock the front gate, which our father will have locked and which he will want you to relock securely. With a grand flourish, Claudia handed the man the keys. He stared at them dumbly.

I twisted the end of my braid. The man's face had a freshly sunburned look, as though they had just come from the far south of the country, or maybe Greece. Here, in Quiesa, it was already fall, with a bite in the night air that awoke me every night. Why these people, this couple with their two young daughters, would vacation now bewildered me. What kind of job did this man have back in the United States that allowed him to leave in October? And what about school for the girls? I would have to dream up my own answers—I knew this as soon as I saw his face go slack at the sound of my sister's voice. The man was about forty, I supposed, well cared for, clean-shaven, a tiny mole where the tip of his mustache would be if he grew one. His face had a bigness that intrigued me—it was as if his face had taken on the vastness of America simply by having been born there. His glazed eyes were a blue like the winter sky, light and clear.

His wife had listened more intently, as if mere concentration would translate our language into hers. This is probably why Claudia kept talking; at first glance, the woman looked as though she understood. But her brow was too furrowed, her lips working in the wrong shapes, her sharp face too tense. Her younger daughter, a girl about five with blond bangs even with her white eyebrows, tugged on her arm, but she merely shook the girl off. I imagined that the woman was the type to read a book without ever being distracted from the text—no shout, no storm, no hunger could sway her. I remembered my own mother reading books with her legs propped up on a chair during the afternoons when it was too hot to work. I couldn't remember, though, whether I had been able to get her attention. All my memories of her were a child's naive and faulty view.

Claudia asked, "Do you want to rent sheets and towels?"

They stared at her: the husband blankly, the wife with an intent squint.

I nudged Claudia. "They don't speak Italian. Your little speech was wasted."

"You've got to be kidding." She turned to the Americans and asked more loudly, "Do you want to rent sheets and towels?"

The wife repeated something back that sounded like a mockery: a child making fun of the way another talks. She was trying to sort out the sounds.

"Sheets and towels!" Claudia shouted.

"I don't speak Italian," the woman said to us in guidebook Italian.

"Well, we don't speak English," Claudia said.

The woman jumped on the word English. "*Inglese! Sì!*"

"*Inglese, no,*" I said. To Claudia, I said, "Time for a little improvisation."

I led the family into the bedroom on the ground floor. I patted the bed and said, "*Lenzuoli.*" Sheets. I pretended to be making the bed. "*Lenzuoli.*"

The woman's face spread wide with relief. "Linens. Yes."

"Ask her if she wants towels, too," Claudia said.

"But they come together."

"I don't care. Less for us to wash at the end of the week if they don't want them."

I sighed. I couldn't wait until Claudia got married in the spring so that I could manage the villa by myself. I made the motions of drying my face. "*Asciugamani?*"

The man laughed suddenly: a spurting kind of eruption that clearly had caught him by surprise. He said something to the woman in English. She laughed, too, but when she looked back at me, she only shrugged.

"*Asciugamani!*" Claudia shouted. "*Asciugamani!*"

The man and the woman snorted out more laughter. The little girls, who had trailed into the villa behind us, looked at them with evident curiosity. The man's face had turned a shade redder, so that his skin looked raw. The mole danced around his mouth like a flea.

"What did we say?" Claudia asked me.

"We probably said something that means something else in English. We probably told them that we had big breasts. And they're laughing because we don't."

Claudia hit my arm playfully. "Stop it, Elisabetta. Just get them the towels."

As we left, I heard the couple break down into hysterical laughter, as the man shouted something that sounded vaguely like the Italian word for towels. Shugurmahmi. As their laughter subsided, a hole opened up inside me that had the depth of a moonless night. I felt homesick, even though I stood on my own property.

"What's wrong?" Claudia asked as she straddled her motorbike.

I shook my head. "You're lucky that you're getting married. Before you know it, you'll be out of here."

The two horses felt the approach of winter; up on the hill, they snorted and pranced away nervously when they saw me approach on my motorbike. The motorbike never frightened them in the spring or summer; then they merely waited, ears pricked, eyes bright and rambunctious. But as the grasses dried into brown, seedy stalks, they seemed to fear that this would be the day that we would lock them in the barn for the winter. I leaned the motorbike into the ground and sat under the pear tree, now picked and rotted clean of fruit, its leaves yellowed. The dew still clung to the ground. With a shiver, I felt the dampness seep into my pants. The horses whinnied to each other. The chestnut mare, Nocciola, took several lanky steps toward me before being distracted by a sage-colored clump of grass.

"Good girl," I hummed. Looking around, I wondered why my father had kept the horses. Everything else had fallen into disrepair since I was a child; even the villa, our most reliable source of income, had jagged patches where the stucco had failed. The day before I had seen the American woman's eyes drift up the walls, above the large horse print, as I made her bed. She wanted me to follow her gaze, I knew, to the dusty cobwebs Claudia and I had not cleaned because we had been unable to reach that high. She wanted me to see the dark blotches on the otherwise white walls—mosquitoes smashed by tourists who had not cleaned up after themselves. (By the time we had gotten to them, the corpses had already fused with the rough texture of the wall.) The husband made a great show of trying to work the stove, a converted gas one which had only one electric burner because my cousin, an electrician, had moved to Pisa before he had finished the job. The main house and the smaller one at the far edge of the property where my brother and his family lived had better interior appointments, but their exteriors looked even more run-down. That's what happens when your grandfather runs off with another woman, and your mother dies too young. Two generations of neglect.

Inexplicably, I wanted to cry. All the pushing, tumultuous emotions were there in my chest, but they would not break free into tears. My life in Quiesa was so small and so limited, and even the steady stream of tourists did nothing to expand my knowledge of the world. Here I was, an adult, and I had never even been into Firenze. My mother had once said to me, or rather, I think she said this, "You don't have to travel to be wise. You only have to set your heart free." As I sat under the pear tree, I thought what ridiculous advice to give a child. She was telling me that I should be happy with what I had, when she should have been instructing me about the world beyond our plot of land. The urge to cry vanished, and in its place, a vague and sad anger settled.

I rose, kissing the air to call Nocciola. When she obediently came, I stroked her nose, purred to her, held my hand an inch away from her neck to feel the heat rising off her as if she were summer sand. On impulse, I climbed on Nocciola, bareback, nudged her into a difficult canter that led us up a path towards the *autostrade* perched high above us on a marble-white bridge. The wind of our motion drove right through my heavy sweater, so that I felt colder than I had since last winter. The ground was brittle with dead leaves and vegetation under Nocciola's hooves, and I imagined that we were racing through purgatory, toward heaven or hell, which I couldn't tell. My legs ached with the effort of staying on, but I clung to the mare, out of breath, happy, my hair falling down until it was almost as free as the horse's mane. *I have wings, I have wings!* I wanted to shout. Finally, my fingers entwined in her mane, I slowed Nocciola, turned her away, and started our descent. As I slipped down off her back, still panting, I saw the two little American girls, hand in hand, at the edge of the field.

"Hello," I said to them in English, one of the few words of their language that I knew.

"Hello," the older one said brightly.

But silence fell awkwardly between us. I wanted to ask them about America, about their vacation, about how my people seemed to them, what their names were, but our different languages caged me. "My name is Elisabetta," I ventured in Italian. "What's yours?"

They stared at me, blinking. The older one appeared to be about nine or ten years old, though with Americans I couldn't tell because they were often big. In any case, she was much older than her sister and regarded me and my foreign tongue with evident suspicion. The younger one, though, seemed more like her mother, her face scrunched up as if it might help her understand.

"Elisabetta." I pointed to myself. "Elisabetta. You?" I pointed to the older girl.

She understood. "Hannah." She pointed to her sister. "Jenny."

"Hello, Hannah. Hello, Jenny." They giggled; I must not have said their names entirely correctly. With a jolt, I felt Nocciola's breath on my neck, then a strong shove of her muzzle that nearly knocked me to my knees. "Nocciola," I told the girls.

They each repeated her name perfectly. I removed an apple from the leather pack at the back of my motorbike. With my knife, I split the apple in two. "Give it to Nocciola," I told them. I put half in each girl's hand. "Nocciola."

The younger one was brave; she marched right up to the mare and held out her hand. I steadied the hand, kept it flat and open so that the horse would not accidentally bite it. Her eyes grew round as the horse's enormous head lowered gently towards her. In an instant, the apple had vanished. Alabastre, our gelding, trotted over to get his share. He was unpredictable and greedy, though, and I pushed him away with my whole body while Hannah fed his rival.

The deep voice of the American man thundered up the hill. "Hannah! Jenny!"

"Go," I told them, suddenly afraid of their father who might think me irresponsible. I had imagined him as a man with a quick temper and an easy laugh, a seedpod that would explode at the slightest touch. He was, I decided, a powerful businessman who had been forced into vacation because of a medical problem—an ulcer or high blood pressure, most likely. He had not wanted to leave his home, but his doctor had said, go on vacation or die before you're fifty. And so he had gone. But he and his wife tackled their holiday as if it were a business: go see this, get this done, count up how many things they've seen. "Hurry now!"

But they were already running down the path towards their father. Their yellow hair flew out behind them like wings. They had sturdy, pale legs and good strides. I wondered briefly what it would be like to have their mother, but all I could picture was the mole twitching on the surface of their father's skin and the warm, musky smell of my own father as he laughingly recounted the stories of his day.

As she ran, Jenny shouted as though to nobody in particular, "Nocciola, Nocciola, Nocciola."

The American girls were so beautiful in features and spirit, the lightness of their voices, that I dreamed a future for them. I had read that American women do not like to marry and have children until it is almost too late, and instead prefer to run whole companies. Hannah, with her suspicious nature and quick mind, would thrive in this man's world. She would become the president of a bank, counting up accomplishments the way her father always had, and then, when she turned forty, she would abandon it all to raise three children, two girls and a boy, who would care for her in her old age. She would cut her hair short for business, grow it to her shoulders when she became a mother. Jenny, I decided, would have more trouble juggling dual lives. Although she would excel when she had only one task at a time, she would not want to do this, because a narrowing of focus would necessarily eliminate many things she wanted to accomplish. She would be a teacher maybe, or, better yet, someone like me running one of those inns in the United States pictured on the brochures the listing service sent us. I liked to see her, her hair still long and golden, waking before the sun rose to bake breads and clean the inn.

She would have several accidental but well-loved children following her. She would own horses and a pond where she would take the children to swim. The Michelin guide would come to her inn and give it three stars. In her free time, she would paint fiercely colorful pieces that would sell as soon as she finished them. Throughout the girls' whole lives, their mother would help them whenever a crisis arose. Their father would understand their needs.

Our renters rarely spent the day in the villa, even when it rained. In the summer, the Belgians, the French, and the few Italians packed up their cars first thing in the morning with umbrellas, beach towels, and hefty lunches and headed for Viareggio. The British ventured into Lucca, Pisa, and Firenze. The Germans and the few Americans we had did everything. We could tell because during the day, Claudia or I would let ourselves in using the extra key.

We had a system that we invented when Claudia was fourteen and I was thirteen. (Our brother Marco was already in love and so we never revealed our secret to him.) When the tourists went by our house in their car, we counted them. If everyone was there, we would proceed, but if we weren't sure, or if we missed seeing them leave, we would wait until the following day. We couldn't risk being caught because the renters might complain to the service that listed our villa, and our income would be lost. For caution, we always waited at least an hour to make sure that the renters weren't on a quick jaunt to Massarossa, or hadn't forgotten something. Then one of us (we took turns) would ride her motorbike up to the villa. The other would sit on her motorbike in front of the main house. If the tourists returned, the sentry would beep her horn as if in greeting but in reality as a warning to her sister. In seven years, though, we had used this warning system only once.

As I slipped through the front door, a suffocating wall of heat crushed me. I hurried to the thermostat on the wall and shut off the heat—it wasn't winter yet. I imagined the argument they would have later.

"Who turned off the heat?"

"You must have."

"I did not. It must have been you!"

"It wasn't me!"

Then there would be a moment when they locked their gazes, both defiant and right, and realized that perhaps someone had crept into their villa when they were out. The husband and wife would rush to their valuables, checking and counting, and would finally breathe their separate sighs of relief (though I imagined this husband emitting more of a satisfied grunt). The wife (yes, in this case, the wife) would shrug and say, "I don't remember doing it, but maybe it *was* me."

Claudia and I had a rule: never steal anything, not even a nibble of food. Rather, this was my rule but only a part of Claudia's. Claudia had ordered the very first day we snuck into the villa, "Never steal anything. Don't even touch their things. We don't want them to even *suspect* that we've been in."

Of course, I could make my own rules once I entered the villa. As I wandered through the rooms, I would select one or two items to move slightly out of place or maybe transport something from one room to another to create just enough disarray to confuse the renters. Enough to make them think that we had been there, but not enough for them to be certain of it. I never told Claudia of my game because she would be sure to put an end to our visits.

I peeked in the pantry. The Americans had bought a lot of groceries, far too many for a single week, for a single burner. Good virgin olive oil, biscotti, three different shapes of pasta, dried rosemary, oregano, basil, balsamic vinegar, chocolate spread, honey, Arborio rice, thin breadsticks, capers, roasted red peppers, a large bottle of Chianti Classico, bread, and a variety of wraps and bags. My mouth already watering, I opened the door to the small refrigerator: four different cheeses, melon, bottled water, grapefruit soda, carrots, lettuce, pears, veal, chicken, cured black olives, fresh red peppers. I hoped that the Americans would, as most of our renters invariably did, decide that returning to the villa in time to cook dinner was too much of a burden. If this happened, the Americans would have food left over. Perhaps, if we were lucky, they would leave it all for us.

I haunted their rooms much the way I imagined a ghost would: wafting back and forth, trying to read incomprehensible postcards fanned out on a nightstand (they had already been to both Lucca and Pisa), touching pillows and clothes with a light brush of fingertips, smoothing wrinkles on the beds. In the girls' room, each bed had a toy tucked in with its head on the pillow. One had a stuffed raccoon and the other a baby doll with a pursed mouth. I guessed that Jenny had brought the doll, because it seemed too babyish for Hannah. The girls had chosen the room with the most horse pictures, prints with pintos and chestnuts, Lippizaners and Arabians, plow horses straining through a field. Standing there, imagining the two girls asleep there under the horses, I shivered. I suddenly did not want to touch this room—it might scare the girls. Kids had a way of knowing exactly how everything was left. As I was leaving, I tripped over a shoe. A scorpion dashed out from under it. With a shout, I stomped on the insect, heard and felt the crunch of its death. I stood there for several seconds, panting, before I finally wiped up the mess and flushed the evidence down the toilet. I then scoured the girls' room for insects—scorpions or centipedes—but found none.

I once placed a scorpion in the bed of a particularly rude German couple. These scorpions are not the poisonous red kind, but the black kind that stings like acid without threatening your life. They are quick, fearless, and frightening. The Italians cope with them rather nonchalantly, but the Northern Europeans who come here in the summer shriek so loudly that we can hear them down the hill. Earlier that summer, as my father and I tended his long row of tomatoes, my father winked at me. "Another tourist wakes up to reality." I smiled back; I liked to think that our renters lived in a fabricated world and only we knew the complete truth. Our wisdom came from tending the earth, knowing the animals, feeling the air as it was meant to feel, while they lived above the ground in their cars, trains, and planes, soaring above what really was.

That evening, as Claudia and her fiancé Giacomo talked in hushed voices in the next room, I sat on the sofa next to my father. He turned on the television with the hope that our satellite dish, with all its wires blowing loose all the time, would come through so he could watch the soccer game. He smelled dry and worn from finishing up the harvest and preparing the ground for winter.

"Papa," I asked before the soccer game started, "why did you keep the horses?"

He sat still for so long that I thought I had not spoken loudly enough. As I was about to repeat myself, he inhaled deeply. "Your mother wanted those horses. You and your sister grew up on them. I consider them part of the land, and part of our family."

My mother. She had been the first to suggest renting out one of the outbuildings. She had bought the first few horse prints, and after her death my father had continued the tradition, saying that it would be a mistake to challenge the established décor. I stared at my father's angular profile. On the surface, his reasons sounded perfectly logical and down-to-earth, but for the first time I realized the hugeness of his emotions for my mother. He had always spoken of her in concrete, unemotional terms as if he had accepted his loss before it had actually happened. Why had Claudia and I bothered to hide our tears those first few years? Why had we believed that he accepted death as easily as they taught us to in church? I unfolded my hand over his. "I remember my first bareback ride with her at my side."

He nodded, but said nothing. We sat there in silence until the game started. I hoped to see a tear, even a tiny one, but his eyes were focused on the television.

In front of the house, the Americans shouted at us. The woman had tears streaming down her cheeks in dusty streaks; her voice was hoarse and deep, guttural. The man seemed angry at first, but as I tried to understand what they wanted, I saw that it was fear that made his eyes wild.

Claudia covered her ears. "My God, that language is ugly. What do they want?"

Then I understood a single word: police. They needed the police. In a breath, I saw that only the older child, Hannah, clung to her mother.

"Jenny?" I asked.

"Yes, yes!" the woman cried, not questioning how I knew her daughter's name. She sputtered some more in English, and gestured broadly, frantically.

"Quick!" I told Claudia. "I think one of the girls is missing. Have Papa call the police. And find Umberto Riccio!" Umberto was the only person in Quiesa who spoke a passable English.

I sprinted up the road towards the villa, with the Americans huffing and crying behind me. Through the open door, I burst in, searching all the hiding places I had discovered as a child and had imagined as an adult: the wardrobes, the crawl space under the stairs, the washing machine, the dishwasher, the space between the indoor and outdoor shutters. I went back outside and jumped off the terrace on the north side where the pump and the main electrical box were housed. Nothing. My throat had closed tight. Jenny's parents shouted her name through cupped hands. They followed my every step with hope, then anguish, as I failed to uncover her. In the tangled passages of my mind, I believed that if I could restore Jenny to her parents, they would be forever together. And I would be freed from my tiny cage. It was like tossing a pebble towards a can and saying, if it goes in, he loves me, if I miss, he doesn't. My superstition did not make sense, but I couldn't let it go.

When Umberto arrived, he found out that Jenny had vanished by the time her parents awoke. "They think she's been kidnapped," he said gravely.

"By whom?"

"The Mafia, I guess."

"They wouldn't bother with a little girl. Unless the father did something down south to get them angry."

Umberto talked in halting English, and the American man fired back a barrage of words. "He said that's ridiculous."

I cleared my throat. Evidently these people had heard things about the Italian Mafia that were not, in general, true. Did they believe that everyone in my country was corrupt? Did they think we were dangerous? I wondered what they knew about our country and its ways, and what they didn't. I wished they could speak my language and I, theirs, if only for a few minutes so they would see that we weren't all that different. I too knew the anguish of losing someone.

The police arrived shortly thereafter. They took over the questioning, with Umberto as a translator. I couldn't listen anymore, and so drifted out to the road and the stone wall where Claudia and my father sat, shoulder to shoulder. A leaf fluttered down from a tree and rested on my father's shoulder, but he made no move to brush it off.

"What's the story?" my father asked. He had his work hat tipped way back on his head so that the sun shone on his tan face.

I sat heavily next to them. "The younger girl was gone when they woke up."

The Tuscan hills, dappled in bright yellow and orange, rose around us like solid parents. Every year I forgot about how warmly hued autumn was because I always thought of it as brown and gray, its aftermath instead of its life. The sun, though low, felt vaguely capable of warmth; it didn't yet have the steeliness of winter. To the north, I could see our three goats running in their hobbled way to a higher pasture. The *autostrade* whined with distant automobiles. Its white, arched bridge was visible even in summer as it passed between mountains, but now its sinuous path out of the distance had begun to be revealed as well. A horn blared; the air carried it perfectly formed to where we sat. Close to the pillars of the bridge, our two horses grazed in a small field that seemed too steep to be comfortable. I leaned forward, squinting, and tried to focus on Nocciola and Alabastre. I had seen Jenny's expression when she gazed at the horses; she had fallen in love.

"I'll be back," I said. My father didn't seem to hear. Claudia glanced at me with evident interest, but then, as if she were too tired, she collapsed in a slump.

No one had brought up a motorbike, so I took to the path by foot. The way was steep and slippery with newly fallen leaves, but I took large strides, then eased into a slow jog, then a faster, more desperate scramble as I went up.

I reached the horses with my breath clawing at the back of my throat. "Jenny!" I yelled. But my throat was too dry for the sound to carry well. I swallowed once, twice. "Jenny!"

"Elisabetta!"

She was squatted under a tree, tossing dried apples at a stack of rocks. She waved with a smile. I closed my eyes. Why did the horns carry so well from the road, but our urgent voices had not? I walked toward her without any outward sign of alarm. I took her small, cool hands and tried to lead her back down the path, but she shook herself free.

"No!"

That I understood. With so many different languages and so many different ways to say yes, ours shared this word. I marveled at this primitive sound, wondering whether its origin contained the key to both our languages. Maybe through this simple word we could discover exactly what made us so alike, and so different. "Come," I said.

"No." She said something else, and I caught the name Nocciola. She stood, held out a dried apple, called the horse's name. Nocciola lifted her head in a regal arc but quickly lost interest. The mare had no use for Jenny's old fruit. Jenny tossed the apple at the pile of rocks.

I used to live for horseback riding. Awake at dawn, saddled up, the long grooming afterwards that forged a bond between me and the animals. The smell of the horses, acrid at first, softening in my stomach like a homesickness. My mother holding them back with her forearm so that they would not step on Claudia's and my feet. The sensation of both terror and power as I commanded the huge animal beneath me. Every night I had prayed for dreams about horses, and when my mind obliged, I awoke with grief that they had to end. I saw all of this about me in the bright, hurt eyes of the little American. She wanted Nocciola to love her, but, with her meager offerings, her affection was unrequited.

I clicked my tongue to get Nocciola's attention. Her head swung upright. Recognizing me, she ambled towards us.

"Here," I told Jenny. "I shouldn't do this, but I'm going to."

She looked at me in confusion, but in a minute, I knew, language would no longer matter.

I lifted her onto a low sturdy branch of the apple tree before climbing up next to her. The mare hesitated a little when I called, but after a few steps this way and that, she drew up close to the tree. I pulled myself onto Nocciola's back with a grunt. Then I lifted Jenny onto the horse's back in front of me. She said something fast and excited, leaned over and kissed the horse's neck so that she almost fell.

"No," I said firmly. "Your parents will never forgive me if you hurt yourself."

Slowly, we walked down the path towards the villa, Jenny and Nocciola caught tight in my arms and the strength of my legs. I gently covered Jenny's head as an overhanging branch came too close. If we fell off, I knew, this would be Jenny's nightmare, but if we stayed on and rode triumphantly in front of the villa, the memory for her would be a sweet dream, almost unreal and yet everyone will be able to tell her, yes, it really happened. *You ran away and returned, rescued, on the back of a horse.* Maybe Nocciola would later be described as wild, maybe I would no longer be the one carrying her to her parents, maybe the horse's color and name would change, but the idea of it would stay with her. This would be her Italian story, and I would have helped her to create it.

"We aren't so different," I whispered in her ear. I wanted to tell her that we were both of the earth and the sky, not one or the other, but the words seemed awkward even before I spoke them. They said too much and too little at the same time. Instead I said, "Have fun, Jenny."

She twisted to see me, that broad, open smile rippling the freckles on her nose.

As we neared the villa, the shouts went up, starting with Hannah, who had been drawing with a stick in the dust, and the two police officers who were smoking under a tree. The Americans rushed out of the villa. The man seemed unable to move or to believe what he was seeing. The woman clapped her hand to her mouth as she ran towards us. I lowered Jenny to the ground, and her mother embraced her with a fierce hug that squeezed a small choke out of the girl. Cheek to cheek, they held each other, the woman in tears and the girl bewildered, probably a little frightened, at this reception.

I slipped off the horse. Claudia sidled over, stroked Nocciola's nose, and said, very quietly, "You stole her, didn't you?"

Shocked that my sister would think this of me, I opened my mouth to deny it, but, a thought occurred to me: in a way, I had. This story was now as much mine as Jenny's, even though from this point on, the two versions would never exactly be the same. Memory had a way of shifting until only a kernel of reality remained. This Jenny, the one I didn't really know, had become mine. "Yes, I stole her," I said. "And now she's an alien just like us."

Claudia laughed. She gave Nocciola's hindquarters a little pat to send her on her way. "And I thought for a minute that you really had done something bad."

My father squeezed my shoulder as he joined us. "Good work, my girl. You saved us." He continued past me, his work hat now shielding his eyes, and did not glance back.

"He actually gave you a compliment," Claudia giggled as soon as he was far enough away not to hear.

I stared after my father. Even after years of hard work, he still walked straight-backed but had the leathered skin of a man who lived in the sun. His gait was deliberate and strong, as if nothing could stop him. I tried to imagine him kissing my mother with passion, but could not; yet, I know he had. My mother used to smile in a peculiar, satisfied way whenever she talked of him. As a child, I had been jealous, because I wanted all of her radiance for myself, but now I wanted to know more about it. Had she liked the broadness of his shoulders? The strong calves? Maybe she had surrendered to his flash of a smile. Or maybe she loved something I could never see in my father simply because of who he was to me. As he disappeared around a bend in the dirt road, I wondered what made it so difficult for me to see my parents as human.

I looked back at the villa just as the American man strode towards me. He extended his hand and I shook it, but quickly he drew me into a tight embrace. Surprised, I hugged him back.

"*Gracias*," he said in Spanish, but it was close enough to Italian.

"*Prego*."

I expected him to let go, but he held me fast. A shudder racked him. I realized he was crying and did not want his family to see. I wanted to shout, "Let them see," but he never would have understood. The sun blinded me, golden brightness, and the fleeting songs of migrating birds filled my head. He clung to me, saying thank you, thank you in Spanish while I responded in my own language, you're welcome, you're welcome. My head whirled with the scents of horse, dying leaves, cologne, and foreign skin. I felt as though transported to another world, my feet not on the ground but flying fast to the soil of somewhere else.

Stone Daughter

I moved to Japan because my husband's father and elder brother Jiro had died in an early morning fire that destroyed the family house. A nephew, two years old, whom I had never met, had also perished. The day after we received the news, my husband woke me before the sun had risen. "Ellen," he said, "I must return to Kasama." I knew he meant for good, though he was afraid to say it. For six generations, his family had been making pottery in their sloping kiln built up the side of a hill; without Koji, the dynasty would end. His mother feared losing the business to a distant relative, one who did not understand that her husband lived on in his clay.

"*We* must return," I told him.

Relief unfurled his dark eyebrows, and I kissed them. I had come to think of a life as a series of little string pieces knotted together, one at a time, to form a misshapen doll. This journey, I knew, could be another bit of string attached to myself, or it could be the first piece of a new doll, one that perhaps would not end up deformed.

Kasama, my husband once told me, is the word for the hat worn by rice paddy workers, that conical umbrella fastened under the chin with string. The mountain overlooking the village has this shape, and thus is called Mt. Kasama, giving its name to the settlement below. Villagers of old—and many modern ones—believed Mount Kasama contained an ancient and benevolent god who watched over them like a grandfather. Stones with unusual shapes that washed down its sides were coveted as they too contained spirits descended, like the Japanese people, from a powerful god. When I learned this, I encountered the first inaccessible door to Koji's culture: How could I, even as someone who believed in protecting the environment, comprehend how my husband's family could genuinely regard a mountain as an ancestor? But I had come to hate who I was—a woman who jarred other people by always saying the wrong thing, who had few friends, who loved a husband she could not fully understand. To be born of mountain stone seemed like the greatest gift one could receive. As I settled my affairs in New Jersey, I tried to envision myself as a Japanese woman, someone who could bow to the authority of a mountain and have no qualms. Someone who could find peace in the order of a rock garden, the way a leaf lay on the water, or the transformation of clay into a bowl.

I could have refused to go. I could have demanded that Koji choose between his family and me. We had careers: Koji his electrical engineering and me, my accounting. But perhaps because of the love between us, we knew that we had to go to Kasama, and we had to do it together. As Koji waved to our house as we drove off, I realized that this leaving was more difficult for him than for me. For me, the ground beneath the house had shifted and softened, unsteady ground to swallow me whole.

Koji did not know it, but inside of me voices cried out, mental demons, the sounds of my children who had been washed from my womb, our children, defective or conceived of a mother enable to nurture them. They haunted me day in and day out. I hoped to leave them in their sewer-graves. But I could feel my abandonment of them as real as if they were still alive. I did not look back for fear that I would see their tiny faces peering out of the darkened windows.

By the time we arrived in Japan, the Tanaka clan had rebuilt the family house with its wood and stucco sides and its tile roof, its windows shuttered with amber pebbled plastic. The new home appeared to be the same house I had visited twice before; it perched on the side of a hill above a valley of rice paddies. Only a faint smell of charred ground and the deep lines around the mouths of the women betrayed the tragedy. Slipping out of my shoes in the vestibule, I waited. Okasan, as we called Koji's mother, petite and stone-faced, welcomed us with her hands clasped at her stomach. Our sister-in-law Reiko bowed quickly and turned away. Her loss of both husband and son visible only in the downward slope of her shoulders, she scurried out, followed by her two shy daughters. Only Koji's sixteen-year-old sister, Michiko, met me with eager eyes. Pretty and enthusiastic, her hair shiny and perfect in a neat bob, her eyes quick but surprisingly direct, her voice lilting: she was the one who charmed me.

Michiko found herself on the verge of womanhood in the midst of societal changes that suggested she might have a freer life than her mother. She wanted to escape, she confided, and not in the arms of a man. She wished for a much more modern path: education in the United States. For Koji, it had been easy, she whispered to me, because he was a man, and he was expected to seek out the best. Especially there, in Kasama, outside of the cities, women did not follow their own dreams. Michiko wanted Westernization, so that she could return to her homeland on her own terms, as an actress and not as a translator and eventual wife, as her schools told her she should be. Following me throughout the house, she asked questions in her singsong voice. I did not want to remember the United States; however, I had goals of my own, not dissimilar to Michiko's. These goals required that I respond to Michiko with all the patience of a wise-woman and give her the courtesy of an honorable answer.

As a child, I did not belong well to groups. The children taunted me and played tricks on me until the hurt cut so deep that I cried. My shell was not hard enough, my demeanor not aggressive enough, my looks so average as to be invisible. For those reasons, I became an instant target wherever we moved. My mother always told me that I simply did not try hard enough to fit in. Start over, she would say as we pulled into the driveway of a new house, this time you can do it, if you just put your mind to it.

Even as an adult, I failed. My co-workers disliked me. I had chosen accounting simply because numbers and columns posed little challenge and because there always seemed to be a glut of accountant want ads in the newspaper. My colleagues, on the other hand, approached accounting with true appreciation. They hated my easy rise through the ranks. They hated that I did not love my profession. They hated that I did not get flustered over deadlines and other people's mistakes. They shunned me by not inviting me out after work. Japan-bashing had become the rage, and they saw my marriage to Koji as dangerous, even traitorous. I could not understand why they would believe this, why they would not tolerate a different culture among them, why they seemed to fear me.

I spoke to Koji about this only once. We had just moved into our New Jersey house, and he was installing a gas dryer himself using the imprecise directions of the manual.

"Does your family hate that you married an American?"

"My family doesn't hate."

"Were they upset? Disappointed?"

"They didn't say." He looked up at me, his hair fallen a little onto his forehead. "Now quiet. I've got to figure this out, or we'll be gassed to death in our sleep."

I understood that indeed they had been disappointed, but that he would not hurt me by telling me this. I wanted his family to admit they had been wrong about me, to love me. "My mother uses us as an example of how she raised me in the spirit of tolerance." I sighed. "People are sometimes uncomfortable here, you know. With mixed marriages."

"Not as bad as in Japan. In Japan, everyone must fit in. Here, we are free to get other people angry."

I wished desperately to be Koji, not to hate, not to be angry, not to fear. If I could not be him, then I wanted to think like him. "Tell me what you're thinking."

"I'm thinking that this dryer is a pain-in-the-ass."

I cringed. Koji, my gentle husband, had learned yet another vulgar phrase.

Okasan kept an old-fashioned Japanese house even as some of her neighbors, not as well-to-do, bought the newest electronics and Western-style beds. We ate food that Okasan's mother had taught her how to cook. Although I saw her wear a kimono only once, at my wedding, she kept a formal black one in a special trunk. She and Reiko forbade television, because Michiko and the two little girls needed to study, even though most others in Kasama owned sets. The family owned a car, but only her late husband had driven it. Now it was declared for emergencies only, perhaps for a family outing, but not for everyday.

I felt as though I had stepped back into another century.

Koji and I received the honor of inheriting his parents' tiny room. His mother scurried across the tatami mats with her meager belongings into Reiko and the girls' room. This move clearly pleased Koji, although he said nothing. I found it difficult to know that I had displaced his mother.

"In the cities," Koji explained as he undressed for his evening bath and knotted his yukata deftly at the waist, "couples save their money so that they can afford an apartment of their own. If the man has a good position, this can be done. Less fortunate couples find themselves locked into the family home. But they hope not for long."

"But what about making love?" I whispered.

He shrugged. "As you like to say, when there's a will, there's a way."

He had once tried to make love to me in my parents' home, but I had pushed him away. I couldn't—the very thought of my parents discovering us terrified me. I felt like a teenager doing something illicit.

Okasan moved through the rooms like a ballet dancer: fluid, careful, light on her feet, concentrated in her expression. My own mother was much bigger and less purposeful. Koji told me that the marriage of his parents had been arranged, as was still sometimes the custom, by a matchmaker who knew the two families. Okasan was the youngest daughter of a once-successful merchant from Mito who had lost much of his fortune before being able to marry off his youngest, and hence, Okasan married beneath her station. Since the age of six, she had practiced the art of the tea ceremony and knew the intricacies of high breeding. Koji's father, on the other hand, came from a well-to-do family but one that worked with clay that made cracks in the skin of their hands. Although he was not coarse, he lacked the refinement of Okasan's family.

I tried to help Okasan with the housework, but she always gently pushed me away. "Never mind. I will do it. You go rest." Still, I watched and learned, studied the movement of each finger, each gesture, so that one day she would accept me as she did Reiko, who bustled behind her in a great show of helpfulness.

After I had been in Kasama nearly a year, I finally had the courage to ask a personal question of Okasan. As she rolled up the futons in the morning, my eyes rested on the gentle, yielding curve of her back. "Forgive me, Okasan, if I ask too much," I said in my hesitant Japanese. "What did you think of Otosan when you first met?"

She regarded me with a light smile on her lips, the most I had ever seen. "I thought him handsome and strong. I liked the way he held himself." For a moment, her eyes looked inside of herself to the memory, and the dreaminess in her expression filled me with my own love for Koji. Breaking away from her memories, Okasan leveled her eyes at me. "And you, Ellen-san. What do you think of gracing this family with another heir?"

I stared at her, horrified that my deficiency might be revealed. Taking a moment to compose myself, I said, in the softest, most even voice possible, "If Koji and I are so blessed, we would be as happy as you."

Reiko, our sister-in-law, hated me, perhaps because she believed that I had taken her place as the wife of the eldest son. She was a dull, silent, brooding woman, but I could not tell if this was because she had lost her son and husband, or if this was a natural tendency. In the beginning, she corrected my Japanese so stringently that I could not complete a thought. However, I soon spoke so well that she could find little fault. I followed her on her daily shopping trips, not because I wanted to be with her, but because I could learn much from her. We went into the stores, Reiko always first, and while she selected her items, I conversed with the shopkeepers.

One day, as we trudged back up the hill to the house, Reiko said to me, "They talk with you because they do not wish to be rude."

I knew her meaning well enough to reply, "I talk with them because I do not wish to be rude."

My shoes with ties had no place in Kasama, for I had not mastered the art of slipping them on and off quickly without undoing the knots. I bought loafers, fashionably Western but practical for a budding Japanese. Okasan nodded with approval when she saw me slip them off onto the mat in the vestibule, but later, when I asked her to teach me how to prepare sushi, she smiled. "It's okay. You go rest."

She did not know that I had only to touch the sushi mat and the ingredients to make it, for I had memorized the technique. I had seen the look of satisfaction on her face when she rolled the sushi, and I wanted it for myself. I could only imagine the pleasure of perfectly cooked udon noodles, or tsukemono with the right, pickled bite. Be patient, Ellen-san, I told myself as I bowed to my mother-in-law. For hours, I sat in the well-tended garden next to the house to find the strength in the angles of branches and in the raked coarseness of sand.

In the dark of the house, Koji and I whispered to each other beneath the heavy quilts; voices carried too easily through the thin walls.

"Your step is becoming very light," Koji told me as he entwined his fingers in mine. "And your voice has become like that of a bird."

"You sound sad. Why?"

He did not say anything for a long time. I could not see his face, only the vague outline of his head. Finally, he took a deep breath. "I like hiking boots," he said.

I cupped our two pairs of hands and laughed into them. "And loud American voices?"

"Maybe not the voices. But brashness. So un-Japanese."

"But Koji, I *want* to be Japanese. Here you have such a *spiritual* society. What do we have in America?"

He withdrew his hands. "Much more than you know."

"Are we two expatriates of different countries?"

"Expatriates," he said carefully. "Yes. Perhaps we love each other as much for our countries as for ourselves." He sighed. "If only my mother would have accepted one of my cousins to oversee the business. I am an electrical engineer, not a potter."

I was already Japanese enough to imagine myself a mountain that refused to be worn down by the rain—enough stone to withstand anything. As Koji told me of his restlessness, I smiled and said yes, I understood how he could be unhappy. It was a very difficult problem. By the way I said it, I had refused to return to America. He looked away from me with such sad eyes that I wanted to cry. But still, it did not dissuade me from my goal.

I visited the pottery workshop on Thursdays when I arrived with two bento boxes of sushi for Koji's and my lunch. Sometimes Koji's cousin Hideo ate with us. Hideo was the third son of Otosan's brother, and he had come to the Tanaka workshop to escape the shadows of his elders. Koji treated him more as a brother than as a worker, and I often wondered if Hideo reminded him of Jiro. We often squatted in a corner of the kiln shed and ate quickly. The kiln itself, tiered and sloping upward on the steep hill, dominated these lunches, for it was impossible to ignore, with its capacity for forty thousand pieces of pottery. Whenever Koji lit the oven, six times a year, I stayed home.

"What do you think of the pottery?" Koji asked me, holding up a newly fired vase and rotating it on his palm.

"It is very Japanese."

He smiled. "You don't have to talk like that with me. Remember, I'm practically American. And I never liked this much myself."

The pottery was plain and primitive, somber with its dark glazes, almost rough on the surface. Many vases were adorned with a sash of clay, simply knotted, permanently fixed, and I did not like this pretense of fabric. I wanted to like the pieces, to feel a connection with the hardened soil of the Tanaka family, but could not.

"But it has a strong character," he said. "Simple. A foundation for good luck."

"I'm not fond of the ties," I finally told him. "It isn't right with stone."

Most days, Michiko arrived home from school early in the evening, and still in her navy blue uniform, she would take my hand and lead me into the bamboo grove across the street from the house, walking, talking, asking. I patiently explained America to Michiko, and, in exchange, she told me about Japan. As we wove our way through the bamboo, both caught up in our excitement, I touched trunks rising shiny and smooth to the canopy of narrow leaves; the trees seemed unreal and plastic, not living, growing plants. For this otherworldliness, I loved them. Koji once told me to run into this grove in the event of an earthquake. Bamboo roots are invasive and hold the ground together, he said. The trunks give and bend instead of falling like heavy maples. Here, he had said, you will be safe.

We had three earthquakes in as many years, not severe ones, but I never ran into the grove. I was afraid of being the only one.

In secret, Michiko and I pored over her college application forms. Her mother would not have approved of her dreams, but once the details had been settled she would accept her daughter's flight. I instructed her on what I thought the universities wanted to know, what points she should stress in her essays and how to exploit her foreignness instead of trying to disguise it. She so feared the anger of her mother that I mailed the applications myself to hide Michiko's embryonic ties to the United States.

Michiko delighted in pointing out the serenity of certain rocks, of the undulating call of a bird, of the precision with which Koji and her mother raked the sand in the garden. She taught me to love shapes and harmony, to find the place within myself that felt still and calm. Soon, I could meditate on a single tree for an hour without becoming bored.

For the first two years, before she turned eighteen, Michiko and I rode our bicycles into town on Sundays to do the shopping. Reiko was always given the day to spend with her girls, who were seldom home during the week, and Michiko and I were trusted to carry out her duties. In that way I learned the language and the bearing, the solicitudes, and the proper way to present oneself. I witnessed the attention to detail and appearance, the carefully smoothed exteriors as hard as the local Inada granite. Michiko did not rebuff my efforts as her mother and Reiko did. The townspeople affectionately called me gaikoku-jin, instead of the more disdainful gaijin, foreigner. When I spoke Japanese, even haltingly, they beamed with pride, as if I were their child learning her first words. "Our American speaks Japanese," they told their visiting countrymen.

I mimicked Michiko and other women until my gestures became automatic and an integral part of who I was. By this careful study, I became a person of great standing in Kasama, a celebrity of sorts, someone with whom many people wished to associate. At the Inari shrine, sometimes Westerners would arrive with their cameras and loud, laughing voices, but they did not belong to Kasama. I could tell that the townspeople regarded them with amusement. Me, they took seriously. They spent much time trying to teach me the ways of the Japanese. By the time Michiko left for the United States, I could feel my new strength.

It would have been fine, to be a mountain under Koji's rain, to withstand his sadness with only a measure of erosion.

This time, the baby within me stayed. I had awaited the blood for so long that I had forgotten about the time that had passed. At first, Koji did not notice. Every night he returned tired and wan, barely able to eat. Sometimes we did not make love for almost two weeks; perhaps he assumed that he had missed my menstruation. When I realized that the pregnancy had progressed beyond six weeks, I went about my chores with light-headedness as if I were ill.

Sitting on his heels, Koji noticed as he ate his supper. He stared at me with his penetrating gaze, a shrewdness I had only seen directed towards me, and I knew he sensed something. Not until we were alone in our room did he ask, "What is it, Ellen?"

"I'm pregnant," I whispered in his ear. I did not want the rest of the family to hear.

He hugged me so tightly that it brought tears to both our eyes.

"We can't tell anyone yet," I said. A flicker of sadness passed through his eyes, and I could see that he too was remembering all our lost children.

"We have time," he said. "Another month maybe, before we have to buy you new clothes. Then we must tell."

I nodded. Part of me wanted to shout the news on the doorstep, but another, darker part, full of superstition and dread, kept me silent. We finished dressing for bed.

Koji, about to climb under the quilts, froze, one knee on the floor, one on the futon. "The baby will be a gaijin, you know. His eyes will be rounder, his hair perhaps not so dark and straight, his skin lighter, his bones bigger. Maybe he will even have green eyes. One look at him, and everyone will know. The Japanese are as racist as Americans. They don't trust foreigners."

"They trust *me*."

He shook his head. "They trust you as a foreigner. They don't trust you as a Japanese. Our son—or daughter—will not belong."

"Nonsense. He will be Japanese." And I will, I finished mentally, be a Japanese mother.

Michiko wrote short, factual letters to the family, which Okasan read to me since I could not read kanji characters. Every once in a while, Michiko sent me a letter written in English chattering about her studies, her friends, her successes and failures in the plays she acted, the wonders she saw. She told me about a boy whom she dated; he taught her to sail and to make sandwiches. I withheld these letters from everyone, including Koji, because I did not want to further wound this family that was bleeding into America. I knew Michiko would not return to Kasama. I missed her deeply.

"The classes aren't bad, but the food is," she wrote. "Too much bread and not enough rice. I wish I could cook in my dorm room, but this is not allowed. People scare me when they look for so long into my eyes. But I become bold. Almost American."

I sent Michiko money to buy a rice cooker and warned her to keep it well-hidden.

Why was it that this family, in the countryside of Japan, a hundred kilometers from Tokyo, could not resist Westernization? I could not, cannot, answer. I had visited Tokyo and Kyoto; those cities were more progressive than Kasama, the children more exposed to gaijin, the ideas of the world flew more freely there—I could understand their leaving. But here, people depended on pottery and rice and granite. Their lives followed predictable patterns. So why did the Tanakas flee not only their home but their country? I could not understand anyone leaving the serenity this countryside offered. Was it the way the Tanaka children had been raised? Or was it a rebellion against the old-fashioned notions of their mother?

Okasan had quick, knowing eyes. She hid her intelligence not with a pretense of stupidity but with her reticence. She had known a finer life than this; perhaps the children had picked up, as Japanese do, on unspoken cues that they did not have to settle for this. That they should aspire for more. I had not known Otosan well. I had visited with him only three times, once before the wedding, once at the wedding, and once afterwards. From what Koji told me, I gathered he was a man dedicated to his career, hard-working and scrupulous in his attention to quality, unyielding but fair. Koji's parents did not seem like the types to drive their children from them. I could only guess that their children's clear intelligence hungered for the unknown, and in this way, they sought out America. I wondered how long it would take Michiko to discover violence, prejudice, and apathy.

I wrote to Michiko, "When are you coming back? I'm glad that you're having such a great time, but Kasama is not the same without you."

She wrote back: "If Kasama is not the same, come here. I carry myself wherever I go." I could almost hear her high-pitched giggle as she covered her mouth with her hand.

In the spring when my belly had grown round and hard, the Tanakas begged me not to go out in public. Okasan even let me put the rice in the cooker, roll the futons in the morning, unroll them at night, anything to keep me busy in the house. She said, "Now that you will be a mother, you must learn how to keep a Japanese house." Slowly, finally, she began to instruct me. The Japanese baby within me had finally brought me to my destination. I accepted the honor of these duties with goosebumps running the length of my arms.

But after I shook off the first trimester exhaustion, I grew inexplicably restless. I paced the small rooms after completing my chores, voraciously read Eastern philosophy, tried to teach myself kanji by poring over the girls' school books, went out for walks and bicycle rides into the town, out to the country, although I never felt as though I had gone far enough. The veins in my arms ached almost as if they craved some opiate. Although I ate enough to nurture the growing life within me, I felt hungry, though for something more than food. I was no longer satisfied with a little work here and there, but wanted everything. I wanted to know how to run the house, how to clean, cook, how to tend the garden, how to manage a child's education: all that the women did. Okasan taught me only a fraction of what I wanted to know.

When I told Koji of my frustration, he said with a small laugh, "You're not only *eating* for two."

He must have spoken to his mother, because she gave me many more time-consuming chores. Even then, as I stepped completely into my role as Japanese wife and mother, my mind ran wild. I refused to be invisible. When I was no longer able to keep my balance on a bicycle, I waddled the half mile into town every day. Okasan and Reiko were mortified. Koji seemed secretly pleased.

I worried endlessly about Koji. His skin had been acquiring a sickly cast since we had arrived in Japan, and he seemed to smile only at night when he splayed his fingers across my taut belly to feel the prod of a fist, a foot, a knee, an elbow. We whispered to the baby. Koji told him jokes and riddles, and I sang to him in my imperfect voice. Invariably, one of us ended up saying or doing something so ridiculous that we would laugh, yanking the comforter over our heads so that we would not wake the others. Every morning I awoke with the hope that the merriment of the night before had cured my Koji, but his feet got out of bed with the same heavy shuffle of the day before.

On one of our Thursdays, I asked him, "What is it, Koji? Are you sick?"

"I would tell you that."

"Then what is it? You don't love me anymore?"

He reached out to touch my cheek, but his fingers seemed to have no strength. "I will always love you."

I thought for a minute. "Is it the workshop? Is it making money?"

He frowned, shifted his weight on the balls of his feet. He broke his chopsticks in two and placed them inside the bento box. He had only eaten half of his sushi. "I don't know."

"You don't know? How can that be?"

He would not look at me. When he spoke, his voice was so low that I could barely hear him. "An old man, the father of one of our craftsmen, records everything. But I can't decipher any of it."

"Did you ask him?"

"He says we have enough money. But he's a very old man. It's very difficult to question him further."

In my other life, I might have yelled at him for being so timid. Or for trusting someone with his family's fortune. Or for not learning the intricacies of finances. But now, I merely said, "Show me the books."

Hidden away in Koji's tiny office, I studied the old man's accounting until I made some sense of it. Unfortunately, Koji's bookkeeper had no talent for math, nor had he been trained in accounting. He used a measure of common sense, which was the only thing between what I found and complete disaster.

"I will help," I assured Koji. And I began to tear through the figures.

Of course, I knew by then that something more than the accounting books consumed Koji from the inside out. The same country that had given us the miracle of a baby was destroying my husband. I began to wonder why Koji's older brother, Jiro, had stayed in Kasama and what he had found there to fill his short life and whether Koji could do the same.

One day I started out on a walk to town before realizing that I had forgotten my purse. When I returned to the house, I found Reiko rerolling the futons I had put away earlier. She rose, clearly surprised at seeing me, bowed a little. "Ellen," she said.

"What are you doing?"

"Oh," she said, "the ends were not meeting well today, and I thought I would save you the trouble of doing it again." Her eyes met mine. We understood each other perfectly. Every day, she had been going over my work and fixing it.

"Forgive me," I told her. "I know I have much to learn."

"You are not Japanese. There is nothing to forgive." She was sincere in this. To my surprise, I saw that she did not hate me but merely found my gaijin ways clumsy and disruptive. For this she could not blame me, because it came from within, not from any laziness or lack of respect.

I bowed slightly. "Thank you." But inside I felt as pale and as wan as Koji's face. As I watched Reiko expertly roll the futons, I thought: there

THE EARTH AND THE SKY

are two kinds of birds—ones that sing beautifully in captivity and ones that cannot. But I had no idea which of us was caged.

During the last months of my pregnancy I spent hours trying to rectify Koji's accounting books. Painstakingly, I copied entries into a new book so that we had at the very least a legible copy. As the baby in me jumped, I found myself thrilled with the order I was creating out of a numerical jungle. I had forgotten the part of me that relished regimentation and precision, the using of my mind to decipher the meaning of numbers and their consequences. I began to wonder if my success in accounting was not a fluke after all and if what I sought in Japan was nothing more than a lifestyle akin to neat columns of black and red numbers. As I worked side by side with Koji, I felt the baby settle into the last inch of space in my womb.

Okasan said, "Do not work so hard, Ellen-san. Let the old man and Koji take care of it. Think of your baby."

"I am thinking of my *family*," I told her. "I don't want you to live out your old age in poverty."

She looked at me in shock, perhaps because I had never before spoken to her so strongly.

Koji came to my bedside after the birth of our daughter. We called her Mari, Mary. I envisioned her name as Japanese phonetics whereas Koji saw in his mind the American version. To the ears of outsiders, we used the same name.

"She is beautiful," he said. He did not point out that her face lacked the characteristic roundness of Japanese babies, that her face was longer than that, that her eyes were wider and her hair too light. I had seen these things, felt a twinge of knowing, and fell in love with the strange creature that had not washed away and instead had come to rest in my arms. She was solid, perfectly formed, smooth-featured.

"You aren't disappointed that she is not a son?" I asked.

He shook his head. "In truth, I wished for a daughter." For Koji to say "wish," I knew that it had been more of a prayer.

I looked at him. Although he had begun eating more, his face was still hollow, etched with too many lines; his voice sounded harder than it had in America. We still whispered under the comforters, still sought out the touch of the other, but Koji had suffered. I knew why he had prayed for a daughter—she would not be obligated to run the family business. "You're an engineer through and through. Will Mari be an engineer, too?"

"She is a girl. It will be difficult. Girls are not often encouraged that way."

I swallowed. He knew too well the American in me that believed in free will and opportunity, in climbing to the top despite what others expected. Perhaps if I stayed the rest of my days in Kasama, I would become a real Japanese, but I no longer knew if that was what I wanted. Mari had complicated matters. I could no longer act only for myself. If I caged her, she would only flee as Michiko had. "Who will take care of the pottery workshop if we leave?"

He blinked, surprised but clearly pleased. "My cousin Hideo has a head for business. He has learned the trade, and the artisans will trust him more than they do me. My mother will just have to accept that her nephew can keep her husband's dream alive better than her son can."

"Then we should go back to America." I closed my eyes and sank back against the hard grain-filled pillow, fearful of Mari's power now that the umbilical cord had been cut to free her.

Michiko took a job near our new home in New Jersey after she graduated. Perky, straightforward, smart: she betrayed her origins only with her accent. Occasionally, I saw her hand instinctively twitch to cover her mouth self-deprecatingly, but she had the control to keep it at her side. Her dream of acting had been put aside, but she found a new one in radio production.

With Mari, Koji and I resumed our lives in America more or less intact, walking around with knotted shoes and eating off brightly glazed dishes, oddly happy. As I raced after Mari, who ran on fat, uncertain legs, I grew thin. The other mothers looked at me strangely and asked how I had adopted Mari, not knowing that she had adopted me.

One stranger dared to ask, "How much did she cost?"

I quickly found the center in me that still lived in Kasama, the part that did not anger and that knew the power of a perfectly placed rock. I answered quietly, "She is as priceless as the gems in the earth and as free as the wind." I could almost see the nods of approval from my Japanese friends and family—even Reiko. I pictured Okasan smiling quietly as she turned back to her work.

One night, as Koji and I, exhausted from our long day, sat with our books in our high-post bed, I was suddenly struck with an inexplicable sadness, a yearning. I tried to think of myself as that knotted doll but could not; there was nothing left to tie. As I thought about this, my sadness dissolved. Somehow I had become a stone daughter, permanently tied with a ceramic sash. A foundation.

I reached out and took Koji's warm hand in mine; the callouses from Japan had almost disappeared.

"What is it?" he asked.

"Let's whisper under the covers."

He looked at me through the glasses slipping down his nose, and smiled. He slid with me under the blankets where we met nose to nose, beneath the mountains of our cultures, and whispered our darkest desires and greatest fears.

Ingrid, Face Down

Ingrid fears the ocean. The water hides mysteries she would rather not encounter: murky water, barracudas, volcanic vents and infectious coral reefs, blind fish that generate their own electric shocks, currents so strong and deep that they can be charted but not conquered, a bottom that drops off to the end of the earth's crust, the smell of disintegrated sea bodies. She likes sand, dry sand, wet sand, the splash of water around her ankles—she is a shore person. But they want her to ride the boat out and snorkel with them. With voices high and shrill, loud, they try to persuade her, though they do not know her except that she holds them up. She squints at the (seemingly) innocuous flat Caribbean, aquamarine, glittering, no tidal waves, though Ingrid knows that tsunamis travel underwater and when you finally see one rising off the ocean floor, it is too late, because no one can outrun a five-hundred-mile-an-hour wall of water. She knows that she cannot dive underneath a tsunami, because its force is also under the surface. Children shout to one another behind her. The ocean has its own noise, a rhythmic wash that never quiets.

No, she says to these strangers on Grand Cayman, I don't want to.

It's part of the package, the guide tells her. Why else come to Cayman?

(Ingrid's boyfriend Max, back in the States, outside of Chicago, who was supposed to come with her, sits down on his bed, about to write her a love letter that he hopes will make amends. His bedroom is tasteless, half boy, half bachelor: red and black plaid bedspread, flat blue walls, bookshelves lined with empty imported beer bottles and baseball cards in plastic sleeves, posters of rock stars and a framed photograph of Ingrid leaning against the newly polished side of his black Mercedes convertible, a desk too small for him. He hates his room, and loves it, because of the

childhood memories. Max is thirty-six and still lives at home, not by con-
venience but because he is afraid for his mother, who has no one else.)

Ingrid has found ordinary expenses on Grand Cayman to be beyond
the reach of her teacher's salary, but she is determined to pretend otherwise. Unlike Max, she could not afford to throw away a nonrefundable
airline ticket. Even this long weekend—four days, no more—a present to
herself for President's Day, seems burdensome. In the stores, she finds
nothing affordable that interests her, only shell sculptures and sea-turtle
T-shirts, junk that she could find in Florida. Meals cost more than Ingrid
thought possible—she doesn't care if all the food has to be brought in
from the United States. She is not sympathetic. Places like this, she
thinks, should make life easy instead of pointing up inadequacies.

The guide, Jewel, hands her a mask and a snorkel. The guide has
bronze curly hair and dark Caribbean skin and green eyes that flash the
way the sky does here at sunset on clear, dry evenings. The night before,
her first here, Ingrid saw such a green-flash sunset, but it seems to her like
a dream, something she may have imagined in the split second of it all.
Without thinking, she takes the snorkel equipment and suddenly realizes
that she has unwittingly agreed to the trip. Reluctantly, she gets in the
boat with the others.

The others: a couple nearing retirement, Kirby and Jill, who appear
in better shape than the younger ones; three women friends, all slightly
overweight, all done up in waterproof makeup and black swimsuits; a
couple in their late twenties, smooth-skinned and white, talking in tense
syllables. Ingrid wears no makeup. That morning she drew her hair into a
short ponytail. She has the best body of anyone there, except maybe
Jewel, she knows it, but wants to cover herself with a towel. The boat
skims along the water to a point Jewel indicates with one finger. Jewel says
something frightening about petting manta rays.

Ingrid remembers a childhood neighbor, Mr. Peters, who had gone to
Hawaii for a vacation with his family and had gone out to swim, never to
be seen again. Ingrid distinctly remembers the horror with which her
mother had said, *and they never found his body.* Before then, even living
within easy distance of the Great Lakes, Ingrid had never once imagined
a body of water so vast and so deep that even dead bodies never returned
to be buried. She remembers the stinging cold of a beach in Maine, one
stop of many on a crazy family trip, and the way the waves crashed on her,

bodysurfing, and held her down, pressing and churning against her back, pulling her away from the sturdy legs of her father, until finally, it let go, and she sputtered upright. In her third grade class, she teaches the children about the way the continental shelf drops off to the ocean floor, about volcanic islands, coral reefs, trenches, and hot-water vents. With shaking hands, she listens to oral reports on sharks, jellyfish, giant squid, and killer whales.

Jewel teaches them to spit on their masks and rub it in, so that they won't fog up when they put their faces in the water. She demonstrates how to blow water out of the snorkel after diving, what to do if they develop leg cramps, tells them never, never, to try to pet a moray eel, do not touch the coral because it is a fragile ecosystem. Ingrid listens warily. This ocean looks as if it is something different from the one that tried to carry her away, and, because of this, she mistrusts it more. She would rather face an honest sea than one that lies.

They all slip into the cool water—even Ingrid, who expects to die at any moment. Her heart flutters at the prospect of depending on a plastic tube for breathing. An old boyfriend had once tried to persuade her to try skydiving with him. He could not understand that it was not the height that frightened her but the dependence on a mechanical thing, the parachute, to save her life. Next to these strangers, who seem not to fear such dependence, Ingrid treads water, begins to warm despite her apprehension. She watches as Kirby and Jill paddle away at once with their faces in the water. The three friends (names Ingrid cannot, and will never, remember) show surprising aplomb and take to the snorkeling after only a few minutes of practice. The tense couple take a few minutes longer. Ingrid, however, tests Jewel's patience—she can hear it in Jewel's steady, repeated directions—by panicking every time she puts her face in the water. Jewel tells her that she can tell Ingrid is, or was, an athlete, that she should be able to do this without much problem, as long as she gives herself the chance.

(Max writes: Dearest Ingrid, I love you wholly even though I have bowed to the wishes of my mother. You are the love of my life. When you look at me with those deep brown eyes and lean over to kiss me, I feel as if a wild hawk has been freed from my chest. I am not the same man I was when I met you. I am lighter, stronger, capable now of everything because of the love you've given me. I know you feel that I have deserted you because of my mother's sense of morality, but I am in true pain waiting for you to return from the vacation that should have been ours. Please, forgive me, and understand my responsibility as an only son. . . .)

Jewel proves to be a capable teacher and counselor, for Ingrid finally manages to put her face in the water and leave it there, her feet floating out behind her, until her breathing slows to normal. She follows Jewel's lead away from the skiff to where the others gently wave themselves across the water. Not until Ingrid forgets to concentrate on taking breaths does she realize how quiet everything is there under the water. How noisy her own life is, with children calling out answers and laughing, she and Max yelling, screaming at each other all the time, the wall of her condo shared with neighbors who like to play music and television too loud, cars, trucks, trains, airplanes that pass low overhead. There, under the water, fish float as if suspended in outer space, weightless and drifting on their own inertia. A yellow and blue striped parrot fish passes beneath her; she boldly stretches out her hand to touch it but the clarity of the water has tricked her into miscalculating distances. For the first time, she realizes how far it must be to the bottom. Surprisingly, this new knowledge does not bother her. The coral stretches beneath her in pinks, yellows, and whites, trees of the wildest dreams her mind can create, and she wonders why she has feared this moment when there is only blissful silence. She imagines that a fetus must feel like this in its floating, muted world where nothing has been seen but can only be imagined.

(On the beach, a shark has washed ashore, and a crowd gathers on the white sand to inspect it, to imagine coming face-to-face with such a fierce creature, though it is only three feet long and clearly dead for quite a while, its eyes white and gashes of flesh eaten from its side. A child, British, tosses ocean-polished stones and pieces of bleached coral at it until his mother, disgusted, turns from the shark and makes him stop.)

Talking inside her head, Ingrid tries to imprint upon her brain every sight before her so that she may tell her students about the marvels allowed by a tiny pipe sticking out of her mouth. She wishes she could tell them about how nothing matters right now, not Max, not her job, not her fears that have until now kept her from this, but the children will not listen, should not be told about adult fears anyway. Still, they might understand that lying face down must feel something like traveling to an alien world. They might understand the thrill of discovering that they have been wrong all along, that this new world has promises they had never imagined, life so enigmatic that they can hope to comprehend what it is like but never really know.

Clown fish hide among the spaces between coral arms, dart out, hide again. A yellow fish, snout-nosed, a name Ingrid refuses to find out because it will mean lifting her head up into the other world, approaches her mask, curious, as if it has more of a brain than it does. Blinking hard, Ingrid wants to laugh at this little fish but holds it back for fear of what a laugh will do to her snorkel. Instead, she pokes at the fish gently, until it twists around, swimming frantically a few feet, before once again drifting towards her. They play this game several times before Ingrid, with a lurch in her chest, realizes that she does not know where the others are. Twisting, she sees Kirby and Jill dive down towards the bottom, both so expert with their equipment. Ingrid kicks four times, then slides over the water to where they are. She sees with a start that they have discovered a manta ray.

(Max writes frantically on his lined notebook paper. He plans to copy everything, once he gets it to his liking, onto cream-colored stock, the kind Ingrid once noted had a certain classiness. He hopes that Ingrid will mellow in the sun so that when she returns she will have forgotten their argument, or at least, how to argue. Downstairs, his mother has awakened from her nap—they seem to be getting shorter—and calls up to ask if he would like a snack with her. The question, so familiar, so comforting, fills him with disgust for himself, because he knows that he cannot release this part of himself, even for Ingrid, though if he works hard enough he thinks he can fool them both.)

(At the same time, outside of Chicago, the school board president, working on the holiday weekend, opens a letter from a parent complaining that Ingrid has irreparably frightened the children by describing what would happen to an astronaut if he stepped out into space without his space suit. Her son, the parent claims, has been having nightmares about his body exploding. The school board president carefully refolds the letter and puts it back in the envelope—she wishes that she had not come into the administrative offices over the holiday weekend to catch up on work. She knows Ingrid, likes her, admires her creativity in teaching the kids. The school board president also knows the parent who wrote the letter and knows that she makes trouble very easily and that her children never excel in school. Regardless, a modest inquiry must be started. The president forwards the letter to the principal of Ingrid's school, who now must talk with Ingrid, confront her, explain the impressionability of third graders.)

Ingrid watches, amazed, as Kirby tries to touch the undulating wings of the ray, but he cannot hold his breath long enough to accomplish this. Nor can his wife. Instead, the ray follows them up near the surface, where he glides, all black undulation, under Ingrid in a sweep of darkness. Ingrid must fight not to panic, not to pull her face up and her feet down and surely kick this dark, mysterious thing that is sometimes called, after all, a stingray.

Now everyone comes over to see the ray—he seems to enjoy their company. He dances a ballet underneath them, and Ingrid cannot believe that she attempted to miss this. That Max relinquished his opportunity to see it. Ingrid feels a surge of triumph, and also a deep sadness, because she knows now that Max will never put her over his mother, not for anything, not for this miraculous display of underwater ballet that most people never see anywhere other than a National Geographic special, not for relaxation, not for love. Ingrid hates Max's mother, who uses guilt and skilled underhandedness to keep her son for herself. Ingrid hates Max, who lets his mother succeed. When she returns home, she will describe this afternoon to Max and then walk away from him, holding back her tears as she does now at the realization of the future.

(Max finishes his letter. He is pleased with what he says. This letter will force Ingrid to like him, to sympathize with him, because he has written so passionately that his hand aches. He firmly believes that he has the power to win over Ingrid despite what they have said to each other. If he has to, he plans to threaten suicide.)

The manta grows tired of them before they grow tired of him, and with a rhythmic rippling the length of his body, he skims away along the bottom. Ingrid watches his steady progress until he disappears from sight and once again the yellow fish looks up through her mask. Her back has burned in the sun—she can feel the familiar tightening of skin between her shoulder blades. She looks at the fanning combs of coral and thinks that her life is like that: spreading out in delicate fingers but seemingly arrested in its progress, fragile, able to be broken off in a turbulent storm. She alternately likes this and dislikes it, because she had once hoped for more animation but is willing to accept the beauty of a coral life. Coral is colored by the algae that live inside of the empty chambers. Ingrid wonders what has colored her.

Their snorkeling time must be nearing the end. Once getting the feel for it, Ingrid has not lifted her face from the water, unlike the others, who have periodically treaded water to talk about discoveries, or to adjust their masks, or to keep visual contact with each other. Ingrid hears their voices as if they are miles away and shouting into the wind. Their legs scissor in the water, remarkably pale and fleshy, coated with fine bubbles that escape into the water as they move. Ingrid remembers a childhood friend, Margie, who once scared a lifeguard into believing that she had drowned because she stayed for so long at the bottom of a pool. Ingrid has always been more cautious. She has never tested the power of her lungs.

Ingrid has never felt as strong and as capable as she does at that moment floating on the surface of this undisturbed sea. To her amazement, she realizes that she has managed to freeze her life so that time passes without her. She wishes that Max had been strong enough himself, because snorkeling feels right now better than any therapy that digs at sores and analyzes them. Here, the absence of weight absolves all. She recalls that her friend Laura, also a teacher, had become a born-again Baptist and had described how exhilarating it was to have her sins washed away in baptism. At the time, Ingrid could not imagine anything other than ordinary dirt being washed away, but now she can imagine a catharsis, an erasure, a birth into a world that both has changed and not changed while she has been submerged. In prehistoric times, this sea might have looked the same as it does now, the view perhaps essentially the same except for subtle rearrangements, certain rock formations washed in, others out, this place a good place for coral instead of over there. But all in all, nothing has changed.

(Onshore, a young woman with pink-tinted zinc oxide striped on her nose covers her eyes with one hand and gazes out across the rippling sea. She fears the stench of the dead shark, and has moved several feet away. Like Ingrid, she has never trusted oceans, prefers murky lakes because no dangers lie below the surface despite the blindness it creates. To her left, she sees the small boat anchored, not too far out, snorkeling obviously, people crazy to taunt the powers of the ocean. She scans across. To her right, she sees what she first believes must be a mirage, her imagination taking shape over the water, cutting through the blue, condensing into a small triangle. But as she stares, incredulous at what she has mistaken for the manifestation of her fears, she realizes that what she sees is, in fact, real. She kicks sand over her boyfriend. Look, she shouts, a shark. People listen, maybe at first thinking that she spoke of the dead one at their feet, but then they see the fin, and they start shouting, all of them, shark, shark, shark. Their eyes collectively focus on the swimmers, and beyond them, the small group of snorkelers. Shark, they scream, shark!)

Ingrid has drifted a little from the others, who are obviously tiring and wish to return to the solidity of the small boat. She does not want this magic to end. She works hard in completing the pictures in her mind— someday she may want to summon this image and hold onto it. The fish, their colors, the way the coral hides them, the dance of the ray, the muted sounds of voices and water washing over her ears, the way life there moves in blue-green silence, the sensation of complete peace and isolation. Jewel, her lean legs gracefully cutting the water below to announce her, taps Ingrid's shoulder.

Reluctantly, Ingrid lets her feet drop below the surface as she pulls her face out of the clarity, water splashing down her mask, sunlight blinding a little, noises, shouting. She shakes her head to remove the tickling drops that stream down. The world below her has vanished and in its place another reality has taken shape, one (she realizes as Jewel calmly explains the presence of a shark) that has not stopped its plodding course.

Rosa's Vision

After Mass on Good Friday, Rosa Canario climbed out of the valley using the trench worn into the earth by the boys of Esmeralda. Her right hand clutched the bouquet of flowers cut from her garden while the left groped for the short, woody shrubs growing alongside the path. Halfway up, her heart beat so fast that she feared tumbling backwards. Part of her wouldn't have minded—*if* she could have been sure of breaking her neck—but her luck had not been good lately. More likely, she would have ended up with a broken leg, or a head injury that caused permanent madness.

Panting, she rested for a moment. Below her, in the basin surrounded by the Andean foothills, the houses of Esmeralda clustered on either side of the unpaved road—Canarios and their workers on the north side, the Livacics and their workers on the south, the small church off by itself. The corrugated tin roofs glinted dully in the afternoon sun. With a heavy sigh, Rosa renewed her climb.

Finally, she burst through the last steps and onto the narrow shoulder of the highway. Up ahead, the old cactus the younger generation called the Devil Man cast its multiarmed shadow across the small shrine dedicated to Hector, whose car had plunged off that very spot. That day Rosa had been away at her sister's in Santiago, and, on the way home in grief, she saw that the workers were already changing the billboard alongside the highway to add the one more death. At least Hector's life had been recorded, she had thought.

She walked to the shrine and laid the flowers across the feet of the plaster Virgin Mary, and knelt. A single tear smeared her vision—Hector had been a good boy. A good young man. She blinked away the droplet; after a year most of her grief had moved to her heart where it smoldered, unseen but still too hot to touch for long. A few cars sped towards her, slowed. With her eyes closed, Rosa prayed for the safety of her other two children, her husband, all of her relatives, anyone who passed by the tiny memorial. She asked forgiveness for questioning God's motives, especially on this holy day. And finally, as she always did, she prayed for Hector to appear to her in her dreams that night. A car whizzed by at her back.

As she turned to leave, she saw a figure standing at the base of the Devil Man. She cried out in surprise, pressed her hand against her chest to steady herself. Hector! she thought. But, as she squinted into the sun, she could tell that this man was a stranger. The brilliancy of the sun behind him made it hard to distinguish his features, but he was broad-boned, almost too tall for a Chileno, with hair as black as a pure Mapuche's.

Rosa swallowed, but the dryness in her mouth had corked her throat. Although her eyes ached from straining against the sun, she did not dare look away. A bus came up fast behind the man, and he did not seem to flinch. Not to be outdone, Rosa stood her ground as the bus passed them with a whoosh of exhaust and dust. "Are you lost?" she finally managed to ask.

The man cleared his throat. "No," he said finally. "Are *you* lost?"

This peculiar training of the question on her caught her off-guard because she belonged there more than anyone. "No," she said, "though I've been lost from time to time."

The man nodded. "The trick is to find a single landmark and use that as an anchor."

She tried to place his accent: Northern, maybe, from the mine, or even Bolivia, so he couldn't be a Mapuche. "Where are you from?"

He pointed to a spot over her shoulder and, despite her earlier instinct not to take her gaze off him, she turned to see where he meant. But she could only see the curve in the road and the Andean foothills that lay around the valley like huge, mangy dogs asleep in the April autumn sun. Few people lived on the hills because the rain water washed almost everything down into their bony ravines, and earthquakes shook everything loose. As for the valley, Rosa knew most people, if not all, by sight. This large man would have certainly caught her eye before now. Puzzled, she turned back to the man, but he had vanished.

She stared at the spot where he had stood, swung around frantically to see where he had gone. She licked her lips. Her mind had otherwise been stable, but could it be that it had turned on her? Had she fallen asleep at the shrine and dreamed not of Hector but of an imaginary man who spoke the falsely mysterious language of dreams? She licked the dust off her lips again. Yes, she decided, she had dreamed it all. The stranger had never existed.

But as she passed the large cactus, when the sun shifted out of her eyes, she saw two footprints outlined in the thin layer of dust. Two perfectly formed footprints, shoes or maybe boots, but none leading towards the Devil Man, none leading away. Rosa studied the possibilities. The man could have taken a small leap and landed on the hard surface of the road. But then where could he have fled without her hearing or seeing him? The only other possibility was the other side of the road. But he could not have gone far on foot, since the road leaned into the steep side of a hill. Maybe he had parked his car there, and she hadn't noticed. But it all seemed so strange and impossible. Miraculous, even.

Although Rosa believed in miracles, she believed that they did not pertain to her. She had seen cows die giving birth, and she had saved others by reaching inside them to free the hooves of their calves. She had seen vultures circling high over a ewe that never died. These things were not miracles as much as luck. Still, as she stood above the village of Esmeralda, poised on the verge of the downward path, she considered that something extraordinary had occurred. She could not discount the coincidence of this odd event taking place on such a holy day. Bernardo, she knew, was across the valley with his brothers overseeing the final shipment of grapes out of the family vineyard, but her surviving son Camilo was mending fences. High above the village, Rosa shielded her eyes until she saw the familiar form of her son, his shirt white and shining against the emerald green of the fertile valley, not more than five hundred meters from where she stood. As she descended, she shouted his name.

At that moment, Camilo, on his knees by the twisted wire of a fence, was thinking how he hated ranching, though he tried not to complain. As he twisted wires together with his pliers, he dreamed of hopping on a bus before dawn and riding it all the way into glorious Santiago, where work did not swallow whole days and nights, where the girls with polished skin could meet him in the park in the evenings, where the city sparkled with vibrant lights that made his head spin. He could make his fortune there. He could work hard in a factory, save everything, so he could open his own restaurant. Not some grimy stand selling *empanadas* and Coca-Cola, but a real restaurant serving fresh fish trucked in daily from Valparaiso, sweet corn, tomatoes so ripe their juices ran freely, good Chilean beef from his family's ranch, and *vino tinto* with a body so full and balanced that his customers would order more food just to accompany it. Camilo sighed. His mother could not survive losing another son, even if he moved only an hour away. At the thought of his mother, he glanced up the hill where he had last seen her struggling to the top. He saw her running down the hill, a knee-high cloud of dust hovering about her. She shouted Camilo's name.

He stood, alarmed. Someone must have defaced Hector's shrine, or robbed his mother as she prayed, or . . . He threw the pliers to the ground and ran to her. She caught his rough hands in hers, and told him the story.

At the foot of the Devil Man, they stared at the perfect impressions. Rosa was beginning to think that someone had played a cruel trick on her, but Camilo believed that his mother had seen an angel. A man could not disappear as easily as a whisper. But why would an angel appear to his mother, who, he conceded, was a good enough woman but certainly not an extraordinary one? Camilo studied his mother's puzzled face: deep furrows, skin still brown from the long summer, eyes bright and probing.

"I think we'd better find Father Paolo," Camilo finally said.

Rosa looked up at her son, who at twenty-two was stronger than his own father. How could this capable creature have sprung from her? He had never seemed so decisive before, so sure of what needed to be done that she wondered if she had missed the moment when he had leapt from boy to man.

News of Rosa's vision spread rapidly through the village. The people called it an angel even before Father Paolo had a chance to make the climb. On Good Friday, they said, there could be only one explanation for a man who appeared and disappeared on a prayer. Aguirre Canario, Rosa's nephew, believed that his aunt had forgotten what Hector had looked like, and had seen him resurrected by the Lord on Good Friday.

"That's stupid," his girlfriend, Isabel, said. "Why on Good Friday? Why not Easter, when Jesus rose from the dead?"

Theories abounded even before people saw the footprints: an angel upset with the naming of the Devil Man, a spirit sent from Heaven to warn the villagers of an imminent catastrophe, Jesus himself testing their faith. Very few dared to oppose a supernatural explanation. One of those who did, Rosa's nineteen-year-old daughter Patria, believed that the man had simply hopped on a bus while her mother's back was turned. Esteban Livacic said, and quite loudly, that he had seen Rosa huffing and puffing up the hill just moments before she came flying back down.

"She suffered from lack of oxygen to the brain," he said, "and hallucinated." Everyone knew that Esteban had wanted to be a doctor but that his parents had not allowed him to go because, with the current government, it cost money.

The villagers crowded around Father Paolo as he examined the impressions in the dust. Children hung back, pressed there by their parents. Some of the adults hushed the children, who periodically broke out into stifled laughter or a small fistfight. Rosa wiped her palms against her skirt.

The priest did not know what to say. He had known Rosa for many years; she was a good, caring woman who had raised three fine children. His hands rubbing flat against each other, he thought about the situation, but he could not chase away the small jealousy. He was not, he realized with sadness, entirely impartial.

Camilo was already erecting a small fence around the Devil Man to protect the footprints. The faces of the other villagers watched the priest intently; Paolo could feel their eagerness to learn the truth. Each one, however, wanted a different truth, none of which he could unequivocally endorse. He cleared his throat. "Tell me again, Rosa, what happened."

Rosa held herself still, braced herself, before beginning. As she retold the story, she was unsure of whether she still told the truth or if it had already mutated. The story sounded to her as if it had not involved her at all but rather someone else. When she had finished, she reached out to Patria, who seemed to be the most level-headed about the whole matter.

Father Paolo ran his finger along the inside of his high collar. This autumn heat still felt like summer. As he perspired, he realized that, although he was nearing forty-five and had been a spiritual man since his late teens, he had not an inkling of exactly what spirituality was. He knew his faith, the words of the Lord, the holy rituals, what it all meant to him, but he could not say what religion meant to his parishioners. He could not understand why these people had instantly clung to the idea of a holy miracle in these times of biological deconstruction. The idea that they were more ready than he to accept a miracle frightened him. "I'll have to call the monsignor," he finally said. "In the meantime, we have to provide a roof over the prints, so that they don't wash away in the next rain. And Camilo, you'll have to build a fence around the shrine, too."

"The shrine?" Rosa asked. "Why?"

"Weren't you praying there just moments before?" he asked her. "Perhaps Hector's shrine has been blessed. Perhaps *Hector* is blessed."

Patria looked over her shoulder at her brother's shrine. Hector possibly a saint? Not her brother, who had thrown stones at her and her friends as they played with their dolls. Not the brother who had snuck out of the house at night to kiss girls under the moonlight. Camilo, too, found this hard to believe, but he was ready to accept whatever Father Paolo told them.

Just then Rosa's husband Bernardo and his brothers came racing across the floor of the valley in Bernardo's red truck. Rosa saw the urgency of the driver, and she scrambled down the hill. Camilo ran past his mother. Many of the townspeople, including Father Paolo, followed.

"What is it?" Camilo panted as he met the truck.

Bernardo, in the passenger seat, swung open the door and stepped out gingerly, with his brother Daniel assisting him. Ramòn, who had been driving, leapt from the cabin.

"Bernardo!" Rosa said. "What's happened?"

"You wouldn't believe it," he told her with a wince. His dark, wavy hair was frosted with dust.

"One of the trucks ran over Bernardo," Daniel said, still out of breath. "He was right under the tire. He screamed and called out Hector's name over and over. The driver heard him and pulled forward right away."

Ramòn picked up the story. "When I heard him call out to Hector, I was sure he was dying. But then he stood up as if almost nothing had happened. Still, he should see a doctor right away. In case something happened inside."

Rosa looked around for the doctor, but he was one of the few who had not come to witness the footprints. She wrapped her arm around her husband, fearing that something had ruptured inside him and that she would lose him that very night. "Come, Bernardo," she said gently. "Back into the truck."

Doctor Salvador Canario, a cousin of Bernardo, had been sleeping when all the excitement of the vision had drawn the villagers out of their routines. Father Paolo would write in his diaries later that neither the doctor nor Bernardo had any reason to falsify their stories since they had been completely ignorant of the appearance of the angel. The doctor prodded Bernardo, questioned him intensely, took his vital signs, looked deep into his pupils. Cautiously, he pronounced Bernardo without major injuries.

Father Paolo stood in the corner of the examining room. As the doctor stated his findings, the priest felt an enormous exhilaration spread inside him like the wings of an eagle. He was no longer jealous of Rosa's vision; he knew he was at the core of something fabulous, greater than any individual. He could no longer deny the coincidences of Good Friday, Rosa's vision, and Bernardo's walking away from death. As the parish priest, he had been entrusted by God to care for this event, nurture it, make certain that its simple beauty was not corrupted.

"Hector's first miracle," he told Rosa and Bernardo.

By Easter Sunday, word had spread throughout the basin and beyond, some fifty miles in every direction, that Jesus himself would appear at the roadside in Esmeralda. Hundreds arrived by car, bus, and truck; they lined the road like a colorful serpent that slunk along the borders of Rosa's life. Rosa chose to ignore the commotion, because the stranger had said nothing about such an appearance. Instead, she attended Mass with her family and set about cooking Easter dinner. As she sliced a ripe tomato, one of the last of the season, Bernardo came up behind her and caught her hand. With a grand flourish, he spun her around and into his arms.

"Oh, Bernardo," she laughed. "That truck didn't kill you. It made you ten years younger."

He brushed her cheek with his mustache. "It made me hungry."

"Not for food, I know! But the rest of the family must eat." Reluctantly, she wiggled her way out of her husband's arms. She liked this new version of her husband who had been frightened into appreciation. She had fallen in love with Bernardo when she was only sixteen, married him only a year later, hated him three years after that. But over the years, she had found a much easier, fonder love for him. Through the children, she was reminded of what she had first loved in Bernardo. As she checked the potatoes on the stove, still sensing the heavy-lidded gaze of her husband, a small thrill danced the length of her arms and back.

She glanced out her kitchen window which overlooked the fields and the highway behind. The sight of the teeming mass of people made her gasp. She wished she knew what she was supposed to do. All she felt was a sickening feeling that reached all the way into her heart. She spun to throw herself back into Bernardo's arms, but he had already left the room.

Camilo and Patria had obeyed their mother and stayed away from the crowds on Easter. The two sat side by side, feeling like small children, on their garden bench and watched the mass of strangers above. Some of the pilgrims had come down into town, trampling the cattle fences, looking for Rosa as if she were a saint herself. Eventually, someone pointed out where she lived. Chanting, a group of twenty or so marched towards the house. At first, Camilo and Patria were amused; their mother did not seem extraordinary to them and the idea of these strangers seeking her made them laugh. One or two of the faithful saw the young adults and started to approach. Before either Canario could react, the whole throng was running at them. Camilo and Patria sprinted towards the house.

Rosa had seen the mad dash for her children unfold but had been too paralyzed to warn them. Camilo pushed Patria over the threshold and into Rosa's arms, then slammed the door behind him.

Bernardo ran into the room. "What's going on?"

"They want Mama," Patria said. "I don't know why, but they want her."

Camilo sat dejectedly on a stool. "They think that Jesus won't appear unless Mama goes up there with them."

"He's not going to appear, period," Rosa said with a firmness that surprised her. "The stranger I saw said nothing about Jesus, or God, or Hector, and anybody coming back from the dead. Now everybody sit down and eat the *empanadas* I fixed to tide you over. I'll make some tea." When no one moved right away, she shouted, "Now!"

Quickly, the three Canarios obeyed. They sat at the table awaiting the small pastries stuffed with chopped egg, onions, and raisins. Bernardo stroked his stomach, where the weight of the truck still branded him a purplish yellow.

The next day, as Camilo mended the same section of fence he had fixed just days before, he felt no annoyance. Instead, the repetition of the repair felt deeply satisfying, as if this were something he was meant to do again and again. He glanced up to the giant cactus, knowing that Hector's shrine lay just beyond it. What had the stranger told his mother? Find a landmark to anchor you. Camilo turned back to the fence with a smile.

Three weeks later the monsignor arrived with several other priests. The monsignor ate lunch alone with Father Paolo in the cool shade of the rectory's small garden while the others interviewed Rosa, Bernardo, and the other villagers. The monsignor had briefly taught Father Paolo at the seminary, and had found him pious but not blind, a quality he found too rare in the priesthood. He had taken upon himself to instruct the young man in matters of caring and faith, often insisting that Paolo accompany him on long walks during which they discussed both theological and secular matters. The monsignor had held great hopes for Paolo, but Paolo wanted only to be a parish priest for a small village. The monsignor was a tall man, with wide bones, and it occurred to Father Paolo that he fit the description of Rosa's vision.

"This isn't a ploy of yours to be named a monsignor, is it?" the monsignor teased.

"Oh, of course, " Father Paolo laughed. "Tell me again what time your day starts. When it ends."

"I sleep between two and three in the morning." The monsignor wiped the cream sauce from his lips and leaned like a conspirator towards Paolo. "The church has grown wary of these miracles. True miracles are hard to come by in this day and age."

"Because God is forsaking us?"

The monsignor adjusted his napkin in his lap. "Don't be sarcastic. It's just that—these people are rural folks." He held up one of his large hands to silence a protest from Father Paolo. "I'm not saying they are ignorant. But the church needs to ask, why here? How reliable are the people? Chile is a superstitious land, particularly outside of Santiago. We have to separate the truly faithful from the heathen."

"How could you say that about your own country? Your own people?" Paolo worked hard to control his anger, and so his words came out tight and hard. "Are miracles only allowed to be witnessed by the elite?"

The monsignor laughed. "Calm yourself, dear Paolo. I haven't said that I've *discounted* the reports. I only said that we have to be careful. Several people who came for the Easter vigil claim to have been healed. We need to interview them as well, get doctors' reports, find out if their illnesses were possibly psychosomatic to begin with. In contemporary times, we've many more tools to confirm and deny such sightings."

The two men ate in silence for a while. Father Paolo wondered about the human tendency to be skeptical of miracles. He guessed that the idea of a spiritual world threatened some people. But for the monsignor himself to discount miracles? Father Paolo did not like to think of the implications. He had not expected this of a spiritual man, further reminding himself of how little he knew about faith.

"Sometimes we have to trust our hearts," Paolo finally said.

The monsignor looked up from his plate and smiled broadly. "I know we do. I know." He folded his napkin into a neat rectangle. "I'm not your enemy. I'm not Doña Canario's enemy. I'm only a man who has to be careful about what I burden my superiors with."

When the monsignor and the others arrived, Patria's hands began perspiring although she could not say why. The priests did not particularly frighten her, despite their pointed questions. They wanted to know about her mother: if she had ever told lies, even small ones, if she had ever seen ghosts or auras before, if she was crazy (we won't tell anyone that it came from you, one of the priests assured her), if she enjoyed flowery stories, a good laugh. They wanted to know about Hector and his short life. Why Patria thought he was worthy of God's singular attention. When she told them that she did not think of either brother as a saint, the priest transcribing the interview jotted something lengthy and furious on his notepad.

After they had gone, when the dusk crept over the wrinkled hills and into the valley, Patria climbed the trench to her brother's shrine. The path was steep, but her young legs took each step with little effort. She strode past the Devil Man (now renamed the Cactus of God, but she would never be able to rid her mind of the original name) and shouldered her way through the remaining people to the shrine. Behind the fence, the small statue of the Virgin Mary stood amid a pile of flowers and bright coins, crumpled pieces of paper inscribed with special prayers. Patria had a picture in her mind as still and as immutable as a photograph: Hector sitting in the garden with a bottle of Coca-Cola in one hand and a book in the other. His mouth was twisted to meet the bottle, but his eyes would not leave the words even for a second to find the bottle.

As Rosa gathered the tea and coffee cups the priests had left scattered outside around her house, she had a sudden, horrible thought: the priests could steal her son. If they agreed that this miracle of the stranger and Hector were linked, that her vision and Bernardo's escape from death were very possibly real miracles, then the humanity of her son would disappear forever. And if the priests denied that anything spectacular had occurred, Hector's shrine and his memory would be forcibly pushed out of everyone's consciousness. Now, he could only be a saint or a fraud. She leaned heavily against the wall, one hand to her eyes; her other, holding a single cup by its handle, hung limply at her side.

The following week the morning chill in the air seemed impenetrable. Rosa hung newly washed laundry onto the clothesline—all the summer clothes to be put away until next year, light fabrics in pastel colors. Rosa smiled. As a child, she had asked her mother why her clothes had to change colors every season, since she always preferred a light, airy pink that her mother told her could not be worn in the winter. Her mother had said, "Because the snow elves would steal them." It hardly snowed at all there at the edge of the Andean foothills, and Rosa had never been told any folk tales involving snow elves. But she had liked the sound of it, and so had not questioned it.

Rosa finished hanging the laundry. She glanced at her watch; the first bus from Santiago would be arriving in fifteen minutes or so. That gave her enough time before the pilgrims came looking for her to run down the street to Paulina Livacic's house. As Rosa shook the last droplets from her hands and wiped them on her apron, she thought angrily, I've become a prisoner. She hated the prosperity and contentment that had invaded the village. Pilgrims bought bread, produce, biscuits to spread with orange marmalade. They bought clothing from the women and handed out coins to the children. Esteban had set up a small concession stand selling, besides Fanta orange and Coca-Cola, little vials filled with Esmeralda dirt. Before Rosa's vision, Esmeralda had been a raisin in the valley, a place no one wanted to stay unless he had no other choice. Now, people were coming to Esmeralda, talking about buying Canario land on which to build houses, great adobe, tiled-roof houses with geraniums in the window pots.

As Rosa neared Paulina's house, she saw her friend in the backyard, her hair tied back under a scarf. Paulina waved to Rosa, then placed the last clothespin on the wash.

"Can you spare a couple hundred grams of flour?" Rosa asked.

Paulina laughed high in her throat. "Lately, you've been running out of everything." She picked up her basket and walked to the front. "I'm buying extra—"

The first jolt of the earthquake threw Rosa to her knees. She looked up to see Paulina half in and half out of her basket. Rosa tried to pick herself up but the rumbling, rattling ground held her fast to its soil. People were screaming, shrieking for their children, as the tin houses began to topple one after the other in thudding booms. The single row of power lines waved back and forth as if made of paper matchsticks.

"Look out!" Rosa shouted, as one of the poles toppled. Its wires crackled as they broke loose, but the pole was held aloft by one or two cables, a few feet from the women.

A red cloud of choking dust rose up into the air as parts of the mountains slid into the valley. Metal clamored, crashed, and with it, glass. Then, as suddenly as it had begun, it ended. Her knees still weak, Rosa picked herself off the ground, offered a hand to Paulina. As they looked at the devastation around them, Rosa prayed for her family, her friends, everyone. She turned, straining to hear cries for help. Then, and only then, because the cloud of dust was just beginning to clear, she saw that every house but one had been demolished. She stared at her intact house. No, she thought, don't let it be. Let me be taken down with the others.

Paulina took her by the elbow. "Do you see, Rosa?"

Rosa nodded, fighting the desperation rising inside her.

"It's Hector," Paulina whispered. "His second miracle."

"Look at Bernardo's house!" someone else shouted. "It's Hector!"

Father Paolo, who had been in the rectory garden when the quake started, hurried towards the center of town. A rivulet of blood trickled down his right cheek, a gash from a small tree that had toppled, scraping his cheek as it fell. When Paolo heard the rising call for Hector, he believed at first that his parishioners were blaming Hector for this tragedy. Then he saw the Canario house and the complete destruction around it. That is faith, he thought joyously, a house that nothing can destroy.

The shouts for her son rose around Rosa, out of the streets, the fields, even from within the rubble. She crumpled to the ground. It will never end, she thought, never. The people will always come, they will take my land, my house, my spirit. They have clung to nothingness and somehow made something huge out of it. If the stranger had been an angel, why couldn't everyone had left him that? Why did they have to consume *her* in their path to redemption? No hell could be worse than a miracle touched by human hands. Down the street, her laundry still hung limply on its line, white, pinks, blues, greens the color of new leaves, seemingly untouched by the copper dust. She had never before felt so utterly, hopelessly, irrevocably lost. Her mouth was so parched she couldn't swallow.

The villagers began the arduous work of sifting through the rubble. Dazed, Rosa picked herself up to search for her children and husband. She shouted their names. Bernardo and Camilo had been in the fields, away from buildings, so she expected to find them safe. But Patria? She shouted her name over and over. Finally, Rosa saw the figure of her daughter in front of their house, staring at the standing walls.

"Patria!" Rosa yelled. She broke into a run to meet her daughter, to see if she was hurt, but Esteban Livacic and his brothers stopped her.

"Please," Esteban said. "You must help us find our mother."

Rosa looked at their tear- and dirt-streaked faces, then at the rubble of tin and wood, and finally, at her daughter, immobile, staring, beyond her reach.

"Please!" Their faces were taut with fear.

She imagined Julia Livacic, half-crushed by the weight of her house. How could she abandon her friend? She closed her eyes. There, in the darkness behind her lids, she saw Hector as he really had been, smiling, teasing, his head cocked to one side as if listening for an answer. With a sigh, she opened her eyes. "I'll help you."

With the Livacics, she lifted boards and pipes, shards of glass, splintered pieces of furniture, until they found Julia still alive. All day Rosa worked like that, from house to house, until her arms and legs trembled with exhaustion. She helped carry wounded people to the doctor, and dressed minor injuries herself. When someone asked her to pray, she did. An aftershock sent her to her knees, but she got up and went on.

By the time Rosa joined her family under the stars—for even a Canario house might topple in the night—they had created a small campfire and had already eaten a simple dinner. Patria, who had suffered a cut to her forehead, sat huddled in a blanket. Bernardo squatted, his hands on his knees, while Camilo poked the fire with a metal pipe. When Rosa stepped into the firelight, they looked up at her, their faces illuminated into shifting, orange masks. She touched her fingers to her cheeks, thinking for an instant that she could touch light, but her fingertips met only flesh. For a while longer, until the embers died and the sun began to rise, she would have to wear this shroud of light.

Snow Angels

Toulouse seemed like a city out of another world with its leather clad students, the old men playing *boules* along the grassy banks of the Garonne River, the gypsy children in colorful, slipping-off scarves begging outside the cafés off La Place du Capitole. You couldn't see change in Toulouse—at least I couldn't—and I loved the city for it. My infatuation and a check from my parents kept me in Toulouse the winter after I finished my fall semester abroad. I stayed behind with three other Dartmouth students, all of whom, like me, had decided that we would never have another chance to live in Europe. We called ourselves *Les Quatre Esprits*, as if by giving ourselves a nickname we assured ourselves a place in history. We spoke mostly French, even among ourselves. Just then leaving my teens, I believed that my mind had no limits, that I could understand anything provided I concentrated enough. My powers seemed to equal the Pyrénée mountains that on a clear day I could see rising up white and jagged against the gentle blue of the horizon.

We found two adjacent apartments near the center of the old city: one for me and the other for the guys. I lived in a tiny, one room, water-stained corner while Matthew, Aaron, and Dave lived in a comparatively spacious two bedroom flat (also water-stained) where we gathered when we weren't exploring the countryside on mopeds, or drinking in cafés, or goading the Toulousiens into an argument. My first night in my own place, I leaned back onto my lumpy mattress and thought that nothing, ever, would be as glorious as being an American in a French city. I fell asleep, already by then thinking and dreaming in imperfect French.

In the evenings we invited French university students to the guys' apartment where we drank beer, sat on the mottled rug, and discussed our philosophies about world politics, literature, psychology, and culture.

Sometimes Matthew played his saxophone for us in sorrowful wails. Other times, Dave, his hair in his fists, started arguments. One evening, after listening to an impassioned discussion about which country contributed most to Western culture, I declared that the French theater, once so fiercely innovative, had died.

"How could you say that, Kate?" Rémy asked. He was a slender, large-headed man, older than us, whose broad, steady hands mesmerized me. "We are very creative here."

I shook my head. "I'm a drama major. I've seen plays and studied them, and all I've seen in Toulouse are derivative absurdist plays. Dada junk. Stuff that should never have been allowed past the sixties."

"Kate's right," Aaron said. His wire-rimmed glasses slipped down his nose, his knees awkwardly sticking straight up like grasshopper wings. He was willowy, tall, always bowing under an invisible weight, thinking and calculating all the time—it wasn't until years later that I realized I had fallen in love with him. His intensity, and not his average looks, made him handsome. "The same holds true for literature. You French succeeded so admirably with existentialism that you seem afraid to try anything new. Fear breeds stagnation."

With that, Rémy promised to take us to an opera rehearsal at La Place du Capitole theater, the overbearing centerpiece of the old city that I had seen as a mere backdrop to the colorful tents of the Wednesday market, or, on other days, as something to stare blankly at across the great open plaza from my seat at our favorite café. On our way to the rehearsal, as we walked across the stone-paved Place, the winds picked up, and we huddled into our collars. The narrow streets leading to La Place seemed dark and distant. We neared the theater with its authoritative white columns, and I realized that not once had I seen someone enter this forbidding building even though throngs of people crossed the square in front of it.

Inside, the seats were upholstered in red velvet, the trim along the balcony and the boxes was ornately carved and painted with gilt, and heavy red curtains guarded the flanks of the stage. I quietly slipped into a seat between Rémy and Dave. Onstage, the company, obviously working through a first dress rehearsal, went through the jerky motions of the final scenes of *Orpheus and Eurydice*. Although the set changes were clumsily executed (at one point the singers ran off the stage yelling and shouting as a backdrop fell too quickly), the arias interrupted again and again, the lighting poorly timed and sometimes downright unfocused, I felt uniquely privileged to watch. These were professionals, I told myself. And they were people not unlike me. I dug my fingernails into the velvet of the seats just to contain myself.

I had no concept of how much time had passed, but Dave hit me on the arm to signal that it was time to leave. Reluctantly, I followed my friends out of the theater.

"Well?" Rémy asked. "Do you still think we do it badly? Oh, look. Snow." Toulouse was located so far in the south of France that it rarely snowed, except for occasional flurries such as these. As we paused on the stone steps of the theater, I tipped my head back to see the twisting paths of snowflakes as they materialized from their background of gray sky.

Aaron prodded me. "You didn't answer Rémy's question, Kate."

Reluctantly, I pulled my eyes from the sky. "I loved every minute. But I stand firm. First of all, Puccini wrote that opera, right? Not a Frenchman. And it was written I don't know how many years ago. It doesn't qualify."

"You Americans." Rémy shook his large head. "And you brag about your Broadway!"

"Americans!" A new voice had joined the discussion. About ten feet away from us, facing the theater, a petite woman about my age stood. Snowflakes speckled her short, sandy hair. She wiped her nose quickly with a tissue. "I can't believe that I found Americans in Toulouse." Her French was technically expert, but her accent was so American that I winced. She sounded as if she had learned French from a book.

"Hi," Dave said, stepping forward, brushing the snow off the curls on his head. "You alone in Toulouse?"

"Actually, yes. My boyfriend left me in Madrid for an Australian, and I'm on my own."

Our shared nationality must have tricked her into believing that we were connected. I stepped forward. "We're holed up in Toulouse for another three months. Living the life as only parentally supported students can. I'm Kate. And these are my friends, Dave, Aaron, Matthew, and Rémy."

"I'm Daria." She stuck out a small, reddened hand for me to shake.

"We're heading for a café," Aaron told her. "Want to join us?"

"Sure. I'm freezing."

And from such an accidental meeting, Daria joined our group of temporary expatriates. She stayed in Toulouse as though she had nowhere else to go, seeming to forget that she had taken a year off from Barton College to see "all of Europe." She had grown up in Kentucky, though she did not have a pronounced drawl. She had a plain heart-shaped face splattered with freckles, and hands so unsure that she always ended up dropping something, a glass of beer in the café, one of Dave's books, a bottle of carbonated *limonade* that exploded all over us when she opened it, Matthew's saxophone, a letter for my parents that landed in a puddle. The only things she took great care to hold onto belonged to Aaron.

Daria traveled everywhere with us. When we took to the countryside outside Toulouse on mopeds, she lagged behind; Aaron started driving in circles so that he could talk with us up front, then check on Daria. Once, we stumbled on a gypsy encampment. Dave, Matthew, Aaron, and I stopped to talk to a gypsy woman, but Daria sped away down the road, eventually getting lost. In the dormant fields of Bordeaux, we sang in French while Daria, drunk, vomited. In Nice, a woman stole the watch off Daria's wrist and we spent several hours in the police station with her filling out the paper work. Even Matthew and Dave were annoyed with her for constantly holding us up because this was supposed to be *our* dream: *Les Quatre Esprits*, not *Les Quatre Esprits* plus one. In Carcassonne, we poked around the old fortress city while ridiculously translating English idioms into word-for-word French. As we walked down the narrow cobblestone streets, I laughed so hard that my ribs ached at the French versions of "I knocked her up" and "I fell head over heels" and "I'm freezing my balls off" and "I'm on the rag" and "Boot up the computer."

Daria did not seem to see the humor. "That's not a good translation. That's not how the French say it."

"Of course it's not," Matthew said. "It's a joke, Daria."

"I just think that you should speak properly when you use a language. That's all."

"For God's sake, we're having fun," I said. "Lighten up."

"*Éclaires en haut!*"

We laughed again, and Daria stomped off, followed closely by Aaron, who told her that we were a bunch of jerks. They looked ridiculous, little Daria running next to hunched-over Aaron, who, though keeping up with her pace, seemed to stride leisurely down the cobblestone street.

"Looks like he's in lust," Dave said. "It can't be love. Come on. Let's find a place to eat lunch."

Matthew pointed to a grassy area just outside the fortress walls. "Come on. Over there." We started down the narrow stairway to the city gates. "Thank God I haven't found anyone. This way, you guys can't make fun of *me*."

I knocked him in the ribs. "We're always making fun of you. Get a grip."

"*Obtiens une prise,*" Dave said.

The three of us huddled against the wall. Matthew unzipped his daypack—it had been his turn to carry the lunch. I stretched out my legs in the weak sun. As he handed out the food to us, he glanced up to a point behind me. "Heads up. Here they come."

Aaron and Daria must have seen us from atop the wall and had come down so they didn't miss out on the food. Across the short, yellowish grass, they walked side by side, easily, as if they had come to some understanding. Aaron moved gingerly, as if ready to catch her at the slightest misstep.

I took the baguette from Matthew and ripped it into five chunks, placing Aaron's and Daria's on top of the backpack. With my peasant's knife, a wood-handled pocketknife with a three-inch blade that I had bought at the Wednesday market, I sliced off some goat cheese and spread it on my bread. "Just in time," I told Aaron and Daria as they reached us. "Your bread is right there. Pull up a piece of sod."

"Brrr." Dave shuddered. "It's too cold for a picnic."

"It's never too cold for a picnic," Daria said brightly as she helped herself to one of the clementines. As she peeled, she sang the Beatles song "Michelle" in a stunning voice: clear, powerful, perfectly resonating. She had the type of voice I never expected to hear outside of a recording. Perhaps because of the surprise of it, she sounded better than the opera singers we had heard the day we met. Matthew had stopped midair with his Swiss army knife. Dave stopped chewing with a lump of food sticking out of one cheek. Aaron looked as though he was going to fall over backwards. When Daria abruptly interrupted her song to pop a clementine section into her mouth, she did not even notice our reactions.

"You've got a great voice," I finally managed to say.

She smiled quickly. "Thanks." And concentrated once again on her food. As she separated another section of clementine, the fruit spun out of her hand and skidded across the ground, leaving her with a single piece in her hand. "Shit."

Later, as the guys went to look for a *pissoir*, leaving Daria and me to ourselves back up in the city, I asked, "Do you take singing lessons?"

"Sometimes. I'm not as disciplined as I should be." She wandered down a narrow alley, and I followed. Every once in a while we caught a glimpse of a courtyard strung with laundry hanging out to dry. We passed an old woman squatting in a darkened doorway, her mouth working as if she were eating or just trying to swallow, her head covered with a red scarf. When we were out of earshot, Daria leaned into me and said, "I hope I never get old like that."

I laughed. "Unfortunately, it happens to all of us."

A faint smell of urine wafted in the air. Daria wrinkled her nose. "I just don't understand why this country puts up with so many primitive conditions." She kicked a stone and sent it spinning down a side alley. "Someday, I'm going to figure out this country."

Impulsively, I took her arm. She stopped, turned to me in open surprise. "What do you sing?" I asked.

"Country music."

"Country?" My disappointment must have been as clear as her voice.

"You don't like country? What do you like?"

"Oh, lots. Rock, mostly."

"I want a civilized career." She turned. "We'd better get back."

As we walked down the alley, I asked her when she first discovered that she had a talent for singing. She smiled and said she used to sing to herself whenever she was frightened. When she was three, her mother heard her in the middle of the night singing a church hymn and thought the angels had descended from heaven to claim her.

"I like singing when I'm nervous," Daria said as they reached the main street. "It makes me feel strong." She looked at me with cold, level eyes. I felt horrible at the way we'd been treating her. As I was about to apologize, Dave, Matthew, and Aaron spotted us, shouting and waving. As we watched the guys coming down the street in V-formation, scattering the French before them, Daria said in a low voice, "I do have a sense of humor. But I also take things seriously."

On the bus back to Toulouse, everyone fell asleep except for Aaron and me. I leaned over Daria's bowed head and tapped him on the shoulder. "Hey."

"Hey. Everyone's missing the scenery."

"Maybe they figured they saw everything on the way there."

He pushed his glasses up his nose and shifted his body towards me. "Stupid."

"Yeah." I gripped the seat back in front of me as we hit a pothole. "I'm sorry we got on Daria's case today. I guess we can get sort of clique-ish. It wasn't fair, and we ended up hurting your feelings as well."

"Mine? Why me?"

"You know. Because of you and Daria."

"You're crazy. There's no me and Daria." He changed the subject to the small church we had seen in Carcasonne and what it must have been like to live in the Middle Ages with virtually no knowledge of life beyond the village walls. I glanced at Daria's motionless head, and wondered if she was pretending to sleep and had heard our conversation.

After that day in Carcasonne, Daria stopped hanging out with us as much. She told us she spent a lot of time at the main campus of the university, in the new, high-rise section of the city, a place where I never felt comfortable, although I'm not sure she did either because every time I saw her she had a lost, uncomfortable expression. To this day, I don't know why she didn't leave Toulouse.

Three of *Les Quatres Esprits* became poorer and poorer as we reached the end of money from home. Matthew, though, had the guts to take weekly trips on his Eurail pass to Paris to play his saxophone in the subway stations. He always came back and treated the rest of us to pastries, allowing us to indulge our fantasies about the masterpieces of baking we passed every day. One day, as we gobbled Matthew's pastries on the street corner, not even waiting to carry them away from the patisserie, Daria came up with her knapsack over one shoulder.

"Just the guys I've been looking for," she said. "I met this guy Martin from the university who comes from a small town in the Pyrénées. He's invited all of us to the mountains for skiing this weekend. He'll drive us to his parents' house Friday afternoon. Whatcha say?"

Dave, who was from Colorado, and Aaron, from Vermont, were expert skiers and didn't even let Daria finish her invitation before accepting. Matthew, I knew, could ski well, too—we had skied together many times at school. But skiing in New Hampshire could not compare to skiing in the Pyrénées, mountains almost as magnificent as the Alps. My heart beat so rapidly that I blurted out, "How can we refuse? It's fantastic!"

"Good." Daria winked awkwardly. "Then you owe me one."

Late Friday afternoon, we all crammed into Martin's Citroen. I had been disappointed with French men, finding them not half as good-looking as people claimed. However, Martin was the exception. While he clearly did not wash his hair as often as an American, he kept it neat, and his jawbone had angles that weakened my knees. When he spoke, his voice had a softness that seduced me—he could have threatened to kill me and I would have loved listening to him. It was obvious that he and Daria had an attachment. She sat next to him and stroked his arm as she talked.

The village Martin grew up in nestled in a valley between enormous mountains. Smoke snaked out of the chimneys and vanished into the thin air above. As we descended to the village from the mountain pass, I thought that it seemed as removed from contemporary times as Carcasonne had. The small, weathered stucco and wood-beam houses crowded the road, hugging it as if the people who built them feared being cut off from escape. The streets, probably four in all, were narrow dirt ways, wide enough for a single car. Every three or four houses, the road widened enough for a car to pull aside until the way was clear. Martin turned into a short driveway between two houses, pulled the emergency brake, and shut off the engine.

"We're here," he said.

Carefully, I stepped out of the car. Even here in the valley, the ground sloped dangerously. I picked my way over the snow and ice and followed the others into the small house. Inside, the house smelled of rich wine sauce and wood smoke. Martin's mother rushed to him with her hands in her apron, gave her son two kisses on each cheek, then listened solemnly as Martin introduced us.

"Come in, come in," Madame Giron told us. "Dinner will be ready in an hour."

I could barely understand Madame Giron's heavily weighted, almost Spanish, accent, but I caught enough to know that Daria and I were expected to sleep in the loft overlooking the main room where evidently everything from eating to card playing took place, while the guys slept by the fireplace. I slung my knapsack over my shoulder. Hand over hand, I climbed the wooden ladder up to the loft with Daria close behind. The space was almost pyramidal from the shape of the roof. The Girons had pressed loose hay, as insulation, along the edges where the roof met the platform floor, but I could still feel the wind coming through the roof.

Daria kicked a handful of stray hay back into the eaves.

I unrolled the two featherbeds, and divided the blankets between us. "Put your blankets on the bed now, so it won't be too cold when it's time to go to sleep."

"We'll freeze to death."

I laughed. "No, we won't. And it'll make a good story to tell when we get back to the States. Come on. If you don't take risks, you'll miss half the fun."

By the time we climbed back down, Martin's grandfather, aunt, uncle, and two teenage cousins, a boy and a girl, had arrived. From what I could tell, the extended family ate at Martin's house every night. The grandfather, a right arm amputee from World War II, sat in a chair by the fire; his daughter covered him with a thick blanket which he angrily shook away. "So," he said to me, "are Americans as crazy as they say?"

I grinned. "We sleep hanging upside down by day and by night suck the blood out of Europeans."

He laughed: a crackly, brittle laugh. He patted the stool next to him for me to sit on. Out of the corner of my eye, I saw Daria slip past us to where the guys stood. "You speak French well," he said. "Is it hard for you to understand me?"

"A little." I sat on the stool. "I'm not used to the accent."

"Then listen to this." With mischievousness in his eye, he began to speak sounds that sounded like neither French, nor Spanish, nor any other language I had heard. I must have looked completely bewildered because he laughed heartily and pointed with his one hand to my face. "That's *la langue d'oc*. Have you heard of it?"

Now no one could have dragged me away from the old man. I pulled my stool closer. "Sure. I've heard about it. It's the language that didn't win out."

"Very good. Ancient France was divided into two cultures, each speaking a different language: the north spoke *la langue d'oïl*, the south, *la langue d'oc*. Modern French derived from the more politically powerful *langue d'oïl*, but in this region, until my generation, they spoke *la langue d'oc*. My parents taught it to me, but, too bad for them, my children refused to learn. They understand some, but *their* children . . ." He puffed air out from under his lips as only the French could do. "They don't know any of it. It's a lost language." He pointed a bony finger at me. "I don't often hear an American speaking French with a Toulousien accent."

Martin came up from behind us and draped his arm over his grandfather's shoulder. "You don't often hear Americans, Grandpa."

"True, true! This is a charming young lady you brought home, Martin. I will light a candle for her tomorrow morning at Mass."

"Thank you," I said, feeling suddenly awkward.

"Do you play bridge?" the old man asked.

"I'm sorry. No."

He patted my hand. His skin felt dry and cool. "They can't all be perfect."

"Come on, Grandpa," Martin said. "I'd like you to meet Daria."

As Martin introduced her, Daria hung back a little, her eyes glancing secretly at the folded sleeve where the old man's arm should have been. When she spoke, her grammar faltered. Embarrassed for her, I went into the kitchen to help Madame Giron.

The Girons fed us an enormous dinner of potato and leek *potage*; "winter" salad made from dandelion greens, watercress, and endive; roast dove; whipped turnip and potato; rabbit in a thick, red wine sauce; three different kinds of cheeses; apples; and enough different wines to frighten me about the inevitability of climbing the ladder to my featherbed. Familiar with typical French dinners, which were always served in courses but not usually in so many, I knew that our visit meant a lot to Martin's family. I made an effort to eat and drink everything served to me, as did Matthew, Dave, and Aaron, but Daria poked unhappily at her food.

"What is the matter?" Madame Giron asked her. "Are you ill?"

Daria flashed a falsely bright smile. "No. I'm fine, thank you."

Even Dave, who had been talking rapidly and without much concern about grammar, had nothing to say. Martin looked down at his hands.

Monsieur Giron looked at her through his spectacles and down the length of his nose. "You need some extra kilos," he told her. "You should eat."

Familiar with this French strategy (the family I had stayed with had unbeknownst to me set a goal, and had succeeded, to fatten me up two kilos by the time I finished the semester), and knowing how Daria would not bow to it, I said, "Americans don't eat as well as the French. We have to build up our constitutions. Daria has not been in France as long as the rest of us."

Madame Giron nodded, but I could tell that she thought Daria simply did not like her food.

As we readied for bed up in the loft, I hissed to Daria in English, "Madame Giron went through a lot of effort to fix us a special dinner."

"Well, then, she should have asked what we like. There's no way in hell I'm going to eat doves and rabbits. They're pets, for Christ sake. What next? Kitten in cream sauce? And that salad. It was a plate full of weeds."

I slipped under the heavy covers. "It's what they eat, Daria, and if you'd give it a chance, you'd find out that it's good."

Daria squeezed herself into a far corner to undress. "What do you care?"

"I don't want you to anger the gods of French cuisine. They might miss you and instead strike *me* with their celestial stockpot."

She sank onto her bed. "God, I hope I didn't make a bad impression."

I rolled over onto my side and wondered why I had covered for her at dinner. I decided that, even with her awkwardness and lack of manners, Daria had charmed me —I wanted her to succeed in her quest to conquer France. But we would never be friends, and as I slipped into a deep, alcohol-induced sleep, I wished that I had not claimed the death of the French theater so we would have never met.

In the morning, we arrived at the ski area. The mountains lay close and steep against one another, a dramatic crumpling of earth that rose like ancient gods into the heavens. Between them, the lodge lay low and flat, roughhewn and no frills, as if acknowledging that no human structure could compete with the force of the mountains. As we walked in to rent our skis, I noticed that skiers couldn't buy much more than drinks and goggles there and was instantly thankful that Martin's mother had packed us a full lunch, something I had viewed that morning as a nice gesture, not a necessity.

As we got into our gear, Daria asked, "Where's the beginner slope?"

Martin pointed to a short incline that could have been used for sledding. "There." Small children, some as young as two and few as old as six, swarmed all over the hill, leaving the rope tow and dashing down the slope.

"Not the *baby* slope. The beginner slope." Daria seemed to think that she had selected the wrong French words to convey her meaning.

Martin laughed, but his voice was taut with irritation. "You learn to ski on that hill, and then you go up there and ski." He pointed to the chair lift.

Aaron pulled his new goggles on over his glasses. "If you want, Daria, I'll ski with you."

She waved him off. "Naw. I'll practice here for a while to make sure I remember everything, then I'll go up. Thanks, though."

As the guys headed off to the chair lifts, I leaned into Daria. "If you can't ski, why did you come?"

"I can ski a little. I've gone on five or six trips to the Poconos." She lowered her voice, looked around. "To tell you the truth, Martin's the first hot guy I've met here, and I couldn't say no. Hell, I'll make snow angels if I have to."

I laughed. "I wouldn't say no myself, even if I had *never* been on skis. You'll be all right?"

"Sure. See you at lunch."

By the time I reached the chair lift, the other three had already gone up. I entered the chair lift by myself and as I rose higher and higher, the ground dropping steeply away and the chair lift seeming to rise forever, I realized that no skiing I had done before would compare to this. At the top of the mountain, a man in dark clothes and goggles made sure everyone successfully exited. I stood a few feet from the lifts to decide which trail to pick. The sun shone brilliantly off the snow, making it difficult to judge the angles of inclines, but clearly they were steep and thick with packed powder. I saw five markers, three black and two red, and laughed. It was a good thing Daria had decided to practice at the base of the mountain since there was not room for intermediates here, at least, not easy room. I selected one of the red trails, pushed off with my poles, and shot down into the brilliance, sailing over moguls, and turning sharply. My heart lurched as I quickly discovered that not only was the trail unmarked but that it narrowed quickly, dropping off twenty or thirty feet on each side, forcing me to zigzag more tightly than I ever had. Vaguely, I saw other skiers making different choices, and wondered anxiously if I was still following the trails. When I sped down the final part of the run, more than half an hour had passed since I had begun. I had never skied such a long run in my life. I stopped in an exuberant spray of powder. Matthew was there waiting for me.

"Can you believe it?" he asked. "I went down an expert trail with Martin, Aaron, and Dave, and I thought I was going to die up there. What *fucking* skiing!"

I tried to catch my breath. "Free fall."

Matthew grinned. "Ready for another run?"

"You bet!"

All morning long we skied. At one-thirty, we all met inside the lodge. We unpacked our lunch and spread it over the table: bread, cheeses, ham, apples and oranges, yogurt, and six large chocolate bars. I thought I would never get enough to fill my stomach.

"After lunch, I'm going up with you guys," Daria said.

"I don't know if that's such a good idea," Matthew told her.

"If it gets too tough, I can always take off my skis and walk."

"Maybe Martin had better watch you on the beginner slope to see if you're ready," I told her.

"Would you?" Daria asked him.

Reluctantly Martin agreed. As we left the lodge, I saw that it had become overcast in that short period of time and light flurries swirled around, the weather now closer to the New England conditions I knew best. I told Matthew to wait up while I bought goggles—my sunglasses would only make skiing harder with the cloudy weather. By the time we made it back to the lifts, Daria and Martin had gotten on three or four cars ahead of us. Daria twisted to wave to us.

I laughed. "She's going to pee in her pants."

"At least she's got Martin with her," Matthew said. He flexed his boots so that his skis went up and down, up and down. "You should see him ski." A minute later, he said, "It's snowing pretty hard."

On cue, the winds howled and rattled the lift. Snow whipped up around us in a stinging swirl. Instantly, my legs went cold. We sat in silence as the cables lifted us higher and higher. By the time we were halfway up the mountain, the skies had blackened as I had seen only in thunderstorms.

"We're rocking an awful lot," I said.

"Let's just pray that the French have good safety standards for these things."

A minute later, the lift stopped. We sat suspended over a deep valley, still rocking. My cheeks hurt from the cold and the wind-hurled snow that blew almost horizontally into us. I turned around. With a small panic, I saw that I could no longer make out the base station. "I've never seen weather like this move in so fast."

"It's a good thing Martin's grandfather lit a candle for you this morning," Matthew said. "I'm going to stick to you like glue."

"Fine with me."

The chair lurched forward, making jerky progress towards the top. Several times on the way up, we stopped, nervously waited, started up again. By the time we reached the top, I couldn't see much more than a few feet in front of me.

"Can we ride back down?" I shouted to the man.

He shook his head. "The lift is shut down. We have two more cars, then that's it. Too windy."

I shook my head, slapped Matthew on the back. "We're on our own. Let's keep within sight of each other." I pointed to a trail. "Let's go down that one. We've done it more times than the other. Remember the drop-offs."

Cautiously, we made our way down the slope, often turning our skis slightly uphill to slow us down, even snow-plowing during large parts of the run where we knew the land gave way to rocky cliffs. We couldn't see the trees until we were almost on top of them. The moguls took us by surprise so many times that we fell and skied, fell and skied. As I picked myself up after a spill, I shouted, "How are we going to find our way out of this?"

"As long as we keep going down, we'll get there."

After what seemed like hours, the land under my feet changed, felt more gentle, and I didn't come up to any trees. I knew we had made it. We skied the rest straight down to the lodge. At the bottom, we hugged, clung to each other, not wanting to let go.

"Come on," I said finally. "Let's get into the lodge to warm up."

Inside, Aaron, Dave, and Martin sat at a table near the fire, their coats stripped off, their bare feet extended towards the fire. A few other people relaxed by the fire, warming hands and feet, but most had already left.

Aaron saw us and leaped to his feet. "There you are!"

"Where's Daria?"

"Coming soon, we hope."

"What? She's up there by *herself*?" I pointed to Martin. "She was supposed to be skiing with you."

"When we got to the top, I knew it would be the last run for the day. I wanted to make it a good one, and Daria wasn't ready for it. I told her to take one of the other trails."

I shouted in English. "You idiot! She can't ski. She's from goddamn Kentucky!"

His face clouded with a panicked confusion—he did not understand what I meant, but he could tell it was significant. "I thought it was time for her to try the real trails. She said she'd walk if she had to. I didn't know there would be a blizzard."

"But you did when you got to the top! Jesus! We'd better tell the ski patrol."

They waited fifteen minutes to see if Daria would come down by herself before sending out a rescue patrol. In the lodge, none of us could get warm.

"I can't stand this," I said finally, pulling on my coats and boots. "I'm going out to see if I can find her."

I stood at the bottom where the two red slopes joined, squinting into the gray white of the blizzard, and I cursed Daria for trying to impress Martin with her courage, which I was sure was what had happened. I wondered how long it would take to walk down the run, find one's blind way through the deep snow to safety. I heard the clump, clump of boots behind me. I turned to see Aaron walking towards me.

"I can't believe this," I told him as we stood next to each other trying to see through the snow. Aaron reached out with his gloved hand and held mine in his. We stood there, numb from the cold, waiting for a bit of color to break through the gray.

Two skiers wearing orange appeared out of the dense snow at the end of the run. A few minutes later, two more rescuers appeared, conferred a few feet from us, but we could not hear them through the wind. Aaron squeezed my hand as we stood waiting.

Finally, one of the men came over to us. "Are you the Americans?"

"Yes," Aaron said.

"We haven't found the woman yet. Are you sure she didn't go home without you?"

I shook my head. "She had no way to leave."

"With a man, perhaps?"

"No. Her boyfriend is in the lodge."

"I'm sorry, but we'll have to wait until the morning. There's no visibility, and it will be getting dark soon." He turned to leave.

Aaron lunged for his arm, almost spinning the man around from the force of the gesture. "Isn't there anything we can do?"

The man thought for a moment. His eyes were invisible behind his goggles. "Pray."

By that time, we could not leave the lodge because of the weather. In a way, I was relieved since no one could tell us to go home and wait. We talked about Daria as if she were our best friend and a heroine, someone who could make it out of a blizzard with a smile and a good story. In my thoughts, I scolded Daria for fearing Martin's grandfather and his deformity, otherwise she might have joined our conversation long enough for him to light a candle for her. And for angering those stupid French gods of cuisine. I cursed her for staying in Toulouse when she was supposed to be seeing the rest of Europe, and for trying to impress Martin. I had made fun of her, had been jealous of her, and hated the way she moved about the world, and still I prayed for her.

They found her the next morning up against a six-foot-high rock she had evidently skied off. By that time she was nothing more than a bizarre contour to the land, snow-covered and frozen to death, sparkling in the glitter of a clear sun. One rescuer said it looked like she had broken a leg in the short fall and could not make it by herself to the bottom. Around noon, they lowered her body down in a stretcher that reminded me of a snowshoe, its cargo wrapped in red vinyl. Dave and I were the only ones who left the warmth of the lodge to watch the progress of Daria toward, finally, the bottom of the mountain.

"I really thought she'd be all right," Dave said. In the brilliant sunshine, he appeared calm and steady, though his voice sounded strained.

"I can't believe it." I bit my lip to keep from crying. I had never known anyone my age who had died. The finite span of life had never seemed as real or as mysterious as it did that moment. I tried to grasp what Daria's death meant, but instead the blankness inside me explained nothing. "We don't even know who to contact."

"I'll look through her things when we get back. We can call the consulate with her passport number and they'll do the rest."

Dave always seemed to know procedure. I thought, he'd make a great politician, and Daria will never get to be a country singer. I turned from

Dave. I hated this sadness and this inexplicable situation of mourning someone I never even wanted to be my friend. I shouldn't have known her, I thought, I shouldn't have this chunk taken out of me. Still, it was there, and I nurtured it, for Daria's sake.

We watched as they loaded the strange bundle into the back of an ambulance. I refused to let myself cry in front of the stoic Dave and instead turned to go back into the lodge. As the snow squeaked under my boots, I imagined Daria's last moments leaning against the rock that had undone her, singing to herself in her crystalline voice until the cold silenced her in this country that never quite liked her.

Back in Toulouse, having disposed of our connection to Daria at the consulate, we tried to piece together our previous lives. I slept with the lights on, suddenly believing in ghosts. When I crossed La Place du Capitole, I walked with my eyes downcast. In the evenings, we continued to invite our French friends to the apartment, but it seemed to me that we argued less strenuously and with more sadness. Aaron developed the habit of simply walking out of the room in midsentence and disappearing into the shadowy streets of the city. One night, curious, I followed him down the single-file sidewalks to the river, over the Pont Neuf, to the flat, grassy bank below the street. As Aaron disappeared under the bridge, I heard him cry out. Part of me wanted to go to him and hold his hand, as we had that day waiting for Daria at the base of the mountain, but another part of me held back and left him to the privacy of his grief. Any day now, I knew, we would surrender and leave Toulouse early in a futile effort to forget what we had witnessed.

Life as a Dragon

Ming-li woke to steely, cold gray. She thought of weathered metal, old asphalt, the façade of her apartment building back in Taipei. Warner had told her about snow here in America, where it drifted hungrily against cars and doorways, and Ming-li wondered if this, her first day here, she would have to struggle against the savagery of winter. Although she had tasted the fleeting coldness of snow, she had never scooped it up in big, icy fistfuls to throw it back at the sky. With her imagination, she created the yin-yang of this. In one version, she tossed feather-light crystals into the air and watched them catch the sun one at a time, flitter down, spinning on their gravitational axes, magical mirrors reflecting the magnificence of the day. In the other, however, the cold snatched at her throat, and the snow fell back to earth as an icy rock. In this last version, she started to die that very moment, one painful cell at a time.

"Warner," she said in a whisper that even then sounded too loud. "I'm getting up."

He groaned and tried to catch her with a sleepy, amber-haired arm. "Come back to bed, Ming-li."

"Today is the day," she told him. "I don't want to be lazy."

He smiled with his eyes closed. "It doesn't matter whether they like you or not. We're still married."

"In the eyes of my family, but not yours." His family had insisted on a marriage "in the eyes of God." They had begun preparations even before Ming-li and Warner's plane had landed on American soil.

And later in the day when the first flakes began to fall, Ming-li was in a store outside of Princeton with her new mother- and sisters-in-law. Exhausted, her nights now days, Ming-li could hardly distinguish among

Warner's sisters. They looked like edited copies of the mother: a smaller nose here, a rounder chin there, bigger bones, wider eyes, thinner hips. The sisters were excitable, talkative, and whenever Ming-li felt as though her head would split like a ripe melon from all the noise, her mother-in-law stepped between Ming-li and them, her back solid and straight, broad like a lacquered screen. "Girls," her mother-in-law said, and her daughters instantly quieted. But they would soon rebuild into their previous frenzy.

The four women touched Ming-li lightly. They carried great armfuls of gauzy white fabric that rustled like dead leaves as they moved. Ming-li looked in the mirror at the first dress she tried on. The bows and lace on the gown dwarfed her small face. The design was too intricate, too elaborate, too heavy, for the simplicity she strove for in her life.

"I don't feel comfortable in this," she said, trying out the boldness Warner had told her she would need in this country.

"This is what we wear when we get married in America," Jill, the youngest and still a teenager, told her.

Sandra touched her elbow with a warm hand. "You look beautiful. You'll get used to it."

Ming-li regarded them with caution. Perhaps Warner had not told them that she had been married in Taipei dressed in a white and airy Western gown. (Her mother-in-law had insisted that Ming-li be married here in new clothes, perhaps out of fear of what she had worn for the Chinese wedding.) They had not seen the photographs, still undeveloped, of her and Warner at the Lin An Tai house, posing in the milky sunshine. Having studied American culture for years at the university, she knew their ways as well as any outsider could. Perhaps they wanted to believe in her ignorance. "It's only that I don't want to make a hasty decision."

They nodded, pleased. Her new mother, in her navy skirt, took Ming-li by the hands to lead her back into the dressing room. "Try on something else. We'll find something for you. You're right—no use rushing into something and then regretting it."

Had Ming-li and Warner rushed into marriage the way a rabbit springs from a meadow? Ming-li thought not. They explored their love for each other like blinded creatures eager for the delicacies of the other senses. The light touch of fingertips, intimate questions, inhaling the richness of each other's scent, a shared sigh. Yes, she thought, they were cautious mice in the dark, only too aware of the huge danger lurking behind their two cultures. The danger at the moment was white fabric draped over generations of traditions and hopes.

At night Ming-li and Warner sat on the window sill, bare soles pressed together, and they watched the sifting of snow from the heavens. Definite shapes became vague as the snow tried to swallow the identities of objects.

"It wasn't too bad, was it?" Warner finally asked. They both knew he meant his mother and sisters.

Ming-li could feel against her feet the pressure of his holding his breath. "No. It wasn't. I'm learning how to tame them."

Warner laughed, shook his closely cropped head. "They can be like tigers, can't they? Imagine me—one son among three daughters."

But Ming-li had returned to the snow with thoughts that said, no, not tigers but dragons. And not the fiercely regal Chinese dragons but Western ones, the kind that incinerated entire villages and ate knights in ferocious, cracking bites. She had read the European fairy tales voraciously and had even taught them to her students, in simplified versions, to demonstrate how Westerners saw the world. These Americans had the ferocity and the magnanimity only found among those with true, unbound power. They frightened her with their speed and their sweeping way of moving through the streets.

Warner's eyes narrowed in the dim light. "What is it, Ming? If you miss Taipei, we'll find a way to go back. I can work for a different company."

Ming-li brushed a wisp of stray hair from her face. "No," she said, "I will stay."

In Taipei, people awoke early, often before dawn. When the sun did rise, it shone with a watery light through all the humidity and air pollution so that the days rarely seemed crystal-bright. And so, when Ming-li awoke to the brilliantly reflected light off the new snow, she, for a moment, believed that in her sleep she had achieved nirvana. She had never before seen a day so bright that she could not even avert her eyes from the sun to the ground, which seemed to have a cold fire of its own. Warner left for work, but he promised he would have a snowball fight with her that evening.

She did not understand the importance of making snowballs and why Warner insisted that they frolic like children; however, she could hear the deeply rooted emotion in his voice when he spoke of it. She knew these snowballs must be a key to his soul.

Due to the weather, her mother-in-law called to cancel their shopping plans. With relief, Ming-li slipped into her new winter jacket and mittens. She wanted to walk through the snow, kick it high, discover which version of her imagined snow would prove to be true. But as she stepped briskly into the white fluff, her feet sprouted wings that lifted her up and smashed her back onto the sidewalk. The pain sprang from her tailbone up through her spine. The first few people stared at her, almost seemed to smile at her public humiliation, continued on their busy ways. Then a woman, big and richly brown, offered her gloved hand.

"You okay?" she asked Ming-li.

Ming-li nodded, though she was not at all sure. She stared into the woman's face—never before had she been so close to such dark skin, never before had she seen such a strong, warm smile. She took the hand and felt herself being hoisted by an enormous strength that almost knocked her back into the snow. "Thank you," Ming-li said. "I've never walked in snow."

"What?" the woman almost roared. "Well, I'll have to give you a few lessons."

Ming-li and Karen Anderson had coffee together in a small gourmet shop as if Karen had nowhere else to go and had intended all along to lift a woman from the sidewalk and carry her to breakfast. Squarely on a rickety chair, Karen told too much of her life as the steam rose up off her cup and cast thin, almost-invisible shadows across her face. Karen surprised Ming-li because Ming-li believed deep-down that everybody had a counterpart in each culture, that you only had to look to find people who could fill the roles of the people you knew well. But Ming-li had never before met someone like Karen, who talked loudly about the most embarrassing subjects, who had tremendous physical strength, and who seemed to care very much that Ming-li had only been in the country for two days. With Karen, Ming-li began to believe that she could survive this new place.

Warner seemed happy that Ming-li had already made a friend. "You see," he said that evening as he packed a snowball tightly with his gloves, "everyone wants to like you." With a quick snap of his arm, he hurled the snowball through the night.

The snowball hit her thigh with a sound whack. Stunned, Ming-li looked down at her leg, where it stung with both the hot and the cold of an infant bruise.

"Oh, my God! Did I hurt you?" Warner ran across the snow without losing his footing. He seemed like a spirit coming at her.

"I'm fine." She rubbed her thigh. "I didn't think it would hurt."

He brought her face towards his face and kissed her there, outside, in full view of the world, with a love that she could hear in his lungs. When he drew away, she swiftly reached inside his coat and shirt and stuffed a snowball there, against his skin. Laughingly she stumbled away with the sense that this painfully beautiful snow contained all the happiness and sorrow of this country. Warner chased after her until he caught her.

As the days passed, Ming-li studied the people and the land, because she wanted to slip in among them without their realizing. She missed the quickly rising hills around Taipei and the delicious aromas of dishes she knew well, but this was now her home. She settled for gentle hills and pizza and french fries and people who didn't know how to move down a crowded sidewalk without touching anyone. In Taiwan, Ming-li had rarely left the city, and so she was used to loud, roaring sounds rattling her all day. But in Princeton there was so much quiet that she feared that she breathed too loudly. The snow made the air even more silent and muffled, as though some great secret were being kept. Three days a week, Ming-li crossed the street to meet Karen and the women Karen brought to meet her, and the cars stopped for her without her having to step in front of them. In this way, America seemed more gentle than Taiwan. The people less aggressive. But she soon learned this generosity was false. Karen had left her purse for five minutes in the coffee house only to return to find that her wallet had been stolen.

"In Princeton!" Karen had said, turning her face away as the first tear slipped down her cheek. "Can you believe that?"

And Warner told her that she must not walk alone at night. He did not have to specify what horrible fate might befall her because her imagination was vivid enough. "It doesn't happen often in Princeton, " he told her. "But it happens."

"You can't trust men," Karen told her. "They only look out for themselves."

"I can trust Warner," Ming-li told Karen.

When Ming-li told her mother-in-law that she wanted Karen invited to the wedding, her mother-in-law said, "You can't trust those black people. Most of them steal when you aren't looking. I know it sounds horrible, but it's true."

Ming-li remembered in the flutter of her heart the kindness with which Karen had picked her out of the snow. "I can trust Karen," she said. Her mother-in-law made her wonder what her husband's family thought about the honesty of her color of skin.

"Trust me," Warner told her when he chose the menu and the music for the wedding feast.

In God We Trust, Ming-li read on the back of a coin, wondering what all the concern was about trust. You could love someone enough to trust him most of the time, but this love would also reveal the precise time when you could *not* trust him. Ming-li believed that nothing in the world was absolute. This land of people who rushed by at frenetic speed proved that. Sometimes they stopped. Sometimes they did not. Sometimes they hated each other, sometimes they fell in love. And Ming-li could never guess what would happen next.

Weeks later, Warner's parents decided that the wedding was costing too much. They wanted cuts, immediate and deep. Ming-li was perplexed. Surely even Americans cared about their image.

"We weren't the ones who wanted another wedding," Warner sputtered over the phone. "We got married in Taiwan. But you *promised* we could have it our way." After he got off the phone, his face was the color of the ice that licked the edges of the snow still on the ground.

"Respect your parents' wishes," Ming-li said in an English that lilted like Mandarin.

"They want us to do it exactly their way," Warner told her. "Or they won't pay." He slumped into a chair. "They've made up their minds. They never back down once that happens."

Ming-li studied him. She saw in his expression that "their way" meant no Karen, none of her new friends, not the roast duck that Warner had wanted on their wedding day, not, perhaps, the red, lucky-colored gowns Ming-li had chosen for her bridesmaids, perhaps not even Warner's friends whom he had known since childhood and who, according to his parents, had never made good. Her own father had spared no expense when planning the extravagant wedding feast they had offered their guests. Warner might be embarrassed for his family to offer less. He had made this second wedding his snowball fight, his moment of fun, and for some reason he had wanted her to enjoy it more than she had their Chinese wedding. He said he wanted her to like America. He wanted her first big memory of her new country to be warm and gigantic and full of high, happy noise.

"I know something about saving face," she told Warner quietly. She called her mother-in-law. "Hello," she said. "How are you today?" They went through the pleasantries that Ming-li now knew so well. "You know," Ming-li said after a while, "I'm learning that sometimes American women are much stronger than the men."

Her mother-in-law laughed. Her voice sounded like the enthusiastic run of melted snow down the gutters. "We let them *think* they're in charge."

Ming-li laughed lightly. Warner hovered over her, about to interrupt, but she held up a single, straightened finger to silence him. Her heart beat like that of a dying bird, but she would not allow Warner and his mother to sense it. "You're like the president of the family. I'm very honored that you have given so much of your time to make our wedding a success."

"It's my pleasure, Ming-li."

"Yes, but it must be a burden. My father saved his whole lifetime for my wedding, and even then he had to borrow money to pay for such an extravagant feast. He wanted us to be happy, though, and in Taipei, it is considered bad luck if either the bride or the groom is unhappy on their wedding day. They must celebrate with their friends and eat their favorite foods. Warner says it's the same here. That's why I know that you're making enormous sacrifices for our lifetime of happiness."

When her mother-in-law spoke, Ming-li could hear the tears choking her voice. "We want you two to be happy on your wedding day."

"And we will be," Ming-li told her. "Because you're in charge of the wedding. I don't know anyone I would trust more."

Her mother-in-law gave a deep, shuddering sigh. "Thank you, Ming-li. You're such a gentle girl. I'm very lucky to be gaining such a good daughter."

After she had hung up, Warner wrapped his arms around her waist. "That was some acting job."

She kissed him. "I think we'll have a wedding of duck and red gowns."

He laughed. "You'll make a good American—and you'll make good Chinese out of us."

By the time the second snow of the winter arrived, Ming-li knew how to walk on ice without much of a slip, how to sweeten her voice to just the right pitch, how to slip her tail without detection around the waist of an enemy. She took pride in the fact that, like a good Chinese, she never once drew blood.

When the album from the American wedding arrived, Ming-li sat on the sofa with the heavy weight of the pictures pressing into her lap. She opened the cover, the new leather crackling at the binding, and found herself face to face with a huge satin print of the wedding party. Their hands clasped under the sprays of red and yellow flowers, her scarlet-clad sisters-in-law surrounded the bride and groom. The ushers, Warner's friends, all stood jauntily in their tuxedos—one red bow tie had already fallen askew. Smiling, Ming-li lightly touched her own image with Warner as they stood side by side, their fingers intertwined. Warner wore an easy smile and leaned, just slightly, toward her. Dressed in a simple white satin and lace gown, Ming-li the bride looked boldly at the photographer without a hint of the fluttering stomach she had fought that day.

Down Under Silver Lake

In March, I think that spring will never come. The snow is crusted and holds me up if I'm careful. I am lighter than air, picking my way six inches off the ground. If the crust gives way, I think, I will die. Suddenly, it does, and I trip, falling to my knees. With thick-gloved fingers, I yank down the zipper of my jacket and hold my hand to my chest, feeling for the faint pressure of a heartbeat.

My mother calls out from the house and asks what I think I'm doing.

I zip up my ski jacket. "Nothing." Reluctantly, I stand and brush the snow off my kneecaps.

At school, they call me Tammy Big Tits. My mother says it's because the other girls haven't fully developed. I sneak looks at my mother when she dresses in her bedroom. Hers hang like stockings filled with sand, just like mine.

If I concentrate hard enough, my breasts will disappear. It's like walking on snow.

The boys always try to touch them. They think I want them to. Harriet says I can have any boy I want; she wants them all. She keeps track inside her notebook of who she wants to kiss. After school, she stands with her books balanced on one hip, praying that someone will ask her out. Let her have Timothy Cremmins who kissed me and then went straight for my shirt. I tell her she should be glad her breasts are still like tiny pyramids. My brother Ed told me that the Egyptian Pyramids are one of the Seven Wonders of the World.

I go inside. The warmth from the kitchen blasts me as I open the door, and, for a moment, I'm walking onto a beach. By the stove, my mother glances up at me. The steam from cooking has loosened the curls around her face so that her hair looks longer in the front. This morning, I watched her carefully comb her hair into satiny ribbons to wind around the white curlers. We waited together for the red dots on the end to turn brown. "You look beautiful," I said with my chin on her shoulder, gazing into her mirror at our two reflections. Now, she looks tired, like she did the morning my father left.

My brother Ed sits at the table, his feet propped up on a chair. He reads the paper. I know he has already read it once, but now, because he's bored, he's paying more attention, counting off the minutes until dinner.

I throw my coat on a chair when my mother isn't looking. My sneakers are wet, and I balance on one leg, squeezing the end of my right sneaker to warm my toes. I should take them off, but then my mother will make me go upstairs to get another pair, and I don't want to move. I stick my head under Ed's paper and wiggle my way into his lap.

"Hey!" he says.

I used to lay awake nights, and pretend that Ed wasn't my brother. We'd fall in love and he'd build us a cabin in the woods to protect me. The flowers on my wallpaper looked like a hundred eyes in the dark, but I wasn't scared. Once, I told Harriet about my dreams, and she said it was sick, I don't know why. I mean, we didn't really fall in love—it was all pretend.

I read with Ed for a while. The paper crinkles in his hands. I try to guess what he's reading, but I can't. His eyes are hidden behind his glasses; I see only the reflection of words. I imagine peering inside his head and seeing only black and white words lined up like soldiers. That's the only thing wrong with him. He doesn't like pictures, only words.

He turns the page, smiles at me, and says to my mother, "You should move south."

He doesn't live at home anymore. No ones does except my mother and me. Ed is so much older than he almost doesn't seem like a brother. I'm old enough now to know I was an accident. At first, I was depressed, but then I didn't think it was so bad because I wouldn't be here if they hadn't made a mistake.

Ed lives all the way in Maryland. He's an engineer and he lives in a white apartment—we visited him once. He isn't allowed to paint the walls. My mother says he comes for more visits than the others because he isn't married. He says it's because he's got New England in his blood. I think it's because he feels guilty about us living here all alone.

"Look here," Ed says. "Some kid fell through the ice on Silver Lake."

"Some kid?" my mother snorts. "It was the Barlow boy."

I shiver. I wonder what it must have been like, hearing the crack resound like gunshot as it spread, and then feeling the ice break up under your feet, knowing that you couldn't run because there was nothing left underneath you. Maybe it happened all at once, so quickly that he didn't know until he felt the suffocating water. The cold would be sharp, excruciating, like snow on bare wrists, but it was his *whole body*.

"You're getting heavy," Ed says as he nudges me off his lap. He stomps his leg; it must have fallen asleep.

The warmth of his lap gone, I wrap my arms around my ribs. "Brrr," I say, but no one seems to hear.

I go into the den to check the wood stove. It's March, and the stove is going full-blast. I hear the hot breath of the flames. Holding the tongs in both hands, I open the door and the heat blinds me. I see, though, that the wood is nearly consumed.

"We need more wood," I call. If the fire goes out, I am going to die.

"Then get it," my mother tells me.

I don't move. I hold my palms up inches from the black stove, spreading my fingers like a fan. If I push up close, my hands will be seared, charred. I imagine the pain. I will feel like Henry Barlow.

When I first heard about the accident, I asked my mother why he didn't just swim to the top and get out. She said it was different down under the ice. You couldn't see where you had fallen in, and the cold made it hard to think, to move. Your heart stops cold, she said. "And if you do make it to the top, there's nothing to hang onto. The ice just breaks away in your hands. You can't help slipping back under."

"Do you think he was afraid?" I asked.

She looked at me strangely, intrigued that I would ask that. With her hands, she smoothed my hair so it lay flat against my head. "When you're dying," she said, "you're only afraid for an instant. Then it gets peaceful as you wait to be taken into God's hands."

I want to know if that's true, or if she said that because she knew it scared me to think about. I wonder if dying is like going to another world, and if God really has hands.

Ed comes in with wood for the stove. His arms are thick under his sweater. Grunting, he lowers the logs into the crate by the stove. When he sees how close my hands are, he takes them away.

I watch him as he slips the logs inside, and wonder about the hands of God holding me up.

Harriet and I go over to the lake. We can walk from my house, but her mother had to drop her off. Even though it's still cool, we wear shorts and T-shirts. My arms are covered with goosebumps, but if we stay still under the sun, they will disappear.

We lie on the beach and hope to get tan. Harriet wants tan lines on her arms so she can show everybody how dark she got. I would rather look like red clay. Red from top to bottom so that everyone at school thinks I've got Mohegan blood. I wear a tiny silver Thunderbird on my pinkie for good luck. The bird has a turquoise heart, and I imagine my own heart smooth and cold, shining under the light of the sun.

Every year the snow melts away the sand by the lake, and they back trucks in, dumping mounds of blinding white under the birch trees. Harriet saw them raking it smooth last weekend, and that's why we're here. We're hoping for summer to take us away, to carry us on silver wings. Today, though, it is not summer, only spring, although it's almost June. We spread out beds on the beach, molding pillows for our heads. We close our eyes, pretending that our arms sting from the sun. I drift to sleep dreaming that I'm falling through the sand.

I hear voices, and I sit up. Harriet is already standing, waving her arm so that it looks like putty, not bending at the elbow but everywhere. A sailboat full of boys pulls close to the shore; the deck rides almost even with the water. It is a Sunfish, like the one we own, only this one is red. The boys dangle their legs over the sides even though the water must feel like frozen needles. They have pulled up the dagger board so they can ride in closer, but the wind pushes them sidewise so they look like a giant red waterspider skittering on the surface.

"Hey!" Harriet yells.

"Hey!" two of them yell back.

I recognize one of them as Timothy Cremmins, and I'm disgusted. I squint against the sun to see who the others are. It's too early for tourists so I must know them.

"Shut up," I tell Harriet.

"No," she hisses back. She has just gotten her hair cut short so that she looks like a movie star. And her mother pierced her ears. The tiny diamond studs glisten like ice. My mother says they couldn't have cost that much, being so small and probably with a big black flaw in the center, but she won't let me pierce mine.

The boys push the dagger board back in and head back out. I think, good, they're leaving. But then they slam the rudder hard so that they come back at us, the wind now at their backs. Timothy yanks up the dagger board and they slide across the sandy bottom to shore. The boat comes to rest with a gritty sigh.

They pile out of the boat. I see that I know all but one. They kick sand at us.

"Hey, cut it out!" Harriet says as she throws a fistful back at them.

"What are you guys doing?" Timothy asks as he sits next to Harriet, eyeing me.

"What does it look like?" I ask, and lie back down on the sand. The sun isn't strong enough yet and the sand is as cool as summer water against my back. The strange boy stares at me. "What do you want?" I ask.

He averts his eyes, blushing. No one has bothered to introduce him, either they don't care or hope that we don't care. He looks kind of funny—his small ears stick out like dried apricots, but he has green eyes so clear I could drown in them. His white hands spread on the sand and then clench, clasping a handful, then losing it through the cracks in his fingers.

"I'm Tammy," I tell him. "This is Harriet."

"Hi," he says, forgetting to say his name.

"He's Mark," Timothy says. He sounds annoyed that he has to say the boy's name for him. Either that, or he's mad that I paid attention to Mark. "He's the new kid who moved into the Smiths' house."

"Oh." Neither Harriet nor I know what to say next. We laugh.

They stay for a while, Harriet flirting with them and me just lying there. One of them suggests that we go into the woods. I know what they want and I'm not budging, no way. Harriet knows what they want, too, and she leaps to her feet. You'll regret it, I think, just wait.

"Aren't you coming?" Mark asks me. I can't tell if he's hopeful or if he's just being polite. He half-crouches next to me.

"No," I say. I close my eyes and imagine him staring at me, thinking about touching my breasts, laughing at the way they tumble down to my armpits when I lie on my back. I imagine him staying there so long that his white face hardens into a birch tree, his fingers in the sand spreading into roots, sinking down so deep that they stretch out and become part of the lake bottom. His green eyes spill into the water like oil droplets, rippling circles of rainbows across the surface.

When I open my eyes, he is gone. So quickly, he disappeared. I sit up and I can't hear or see any of them, and I feel like the ground beneath me has melted into quicksand. Will Harriet allow them to reach under her shirt? All of them, or just one? Or will she fend them off, laughing, blinding them with the diamonds in her ears? I lie back down, and try to guess the answers.

A wind picks up and scoots across the melted ice in the lake, trying to freeze me, but I lie still, so still that someone might think I've died. I breathe in whispers.

I try to envision my father dead. I imagine him unshaven like he was Saturday nights, lying in white silk in an ebony box. His eyelids are shut like he's sleeping—or thinking—but the sockets are sunken as if someone, my mother, had plucked his eyes right out, leaving only the lids to pretend they're hiding something. This is how he should look.

When my father left us, my mother told me he had died. She poured milk on my cornflakes and said he had died during the night. At first, I believed her. You're so dumb sometimes, Harriet tells me.

I may be dumb, but I can see things that she can't see, things no one can see. I know what the boys want; they don't want her. They don't want me, either. They want themselves. When they kiss me, it's for them, not me.

I tire of the waning sun. Standing, I shake the grit from my clothes. I jiggle the bottom of my shorts. Some of the sand has worked its way into my underwear.

Silver Lake looks like a sea, with a new wind whipping up tiny white-caps, and the sailboats listing. The color is not silver, though, but pewter. Deep down, in the middle, there is another world, I can feel it.

I walk home alone, counting my steps until I lose count. My mother meets me at the front door. Her hands are white from ammonia; I smell her as I pass.

"Where's Harriet?" she asks.

"With some boys, " I tell her. I know Harriet will come to my house when she is finished because my mother has to drive her home.

She reaches out for my arm and spins me close to her. I smell ammonia and coffee and a funny dry scent I know is only hers. I relax against her soft warmth. "Of all you kids, you're the prettiest," she says. I don't know if she says that because I look just like her.

We stand like that for a while, not talking. Harriet walks in. She has red lines drawn across her face from the brambles. Her eyes are puffy as if she has been crying, but I can't tell. From the way she flexes and relaxes her hand, I guess that she tried to punch one of the boys. She doesn't even say hi, just watches us.

We separate, my mother drifting towards Harriet. She touches Harriet's cheek, but Harriet covers the filaments of blood with her fingers.

The air burns like cayenne pepper. Barefoot, I gingerly step over the sizzling stones in the driveway to get to the clothesline. I pick out two beach towels, one with a Mickey Mouse for Ed and one with a smiling rainbow for me. Inside, he and my mother argue about the money he wants to give her. It never gets this hot, I think, why doesn't it just cool down?

When I get back inside to where the dark air feels like water, Ed is gone.

"Where's Ed?" I ask.

"Changing," she says. The edge of a bill sticks out of her apron, and she slides it back in with her thumb.

I wish that she'd come to the lake with us. Once, she loved the beach; she stayed sprawled in the sun until her skin blistered and, days later, it would come off in white sheets. She's afraid that the other women will laugh at her because my father left us. I can't tell her that they laugh more when she doesn't come out.

Ed clonks down the stairs. He's wearing basketball sneakers that make him seem like a clown, they're so big on his bare feet. His legs are white with black curly hairs all over them, and I have to laugh.

"What's so funny?"

"Nothing. Come on," I say, tugging at his hand.

Outside, we load the Sunfish on top of Ed's car. We used to keep it down by the lake, but our neighbor's boat got stolen, and now we have to take it down every time we want to use it. Imagine that, my mother said, stealing on Silver Lake. Ed didn't seem surprised; he's used to cities. I'm only mad because I have to wait for Ed to visit before I can sail.

"We have to pick up Harriet," I tell him as I lay my towel over the seat.

Harriet waits for us by the side of the road. Her towel is slung over one shoulder, and she clutches a bright pink bag.

"Hey, Chicken Little," Ed says. He calls her that because she's so skinny.

Harriet and I sit facing each other in the back seat, our legs across the seat between us. We tell Ed about this girl we both hate, Monica, and how she has all the boys. Ed doesn't care about Monica. I hear him sing lightly under his breath. His lips don't move, as if someone else is throwing a voice into his mouth.

At the lake, we scramble to unlash the boat from the car. With Harriet and me up front and Ed in the back, we carry it down to the water on our shoulders. The sand gives way under my feet, and I almost trip, but I trudge forward, struggling with every step to keep my balance. The sand burns like fresh ashes.

The air is thick with the scent of coconut oil. Tourists and people I know crowd the beach; their sharp voices bounce off the lake's surface, sounding distant as if I'm enclosed in a bubble listening to them. We put the boat down by the shore, and I run to Ed, hug him, and then lightly punch Harriet in the arm. Harriet catches my wrist and we wrestle, laughing.

Ed gazes out at the sailboats as upright as perfectly driven stakes. He shields his eyes as if saluting them. "Not a breath of wind," he says. It's too hot for a good breeze.

Harriet and I don't care. We know that you can get the best tan out in the water. Without wind, the boat moves so slowly that one of us can swim alongside to cool down. The three of us put up the sail.

Ed decides to stay in for now. We find a good spot not far from the launch area. Ed snaps his towel and lets it settle on the sand. "Be careful," he says, kicking off his sneakers.

A couple of girls who know him from the old days come over with their hips swinging. They have flabby thighs with pockets of white fat, but they aren't bad looking. Harriet and I nudge each other, giggling, until Ed chases us to the boat. The girls think it's hysterical.

We wade out with the boat between us. The sand that washed from the beach sucks at my toes. Soon, I know, the sand will surrender to muck and to weeds that tickle like hungry insects. We hop aboard with me at the rudder and Harriet wrapping the mainsheet around her fist. The boat slides gently from the momentum of our first push, but then we slow. I take the mainsheet from Harriet and try to pick up a breeze.

It seems to take hours, but we float to the middle of the lake. Harriet lies on the deck so her body twists around the base of the mast. When I tack, she waits for the sail to swing over her head, and then she repositions herself on the other side. I don't care that I've done all the sailing. I stretch out my legs so the sun can catch them. I imagine them melting into silver puddles and spilling over into the lake. I rub the stone in my ring for good luck. The smooth turquoise dancing across my fingertips soothes me.

I watch Harriet and think that if a gust would suddenly fill the sails, she would topple into the water. I find it funny to imagine her rolling off the deck like a loose sausage, and I shake the boat to scare her. She clings to the mast, and, when she sees what I'm doing, she says, "Hey!"

I notice that she no longer wears her earrings. "Where are your diamonds?"

She grins at me. "I threw them out."

"Threw them out!" I could have saved them in a tiny box until my mother let me pierce my ears. "What did your mother say?"

"She doesn't know yet."

I wonder why she got rid of them. Did they hurt? Or did they blind too many boys? The lake sparkles like a thousand white diamonds, offering itself to me, but I scoop up a handful and catch nothing.

"Oh, no," Harriet says, pointing.

I twist to see behind me. A red Sunfish gains on us, and I know it's the boys. There are only two of them instead of five, and they paddle to catch up to us. I can't get enough wind in my sails to drift out of their reach.

They pull up alongside us. Timothy is at the rudder, though I know he's not a good sailor. He squints at us, his face scrunched up like a bulldog's. Mark lifts up the paddle and puts it in the hold. He sticks his leg out so his toes touch our boat. I am afraid we will collide, but his foot mesmerizes me: the perfect crescents of his toenails, the tensed arch, the patches of light brown hair glistening like amber glass. As we ease ahead a little, his foot slides towards me, slippery and wet. If he touches me, I will die. I head into the wind just a bit, not enough for Harriet to notice, but enough to keep the boats even.

"Get lost," Harriet moans.

I look at Mark. He wears a red bathing suit. Suddenly I'm embarrassed that he doesn't have anything else on, even though I've seen a thousand boys in bathing suits. The blush ignites in my cheeks and spreads like a brush fire over my whole face and neck. Fortunately, I'm already sunburned a brownish pink.

"Want to race?" Timothy asks.

"You've got to be kidding," I say. A light breeze has begun to pick up, but there's nothing in the air to race with. The heat suffocates me. I need to drench myself in the lake, but I can't, not now with the boys watching. "We're just about to head in."

"Yeah," Harriet says, sitting up and nearly conking herself on the boom. She inches her way to the back where I am.

"Us, too," Mark says.

I'm better at catching the wind than Timothy is, and we sail ahead of them.

"Can you believe this?" Harriet asks.

I'm thinking: things. Diamonds, wings of silver, and turquoise. Ice and amber glass. I wonder, if these things were to disappear, would I still be alive?

We slide into shore. Harriet curses as a canoe cuts in front of us. "Stupid!" she yells.

I know she's mad because of the boys close on our heels. We remind me of the fish I once kept in an aquarium lined with pink pebbles. I had three black mollies, two silver-tailed platys, and four swordtails. The males were relentless in their pursuit of the females, and the females spent all their time trying to avoid them. Harriet is a black molly, I'm the silver-tailed platy.

The boys dock with a splash as they leap into the water, shouting.

I link elbows with Harriet and lead her away towards our towels.

"Hey! Wait for us!" Timothy shouts.

I hear the sand kicking up as they run towards us, their knees giving way as the sand shifts beneath them. Mark gets here first; he stops in front of us and walks backward.

"Where are you going?" he asks.

"Right here," I say. I spot Ed's Mickey Mouse towel. Ed isn't there, but his glasses are folded carefully over Mickey's eyes, and I know he can't be far. We—Harriet, the boys, and I—sit down. I dig my feet into the sand until I reach cool, moist velvet.

Mark claws the sand, digging holes and filling them in. I take a handful of sand and pour it over Harriet's bare leg, my back to the boys. I don't know what to say, so I listen to Harriet who has rekindled her flirting.

I notice clouds building up across the lake. A wind, still gentle, sweeps across us. The sailboats are finally skating across the water, not fast, but enough to interest me. I wonder if a storm is on the way.

Ed comes up, dripping with fresh water. He smiles at the boys and says to me, "You're getting burned, Tammy." He searches through the canvas bag we brought and finds a bottle of sunscreen. "Put this on." He tosses it to me, and I catch it by the neck.

"Do I have to?" I wrinkle up my nose.

"You bet," he says. "The wind's picking up. Do you want to go out?"

I shake my head. "We just got in."

"Harriet?"

Harriet considers but then she shakes her head.

He shrugs and scoops up his glasses, and goes over to the boat.

Mark asks, "Is that your father?"

"My father!" I laugh. "My *brother*." But then, after a moment, I think that it's not so funny after all because he is almost my father. I watch him rotate the boat so that it heads out to the lake. He pokes at the skin on his back, looking over his shoulder, checking for sunburn.

"Tammy!" he yells up. "Bring me my shirt."

"Jeez," I say as I take his shirt with me. As I'm walking away, I wonder if Mark has a mind full of pictures or of words. Harriet runs up next to me. She doesn't want to stay alone, even for a minute, and we walk side by side to Ed.

"Found some boyfriends, did you?" he teases as I hand him the shirt.

"They found us," I tell him. "See you later." We watch him wiggle into the shirt before we head back.

As we draw near, I hear Timothy say, his hand covering his mouth, "Tammy Big Tits." The words cut through the air and lodge against my turquoise heart. Mark laughs and then sees me, staring, and shuts up. His ears are pink, stubs of ugly flesh.

"Jerks!" I yell and kick sand in their faces. I turn and run back to Ed, who has just pushed off. The sail fills with wind, and I yell, "Ed! Wait!"

I dive into the water, the coolness slapping my burnt skin, and stroke hard, gasping as I roll on my side for air. I see that Ed has turned into the wind, stalling the boat for me. Panting, I pull myself onto the deck. The wind, strong now, whips the boom back and forth, and I duck, settling. With a little maneuvering, Ed gets the wind in the sail and we shoot forward, nicking the waves like a dull razor. The wind gets stronger every minute.

"What changed your mind?" Ed shouts.

"I hate boys," I yell. Tammy Big Tits. Words. I should have called them names that would have hurt them more than the pictures I paint in my head: fish with scales rotting from their sides, drying in the sun, their eyes bulging and dull, stinking.

There will be a storm, but we guess we have another hour. Ed lets me take over. I pull in the mainsheet, hugging it to my chest, and the rope cuts into my hand, numbing it, but I hold fast. We tip with the weight of the wind, precariously balanced on a thin edge of the boat. The soles of our feet almost skim the water as we lean backwards away from it. The lake splashes up, trying to swallow us. We are walking on water. Tighter, I pull the mainsheet.

"Yee-ha!" Ed cries. His glasses are sheeted with water and I can barely see his eyes.

A gust of wind collides with us, and I hold the mainsheet tight. Ed, surprised, looks at me with wide eyes before we tumble into the water.

I fight the urge to kick, and allow myself to sink. At first, I see only yellowish bubbles, then, as I sink, Ed's legs treading water by the boat. I am absorbed into this other world: now silent, greenish brown, cold, no longer a glittery silver. There is a threshold where the cold intensifies, a line dividing the lake I know from the other, but I do not sink much beyond it: the hands of God are holding me up. Vague outlines of weeds darken the water around me. There is no light, no pictures to paint. I float suspended, and my lungs beg for air but I cannot kick. I am transfixed by this muted scene.

Something grabs me, and I start. Ed has taken hold of me; his bloated face wild with panic. He tugs me up and suddenly I can no longer hold my breath. I gasp for air and only draw in choking water. My heart races, I struggle, get me to the top, steal me from the hands of God, help me, I don't want to die. My lungs are screaming and what little light there is recedes from me.

Ed slaps me on the back and I come to, gagging, sucking in air and water. I can't breathe, no air comes in, and I vomit. He has pulled me up onto the underside of the capsized boat. I pant, I'm weak. The choking deafens me.

"Breathe, breathe," Ed yells at me.

We've attracted attention, and several boats come to help Ed. Men dive into the water, swimming towards us. They hold me on my back in the water as Ed rights the Sunfish. All I can think is that the clouds are coming fast. On my back, I can see only a small patch of sky, but I can tell that it's blue like spring forget-me-nots.

They lift me onto another boat, a bigger one in which I can lie. I cannot bear to move, to talk, and my lungs work as if giving birth to some monster.

By the time we get to shore, I think I can stand, but a man lifts me up and carries me, running to a clean piece of beach. I want to tell him that he doesn't have to be so dramatic, but everyone is watching, shouting. Ed skids in the sand next to me. His large hands are shaking and cold as he touches my arm.

I really could have died, could have stayed in that other world forever. I shudder.

"What happened?" Ed asks. He knows I'm a strong swimmer.

"Cramps, " I say, not meeting his gaze. How can I tell him that I just wanted to disappear into another world, even if for only a minute? How can I tell him about wanting to be held up so that I would not fall? Drowning, I think, is like walking on snow.

People circle me. All kinds of eyes, like those on my wallpaper, vacant, distant. I see a pair of green eyes, and I squeeze my eyes shut, hoping that I won't drown in them. When I open them, I see Mark, but I don't think that I will drown anymore. I'm in another world, my own. "I'm okay," I tell everyone.

Ed helps me to my feet, holding me up, but I shake him free.

"I can walk," I tell him.

Harriet runs up and holds onto my fingers; she could have been mad at me for leaving her alone with the boys, but she isn't. As Ed takes down the boat by the shore, we look out and watch Silver Lake tarnish black with the storm. Thunder rumbles in the distance and I think of good luck. A single bolt of lightning ignites the clouds, spreading veins of white fire throughout them. Another clap of thunder cracks in our ears. People scurry towards their cars, deserting the beach, and I think that I can't wait for autumn when everything will be quiet again.

Core Puncher

Lillian pressed her foot on the accelerator and sped at ninety miles an hour down the deserted Oklahoma road, her four-wheel-drive Subaru wagon whining with the strain. In the sky a hazy line stretched across the muted blue. The dry line. In this heat, she guessed, thunderheads could erupt in towering black billows by two o'clock. Faster and faster she sped towards the line where warm Gulf air met cool air from the Rockies—she stopped only now and then to consult the map taped to the dashboard. She wished she could see a visual of the incoming front, to see where it might intersect the dry line where winds and moisture and pressure could build up to a spinning frenzy. She popped open a Diet Coke and drove, alternating her gaze between the sky and the flat land where the smallest tree or shack might hide a state trooper. Oil derricks pumped and clanged in the fields, mechanized farmers toiling over a tender crop. Damn machinery, Lillian thought, can't keep a person alive but can spit up oil for all eternity.

Around two, she crossed over into Texas, a remote area with nothing but prairie grass. She chewed a doughnut that had soaked up the heat and humidity and sweated beads of sugar in her hand. After a while she got out of the car to set up a large antenna, and listened to the radio. Damn. The most severe thunderstorms were predicted at least a hundred miles north, maybe farther. Back in the car, she opened another Diet Coke. Her hunger gave her the edge she needed as she sped to the northeastern section of the line. In the distance, the cumulonimbus clouds made their towering ascent into the sky, not yet black but flattening out across the plains like the palm of a malevolent god.

The clouds were moving quickly, growing visibly darker. Yes, she thought, yes, if only I can get there. She turned onto a road to intercept the storm. The sky ahead had grown black, but the sheer levelness of the ground and the absence of trees or buildings enabled her to see the entire storm from billowing top to low, flat bottom. As she neared the storm, policemen stood alongside the road ready to radio in any sign of a tornado. Cowards, she thought. From where they stood far away, a tornado might appear no more lethal than a twisted skein of yarn. In her rearview mirror, she could see another storm gathering in the south, but she stayed on course. She had learned that changing storms was no different from changing check-out lines at the grocery store—something would happen that would make her regret the move.

Up ahead, three trucks, one with the spinning weather beanie of the National Weather Service, sped down an intersecting road, turned in front of her, joined in the pursuit. Lillian turned on her headlights—the sky had darkened to a yellow-green. Lightning splintered the sky. The winds had picked up and swept across the open land, trying to push her car with them, forcing her to steer with two hands. The weather beanie truck and a red pickup that Lillian recognized as belonging to a Texan chaser pulled over to the side of the road. The third truck sped towards the storm. Idiot, Lillian thought as she parked behind the pickup, no sense in core punching when you've got a great view. Driving through the middle of the storm would ruin visibility—it was only worth it if you were in front of the storm with no chance of seeing through to the core.

Lillian stepped out of the car. The air had cooled. She wrapped her bare arms around herself. The Texan unfolded himself from the pickup, recognized her with a nod, then faced the clouds. Lillian remembered him because they had met in a diner the year before after core punching a storm. Like her, he preferred to chase storms alone, while most others paired off in teams, a driver and a navigator. Lillian had not said much to him, except to tell him that she came from Rhode Island and planned on spending her vacation time every spring in Tornado Alley. He had laughed. "I moved here from San Francisco just to be near the twisters. Earthquakes, no thanks, can't predict them at all. But tornadoes—now there's a beautiful natural disaster. I'm an engineer in Houston now. Spend my vacations chasing—and every weekend, too." His face had the cragginess of a ranch hand, the crinkled eyes from squinting against the sun, a hugeness of frame, that forever made him a Texan in Lillian's mind, no matter where he had originated. He embodied the cowboy spirit of the storm-chasing subculture. Lillian did not think she could ever move to Tornado Alley, as he had, because she knew in her heart that the storm-chasing would swallow her whole.

With her video camera up against her eye, Lillian scanned the base of the storm for a wall cloud. Lots of cells—bulges in the clouds—showed good up- and downdrafts. Now she needed the wall cloud to drop. The lead of the storm, the base of the anvil, suddenly unleashed a blackened curtain of rain, but they stood behind it, where lightning shot in every direction, the winds whipping ruthlessly into them. Lillian had cut her hair short just the week before in anticipation of the winds—last year her hair had slapped across her eyes and scratched her cornea.

"There!" one of the weather service guys shouted, his voice almost lost in the wind.

In the center of the storm, a portion of the clouds had dropped out of the perfectly flattened bottom. Four years ago, Lillian would have thought nothing of it, just a low cloud. But now she prayed for it to start rotating. Spin, baby, spin—her personal mantra. She saw the men standing in the road next to her glance at the ditch alongside the road, ready to throw themselves down into it if necessary. The storm shifted direction slightly, still heading east but dropping to the south toward them. Rain started falling in hard pelts, intermixed with pea-size hail. Lillian's arms stung. No, she wasn't going to flee. She had held death in her arms and no longer feared it, for if her child could face it bravely, then so could she.

"It's turning!" the Texan yelled.

Sure enough, the wall cloud began to move. Spin, baby, spin, open up straight into the heavens, hollow out that tunnel to suck up the earth and everything on it. Lillian shielded her eyes from the rain and hail, shivering, waiting, watching. Her heart beat in her ears. But just as suddenly as it had dropped, the wall cloud dissipated, lost its momentum, drifted away in gray vapor.

"Shit!" Lillian said aloud, though the wind was too loud for anyone else to hear. They watched the storm for another few minutes, hoping for another wall cloud, but the storm lost energy as it swept across the land. No sense in chasing this one. Disgusted, she got into her car. Once again, she had been cheated.

Her co-workers back in Rhode Island thought she was crazy. Who ever heard of spending a vacation chasing tornadoes, they asked, a little uneasily. Go to the Caribbean and lie out in the sun, visit the great cathedrals of Europe, go to Disney World, for God's sake, at least you can get thrills there while the staff checks out the safety of every nut and bolt. Her brother called her trips pathetic death wishes. But no one she knew had ever set foot in this land that went on forever, with only a tree or two in sight, a clump of buildings here, another clump twenty miles beyond it, and a sky so low she almost believed she could reach up and touch it. She could not explain to them how exhilarating it felt to be a small speck against such immensity. How loneliness and yearning seemed as natural as the emptiness of the land.

Her estranged husband was the only one who seemed to comprehend, if only a little. "Do what you have to do," he said. "I don't care."

Lillian was drawn to tornadoes first because she had unwittingly lived through one. She, John, and Marguerite had been in Florida, fulfilling what none of them wanted to acknowledge as Marguerite's dying wish. The trip had been full of laughter and stabbing, silent pain, creating memories that were bittersweet even as they formed. Every afternoon, thunderstorms rolled through, as though reminding them of the fragility of the waking dream they struggled to maintain. Their last afternoon there the storm had been violent and long, electrically turbulent. They waited out the weather holding each other in a steamed-up shop. As they were returning to their hotel, they drove by some houses torn apart by a tornado. Lillian knew that her child could have died then, that very day, from something other than bone cancer. That she and John could have died with her, or could have perished before their daughter even though they painfully expected to outlive her. That night Lillian slipped into bed beside Marguerite to hold her frail, curled body against her chest and to cry for all the unexpected things that had befallen them. What were these unpredictable forces that tore people apart, Lillian wondered, and why did humanity have to endure them?

Lillian never would have thought to seek out tornadoes, however, if a man in her office had not subscribed to a weather magazine. What an odd, specialized thing, Lillian had thought when she had seen it on his desk. She could not imagine the function of such a journal. "Hey, Brian," she said, "does this make it easier to talk about the weather?"

Brian, a burly man who never seemed to be paying attention, looked up. Maybe because Lillian no longer had a defined sense of humor—she couldn't even tell a good joke anymore—or because Brian was sufficiently dazed not to understand that she teased him, he said, "Yeah. Take it home for a few days, if you want."

Having failed at humor, she was obligated to pick it up. As she flipped through it, a looming picture of a tornado caught her eye: an immense, black thing bearing down on a solitary farmhouse. What magnificent, unyielding power, Lillian thought. The tornado in the picture looked less like a funnel and more like a column of horrid blackness that had slammed into the earth. Ignoring her work, she read the magazine from cover to cover, returning twice to the letters written by storm-chasers retelling their exploits much the way lecherous men did theirs in pornographic magazines. She found herself driven to face one of those twisting monsters, to feel its force, to stand in its way and defy it.

As the light began to fail, Lillian walked into the Mom's Oklahoma Eat 'N' Run. The Texan sat in the far corner, bent over his meal and a torn map. She liked his build, the way he sat there squarely on the chair, one hand tapping impatiently on the table, as if he had found the perfect balance of confidence and skepticism.

As she pored over her own map waiting for her meal, a voice said, "Miss Rhode Island, right? Without the hair?"

She looked up into the lined face of the Texan. She was so shocked that he remembered her that she almost forgot to answer. "Yeah. And you're the Texan."

He laughed. If storm-chasers recognized each other at all, it was by their favorite vantage points, or by their home state, or by their cars. "Bart McDonald." His offered hand was strong and veined, thinly wooled with dark hairs. His smile seemed easy but guarded.

She shook his hand. "Lillian Macintosh."

"Ah. Two Scots in Oklahoma."

"My married name."

"Oh."

"We're separated."

He nodded, looked down. "I've been there. Divorced now for eight years." He sat down across from her without asking. He pointed to her map. "There was a small twister about fifty miles south of where we were today."

"I was down there afterwards. The path cut right across nowhere and flattened the grass for about a mile."

"So, where are you headed tomorrow?"

"I thought I'd head north, almost up into Kansas. The next front is a lot stronger and it's supposed to come through late tomorrow. I'm betting that this one won't drop as far south."

He leaned back, crossed his arms, balanced on the back legs of his chair. "Are you a gambling woman?"

"You're asking a tornado chaser if she gambles?"

He laughed. "With your money, not your life. *I'm* thinking the front falls further south. I'm thinking the hot spot will be the Texas-Oklahoma border. I'll bet you a hundred dollars that I find a tornado tomorrow and you don't."

She narrowed her eyes at his smug grin. Oh, he thought he had the bet won even before the atmosphere set itself up for the next day. He was probably like half the other storm chasers, thinking she couldn't predict any better than an eighth grader. But hell, her first year she came back with photographs of two tornadoes. Even though last year did not pan out—it was a quiet last two weeks in April—this year she had a video camera and already, just three days into her vacation, had a picture of a wall cloud beginning to rotate. No scientist could accurately predict the emergence of a tornado, but her record was as good as any serious chaser's. "Twenty dollars, and you're on."

"A *conservative* gambling woman," he said. He leaned over her map. "Okay. We'll meet in Oklahoma City." He tapped the map with his index finger. The spot was well south of where Lillian intended to watch, but hell, she drove hundreds of miles every day. "You know that steak house outside town with the Angus in the parking lot?" She nodded. "We'll meet up there."

She clicked her tongue. "And how do we trust each other? Scout's honor?"

"Something like that. But pictures never hurt."

The next morning, Lillian watched the Weather Channel in her motel room. Bet or no bet, she would go wherever tornadoes were likely, even if it meant heading south. The front could go either way, or spawn tornadoes at both sites. She decided to stick with her original plan. After a quick breakfast of coffee and toast with jelly, she got into her car for the long drive. The sky had a light overcast of clouds, nothing nearly potent enough to drop even a few showers, nothing to rivet her attention. She hated these long drives without something to make her stick her head out the window because she always ended up thinking of Marguerite and the instantaneous, powerful vacuum her death created that sucked Lillian and John in, then spit them out miles apart. Without Marguerite, they could not return to being a couple—they had relied on her for their balance, someone to focus on when they did not want to focus on each other. The strangest part of it all was that Lillian had loved John. She bit her lower lip. Marguerite had been *real*, but now everything about her seemed unreal, as if she had been nothing more than a gloriously vivid dream that Lillian could not let go.

As Lillian traveled north, the land appeared more fertile and spring-like. Around four, she still had not found any violent thunderstorms, though the weather seemed right. As she turned the car south again, she saw the thunderhead well to the west, a purple-black mass thrusting upward into the sky. Lightning jagged through it like hot veins, lighting up the whole cloud mass in frenetic beats. Frantically, she looked at the map to find the closest road that would take her toward it—even now, with a bet, she refused to be as inconsiderate as some chasers who simply drove their Jeeps and Broncos and Jimmies across fields to get where they wanted. If she went north about ten miles, she would intersect an east-west road. Turning around once again, she sped towards the thunderhead.

By the time she neared it, the thunderhead was bearing down fast. If she wanted to possibly see a tornado, she had to core punch, drive right through the heavy rain towards the center of the storm, because she had no other chance to reach a good viewing position. A weather service man had lectured her alongside a road, "Don't ever core punch. If there's a tornado in that storm, the odds are against you." But odds never applied to Lillian. One in a hundred, one in a thousand, one in a million—statistics had no bearing on real life. It didn't matter that tornadoes usually hit a specific spot in Oklahoma only once every two hundred and fifty years, or that x-percentage of marriages ended in divorce, or that bone cancer was a rare childhood disease, because what happened, happened. And so, with gritted teeth, Lillian drove through the front of the storm towards its heart.

Rain fell in heavy sheets that the windshield wipers could not clear. She slowed the car to twenty-five and even then could not be sure to stay on the road. Even the lightning could not cut through the rain. Hail clattered on the car roof, grew bigger, louder, the farther she drove. Lillian's heart pounded, sometimes she forgot to breathe and then air came out of her chest in a startling hiss. She leaned forward over the steering wheel.

The hail suddenly hit her hood with a bang-bang-bang that caused her to slam on the brakes, sending the car into a brief skid across the slick road. My God, she thought, as she saw that the hail was almost the size of tennis balls, it really does get that big. Then she knew: she had to get out of the storm. Before she could turn the car around, a huge roar shook the car, as if an eighteen wheeler were speeding towards her, louder, a train. And she knew. Shit! She had no way of knowing where the tornado was, which way it was headed, because she could not see it. The rain and hail swept ferociously towards her. With a prayer, she accelerated the car and headed perpendicular to the direction of the rain, into a farm field not caring what damage she did to the crops, or the land, as long as that tornado, wherever it was, went on by her. It doesn't matter, she said to herself, whatever happens, happens. But she did not want to die, not yet. The roar grew louder, deafening her, the wet ground slowed her car, heaved it up and down, instead of letting it race to safety, the four-wheel drive failing her. She stopped. It was close, it wasn't getting any quieter, and the air grew thin, hard to breathe. Lillian looked frantically into the dark rain to find the tornado. Something large rushed out of the darkness at her. She screamed. The object smashed into the side of her car, broke through the passenger window, hung there for a instant, a cow, brown and white, its face bloodied, eyes bulging, lifting her car up on the opposite two wheels with its impact, before dropping down out of sight. The noise moved away from her, still screaming into the darkness, before disappearing altogether.

Lillian sat in the field until the rain had passed and a line of sunshine slowly advanced towards her. Only then did she realize that she had survived the close pass of a tornado and had lived to tell about it. She twisted around in her seat to see whether she could sight the tornado still spinning down from the thunderhead, but it was gone. She threw her still camera over one shoulder, took the video camera with her other hand, stepped gingerly out of the car. The cow lay dead in the field, its body's rough imprint embedded in the side of her car, its blood already drying there. She bent down to touch the animal, wondered if it had lived within the swirling winds, seeing the miraculous force of its killer before being tossed to its death. Here was something that had seen the inside of hell. She sighed, straightened. Boards and wires and cast iron pots lay strewn all over the field. The video camera at her eye, she panned across the aftermath as the sun washed over the field in an incongruous brightness. There. Not fifty yards from her car, a swath about a hundred yards wide cut into the vegetation as if an immense lawn mower had made a single pass and had bagged all the clippings. Excitedly, she climbed on top of her dented car—the hail had pocked the sheet metal—and videotaped the straight path of the tornado from the southwest towards her car to the northeast where it twisted and skipped, then disappeared from the ground. If only she had seen it!

She considered driving to the nearest town to have her window replaced, but she couldn't wait to see the Texan. By now, he would have heard about the tornado passing through her area, unless, that is, he was in the midst of his own. She arrived at the steak house at nine that evening. In her rearview mirror, she tried to straighten her hair. With a handful of tissues she scraped off some of the mud from her shoes and jeans. No use, she thought as she looked down at herself, I look as though I've lived through a tornado. Laughing aloud, she got out of the car.

She found the Texan in the back of the dimly lit restaurant. He had evidently already eaten and now looked drunkenly sloppy as he stared after a waitress. If he had been a date, Lillian would have turned and left the restaurant without a word, but, as it was, he was the only person she knew who would understand her thrill. She stood in front of his table.

His face grew suddenly alert and intelligent, not so much drunk as exhausted, questioning, waiting.

"Just another day core punching at the OK corral," she said.

"You saw one! I knew it! As soon as I heard the report, I said, Miss Rhode Island was there!" His face grew animated without the mean jealousy Lillian had expected.

She sat down, perched on the edge of the banquette. "I didn't see it, because I was core punching. But it threw a cow right into me." She sat down. "I was fifty yards from the Wizard of Oz."

"Holy shit!" He lowered his voice. "You've gotta tell me the whole thing."

As she talked, he did not take his eyes off hers. He interrupted with questions, took her back over some point, let her go on for another minute before interrupting again, but he did not look away once, not even to reach for his coffee, his eyes steady and blue, unflinching. When the waitress took Lillian's order, he rapped the table impatiently until Lillian was able to continue. After she had finished, he sat back with a satisfied look.

"Part of me would give anything to have been there, but another . . . My kids hate that I do this. They're always dreaming that I've been sucked up by a tornado. My ex calls me from San Francisco every time they do it—to make me stop. Of course, you never really think it'll happen." He hesitated. "You don't have kids, do you?"

"No."

"I figured you wouldn't be out there if you did. I'm hoping my kids will understand in a few years. My oldest—I wouldn't be surprised if he asked me to take him out in a couple of years. He's eleven, and the biggest kid you've ever seen at that age. Growing and eating and growing—"

"I had a daughter. She died four years ago." She had to say it, to stop him from going on and exposing the raw grief still in her.

A quick twinge pulled at the corner of one crinkled eye. He wanted to say something—she could tell— but did not have the words to express himself. Please, please, don't try, she thought, because then I'll probably hate you.

Finally, he said, with a softness that betrayed a fear of his own, "I'll shut up."

She wished she could tell him that he did not have to stop talking about his children, but she could not. Instead, a heavy silence fell between them.

The Texan paid his twenty dollars debt. In the parking lot, he whistled appreciatively as he ran his hands over the dent. The light of the parking lot cast a golden glow on him, and Lillian wondered how his wife had fallen in and out of love with him. Had it been predictable, or sudden, or against all odds, or expected? She wished she knew what it was that made love live and die. What was it that made one person fall into the embrace of another?

"Where're you headed tomorrow?" the Texan asked.

"Nowhere. I've got to get my window fixed."

He sighed. "Sure was hoping you could bring me some of your luck."

"You don't want my luck, believe me," she said as she went around the car to get in. He followed her. She could feel the heat from his body, the solidity of it, and its awkwardness. She almost reached out to touch him, but forced both hands into her pockets. "Well, I'll see you around." She did not allow even a pause for a response and slipped inside her battered car, locked the door. "Bye!" she called out, and drove away. In her rearview mirror, the Texan stood tall and lost, the only figure in the parking lot.

The air during the next week dried out—the nearest front seemed stuck in California. The heat built up without a tangible hint of humidity, so when Lillian took to the road again her perspiration seemed to be whisked away instantly by the hunger of the air. For days she drove all over Texas and Oklahoma in search of storms. Although she found an occasional afternoon one, the clouds threatened no more terror than an overcast day in New England. Rain was sudden and quick, and it evaporated almost as soon as it fell. By the end of the week, dust swirled under the tires of the farm machinery in huge lingering clouds that captured her attention more completely than those in the sky. Not once did she catch sight of the Texan's red pickup—she should not have been surprised given the vast territory they both covered, but she was. At night she watched the Weather Channel and the disgustingly slow progress of the front. And the disappointing absence of severe thunderstorms leading the way. She could only hope that in the upper reaches of the atmosphere, moist, hot air poured over Texas.

By the morning the front was due to arrive in Tornado Alley, Lillian had grown so impatient that she had driven the day before into western Oklahoma, almost into the panhandle, to meet it. The winter wheat stretched on for endless miles, bending green and supple against the slightest breeze with only an occasional farm complex to oversee the acreage. The dryness had already touched the crop with golden tips, too early, Lillian thought. They needed rain. The puffy cumulus clouds, white and pure, drifted in the sky, betraying the humidity up high. Perfect. As she sang along with the car radio, she spotted a weather beanie car up ahead, another good omen. At least the scientists thought her position was right.

Not wanting to get too close to the edge of the plains—for the best tornadoes formed over level expanses of land—she stopped for lunch in a diner that served rancid fried chicken. Two men, whom Lillian recognized as fellow storm-chasers, ate voraciously and noisily, talking about the front with swaggering bravado, as if they wanted everyone to overhear. From their conversation, Lillian guessed that she would have less than an hour to find a viewing position. She studied her map, picked her spot, and left.

Already, clouds, thick and gray, advanced towards her from the horizon, leading the way for the front behind them. Lillian had gone so many days without seeing a storm that she gripped the steering wheel with aching excitement. As she neared the storm, lightning flashed in the charcoal gray sky. At a junction in the road beside a sprawling farm complex, the farmers hurrying the machinery and animals into the barns, Lillian drove onto a dirt track that seemed to lead directly into the darkest, most turbulent part of the storm. She stopped about a mile down the road and got out of the car. Standing with her arms crossed against the chill of the winds, she squinted into the oncoming darkness. Even as a child, she had stood riveted by the uncontrollable sorcery of a thunderstorm while her older brother and sister had huddled against their mother. Although she understood the mechanics of a storm, she could never fathom the existence of this force on a world people were supposed to control. The clouds dwarfed humans, laughed at them, swept over them with unstoppable devastation. The first clap of close thunder startled her into grabbing the outside mirror, and at once she was taken back to the cow hurtling out of the darkness. She looked behind her, around, for a place to take cover in case a tornado formed. Like most roads, this one had a drainage ditch alongside, not certain shelter, but hope. Along the main road, the one she had turned off, about two miles across the fallow fields, a red pickup truck had parked. Lillian got her binoculars out of the car, looked into them. Sure enough, it was the Texan, looking at her through his binoculars. He waved, and she waved back. As she lowered the binoculars, a brilliant thrust of lightning shot towards the ground in the distance, hitting it with a deafening explosion. Lillian moved a few feet from the car, crouched low, lifted her video camera toward the storm. The wind picked up, blowing first one way, then another. The sky darkened so completely that the low-light warning came on in the camera and flicked off whenever the lightning burst across the sky in venous starkness. She set up the video camera on its tripod, readied her still camera around her neck.

A wall cloud formed a few miles behind Lillian. She swiveled the video camera, then snapped a few still shots. It had not yet begun to rain—the ground air was so dry that the first droplets could have instantly evaporated—but the fury of the storm, with violent lightning, thunder, and winds, was right on top of her. Spin, baby, spin. If she had not turned to alert the Texan to the wall cloud, she would have missed the second wall hanging overhead, already rotating. Its path carried it between her and the Texan, not far enough from either if a tornado formed inside it and happened to snake to one side or the other. She was afraid, yes, the instinct to run still strong and high in her chest, but she had that unwillingness to let go, her fascination was too powerful. Quickly, she aimed the video camera at the spinning cloud. The red pickup raced farther away down the road, then stopped.

The cloud had begun to rotate faster and faster, forming into a funnel that Lillian prayed would drop to earth, killing her if it had to, so that she could witness the complete evolution of a tornado, videotape it, capture the most powerful winds on earth, understand at last what such destruction meant. The cloud was spinning exactly as it should, but no tornado had formed. The winds hurt her ears with their furious noise. Lillian felt light-headed as if she had forgotten to breathe.

"Where is it?" she shouted in frustration. "Where the hell is it?"

Just then a tremendous wind hit her, almost knocking her over, and up from the ground rose a sudden red, twisting tower in a roar that reached up miles into the clouds.

"God!" Lillian meant both the expletive and the deity, hanging onto the last. The tornado had been there all along, coming down at them, but had been invisible in the dryness until it had touched down and sucked up the red earth. Lillian was paralyzed. The twister churned and roared toward the farm complex, moving slower than Lillian had expected, although in sight of this invincible column that ripped across the soil she could not be sure that time existed at all. The tight winding of the winds had muscles—red, defined coils of dust: a Titan come down for vengeance. The column was so immensely tall that Lillian felt as though she were falling backwards, even as she snapped her pictures. The tornado leaned toward the Texan, and all Lillian could think of was his children, angry at him for chasing something that could kill him, the great vacuum they would feel in his absence.

"Kill *me!*" she shouted. "*Kill me!*"

She half-feared it would listen and leap towards her, but what a triumph if it did! For once, she would have changed the path of destruction. But the tornado followed its own path, skirted both of them and plowed into the farmhouse. It roared on with boards and pipes rising high into the sky with it, cutting a wake in the fields beyond and tossing its litter about with abandon. Lillian pressed her eye to the video camera to make sure she caught every moment of its life.

Not until the tornado had lifted from the ground miles away did Lillian raise her eye from the video camera. As she saw the destroyed farm without the distance of a lens, her legs began to shake. She had forgotten about the farmers. Throwing her equipment in the passenger seat, she scrambled into her car and sped toward what remained of the farm complex. By the time she reached it, the Texan had already arrived, though not much before, because he was only then leaping from his truck.

The silence and stillness frightened her. Some people had already climbed out of the storm cellar and stood in a small group around something lying on the ground. Lillian swallowed as she and the Texan approached them. She could not muster a voice. The Texan slipped his hand in hers, and she accepted it gladly as they reluctantly walked to the group. The tenderness of his grip seemed so different from what she had expected that she wanted to cry.

"Is everyone okay?" the Texan asked, his voice raspy.

The group dispersed to reveal a yellow dog lying motionless on the ground. A metal pipe had been driven through his body. One by one, the men and women turned from it.

"Just the dog," a man said to them as he passed. "Just the dog."

A woman had drawn the two children toward what remained of the house, comforting them with her arms spread wide around them, speaking softly to them but unable to take her eyes off the devastation around her.

Lillian felt a clenching in her chest. As much as she feared it, she was drawn to the dead animal. She walked toward it. As she stood over it, she saw the horrible wounds; yet, nothing in the dog's final expression showed agony. She sat on the ground next to it, reached out to touch its soft fur which felt as alive and as soothing as any dog's—she almost expected the dog to lift its head to see who had touched it. But nothing stirred under her fingertips. New death always felt so close to life, she thought. It felt soft with its waning warmth, unreal, something that could be reversed. She had sat with Marguerite's limp hand in hers and had thought, this isn't real, it can't be. Across the hospital bed, John had turned from Lillian with grief crumpling his face, the tears streaming down, the control finally crumbled away to a guttural sob. Only then had she sensed the finality of this last moment with her daughter. She stroked the head of the dog. She had prayed for a bridge between life and death, where she could lean over her daughter for a parting kiss, a hug, a few words, but death proved discrete, a perfectly sealed and impenetrable box. Now, as before in the face of death, the tears came hot and fast, acid, and they dropped red with dust onto her T-shirt.

She felt a hand on her shoulder. Through the blur of her tears, she saw the Texan. His face had a tautness around his mouth that perhaps betrayed his own sorrows, but the rest of his expression was stolid and factual, unanalytical. To her relief, she saw that he did not expect her to smile through her tears, or even to acknowledge him, but only to allow him to touch her for those few moments. The warmth of his touch had a peculiar strength to it, a force that gathered her in and held her tightly. For the first time in years, she no longer found it necessary to make sense out of the unexplainable, but instead accepted it for what it was.

When Lillian finally climbed back into her car, her hands were still shaking. She could sell the video tape to a news station, to other storm chasers. Years from now meteorologists might be shaking their heads at her stupidity for not seeking cover, pondering her wish for death, even as they relished the film and played it over and over like pornography, unable to get enough of it.

She inched the car down the road, raindrops pelting the windshield. She could see the Texan in her rearview mirror sitting straight and intent, hands together in fists on the steering wheel, shoulders squared, seemingly drawn to the mysterious emptiness of her heart.

The Advancement of Dawn

Wrapped in her comforter, eight-year-old Jen-mu dreamed child dreams: flying, breathing underwater, vast forests of sweets, dragons lurking in dark corners, things she could not explain, not even in dream language. The fragments, almost instantly forgotten but hovering nearby, confused her when she awoke. Near dawn, she dreamed that she had grown into a giant adult who could reach into any part of Taipei and have what she wanted: toys, sweets, firecrackers, dresses in colorful silks. Her eyes opened, and the grayish predawn light forced them wider. Quickly, she covered her head with the quilt with the hope that it would carry her back to the magical world of grown-ups.

A half hour later, in an apartment across the city, Bao Mei-fang awoke. At first, she stretched slowly, one arm at a time, but then she realized she wasn't at home. *Jen-mu!* Already, the sky glowed orange behind the thin curtains. She had never before stayed at Lan Liang-fan's this long. Poor Jen-mu—if she woke up and Mei-fang had not returned home, she might panic, believing that something dreadful had happened to her mother. Mei-fang's heart ached. At the very best, Jen-mu was still huddled under her covers, sound asleep, and would undoubtedly be late for school. *Jen-mu.*

Mei-fang slipped from under the covers, careful not to disturb Liang-fan, who snored softly with an open mouth. Fang-hsin had been right—Liang-fan had not cared about Mei-fang's great life mistake. For that, Mei-fang thought him the most honorable man she had met. She dressed quietly and quickly, pausing only briefly to gaze at her lover's serene expression. His strong, broad hands looked helpless against the comforter. The scar across his cheek had whitened in his sleep and now reminded Mei-fang of a pale twig laid gently across his face.

She wanted to wake him, but remembered Fang-hsin's warning: never make demands on a man like Liang-fan. He could have any other young woman just like her—prettier even—and she could be tossed away like rotten food. She wanted to think that Liang-fan would never do that, even though the night before she had seen him punch a man who had accidentally bumped them in the nightclub. But he had been drunk. If she were lucky and patient, he might fall in love with her the way she had fallen in love with him. If she were *very* lucky, he would marry her. Mei-fang opened her purse. She took out one of the cloisonné earrings she had worn the night before and laid it on the pillow next to Liang-fan. Quickly, she turned. *Jen-mu.*

Mei-fang hurried down the three flights of stairs and onto the narrow sidewalk. She coughed at the smog heavy in the air. The whole city had been awaiting a good wind, but she heard the night before that it would not happen for at least two more days. *Jen-mu.* She muscled her way across street after street, stepping in front of cars and praying that they would not hit her. Her heels clicked against the pavement. *Jen-mu.* Faster, faster, Mei-fang, she told herself. She should not have stayed with Liang-fan. Although Mei-fang's sister You-lan had promised to stay with Jen-mu until she fell asleep, she could not stay the night—You-lan had been forbidden to speak Mei-fang's name. Mei-fang's heel caught in the design of the sidewalk. She tumbled forward and only barely caught her balance again. *Jen-mu.*

She moved away from the new neighborhood where Liang-fan lived and into the one she knew well: low, two-room houses, put together with loose boards, pieces of plastic, anything that would hold together. Her stomach growled at the breakfast smells. The doors to several of the houses were open, and Mei-fang waved to the families there, called out to them by name, still hurrying along. *Jen-mu, Jen-mu, Jen-mu.*

Mei-fang burst, out of breath, through the door of her two-room house. Jen-mu looked up from the small stove where she was finishing the rice porridge for breakfast. She had already dressed in her pink class uniform and had pulled back her hair into a neat ponytail.

"Hello," Jen-mu said.

"I'm so sorry," Mei-fang said. "I—"

"I'm okay on my own." Jen-mu handed her the pot. It was so heavy with porridge that Mei-fang almost dropped it. "I'll get the bowls."

Mei-fang could not speak, she was so proud of her daughter. Only a child, and able to fix breakfast, get herself up on time for school, keep her head about her. Silently, she scooped out a bowl of porridge for each of them.

"Did you have fun with Mr. Lan last night?" Jen-mu asked.

Mei-fang smiled at Jen-mu's new adult way of talking. She sat down across from her daughter. "He took me out to a fancy restaurant, and then we went out dancing. It was very elegant." Just like the old days, she thought, when she was only a child, and a naughty one. Why, if she hadn't gone to all the parties, if she hadn't fallen in love with Hsia-hsia, and gotten pregnant, if both their families had not forced them to marry while renouncing them, if Hsia-hsia had not taken his own life before Jen-mu was born, then . . . It had all started with the parties. "Promise me you won't go out with men until you're an adult."

"Don't worry," Jen-mu said. "I'll never like boys."

Mei-fang sighed. Then she remembered that she had brought treats for Jen-mu. She took out the sweets from her purse, where she had hidden them wrapped in a delicate napkin, and placed them next to Jen-mu's bowl.

"Thanks!"

Mei-fang watched with pleasure as her child devoured the sweets. Jen-mu didn't know whether she was a child or adult, Mei-fang thought with a smile. And instantly she was saddened. People in the neighborhood took Jen-mu in during the afternoons, fed her bean cakes, bits of pork, whatever they could spare, while Mei-fang worked. When she and Hsia-hsia had first married, all had seemed bright and hopeful. They had not cared about the bills they were recklessly accumulating. Even though their families had refused to allow them over their thresholds, they had each other. All that mattered was that Mei-fang had a fresh life growing inside of her. She and Hsia-hsia had even celebrated their freedom from their families by taking a public bus to see the Taroko Gorge.

"You see?" Hsia-hsia had said, stepping so close to the edge of the cliff that Mei-fang's stomach fluttered. "It's not so difficult to cast off the burden of family obligations."

"You're too close!" Mei-fang laughed nervously. "Please."

Hsia-hsia crossed his arms over his broad chest. "Do you believe I've just cursed myself?" He stepped toward her with glittering eyes. "Are you telling me that you believe in superstition?" With the quickness of a snake, he lunged for her.

But she skipped playfully out of reach. "No, Hsia-hsia! I am not. Because we are free!" She had never confessed her fear of becoming the new daughter of his scowling mother. Now, she thought, she was *no one's* daughter. "Free, free, free!" And Hsia-hsia laughed for a long time, holding his rib cage tightly as though his happiness might split him open.

A few months after that day at the gorge, he had given her a clock wrapped in tissue paper. She gasped and clapped her hand across her belly that danced with their child. Yes, she thought, yes, yes, the baby is still alive.

"What's the matter?" he asked, his face as unreadable as stone. He sat next to her and peered into her eyes. She could not look away. "I thought you weren't superstitious."

She straightened and forced herself to cradle the clock instead of the baby. "You're right," she said. "I'm not." Then she felt her natural smile return. "It's not easy to rid oneself of old habits."

He nodded. "Very smart, Mei-fang. You're a good, smart woman. The baby will be fine." With his palm flat, he ran his hand once through his short hair. "It's just that you're always late."

"You're right," she said. "Of course."

But she had not been so smart because she had failed to see Hsia-hsia's warning. The clock had been an omen of his death and not the baby's. Looking at Jen-mu now grown, Mei-fang wondered what other signs she was destined to miss. Be more vigilant, Mei-fang, she told herself, watch out.

Jen-mu slipped on her backpack. As she stepped out of the door, she cast a quick backwards glance at her mother to make sure she was all right. Her mother sat straight-backed and poised with her chopsticks in midair, obviously lost in some far-away thought. Jen-mu hopped into the street. She knew that her mother hoped to marry Mr. Lan. But why? Yes, he looked handsome, but he was a gangster. Jen-mu wished that her mother had the ambition to work herself out of the typing pool, the way old Mrs. Hung said she should. But Jen-mu knew what her mother would say: she was not raised that way. As if she were still an aristocratic young girl with translucent skin! Jen-mu knew all about how spoiled her mother had been, but she didn't understand why that made a difference *now*. She leaped over a gaping hole in the sidewalk, the one she had tossed bits of garbage into just the day before and that smelled of sour food. She would like to toss her mother's gangster in there, she thought, and let him rot. She swore that when she grew up, she would tell her daughter everything about adults, so that her daughter would not feel so left out.

All day Mei-fang typed without comprehending the words that her fingers created, as though she suffered from a fever. Her neck ached from not moving it much, always staring at the documents placed squarely on her right, only moving it to proofread her work on the computer screen, to acknowledge the occasional comment from her supervisor. This was what the rest of her days would be like, she thought, never quite enough money, but always work, work, work. Soon, Jen-mu would be grown, a woman, and Mei-fang would have done nothing more than type all day to get her there.

Just before lunch, her friend Fang-hsin, who worked at the desk next to hers, slipped her a page ripped out of a newspaper. "You're lucky your Liang-fan is not like this."

With damp hands, Mei-fang read the article about a man, identified by the paper as a "gangster," who had beaten his new wife's son to near-death because the boy had disobeyed him. The boy was not expected to live without brain damage. Carefully, Mei-fang tucked the article into her purse. She had met this horrible man—Liang-fan had introduced him as an old friend, a Mr. Wu. Mr. Wu had looked at Mei-fang out of one narrowed eye, as if he could tell all about her if he squinted just right, and had smiled. He had a gold tooth, and expensive clothes. She had never seen him hit anyone, or even raise his voice, but she had only spent an hour at his side. Could Liang-fan be this way? she wondered. How well did she know him? She thought of her delicate but independent Jen-mu and wondered if Liang-fan could love a child not his own. She stared out the window at the hazy afternoon light that seemed too diffuse to be sunlight at all. Oh, what she would give for one clear, brilliant day! Instead the air looked dirty, dusty, cursed.

A few hours later, Mei-fang became aware of a figure standing to one side of her desk, not moving, just standing. When she looked up, she saw Liang-fan smiling down at her. She cried out with the shock. Although he had called her at work, he had never come before—for an instant she believed that he was a ghost instead of the real man.

"Liang-fan! I didn't expect—"

He slid onto the edge of her desk and dangled her earring from between his thumb and index finger. "This earring missed you so much that I could not keep it away."

Blushing, she took it from him. She could feel the eyes of some of her co-workers on them. "It must be a terribly loud earring to convince a busy man like you."

He laughed, loud and rumbly, not at all self-conscious of the fact he shouldn't be there. It was his confidence, Mei-fang thought, that reminded her so poignantly of Hsia-hsia.

He leaned close to her. His breath smelled of sugar cane and ginger. "I forgot to tell you that we're going to the Liu party tonight. With only the most important people in the city. And of course, that includes you."

She smiled. The way he looked at her, his eyes bright and intense, made her want to do anything he said. "I'll need to find someone to look after Jen-mu."

"Jen-mu?" He frowned. "Oh, yes. Your daughter. Do what you have to. I've arranged to have a dress sent to your house. A driver will pick you up at eight." He glanced mischievously at the women around him who watched and kissed Mei-fang on the hand as if he were an elegant European. "I want to have you all day and night," he whispered.

Mei-fang stared after him, praying that she had misread the change in Liang-fan's voice when he spoke of Jen-mu. Hadn't it sounded as if he thought of her as a bother? Something in his way? No, she told herself. He had so much on his mind that he probably forgot Jen-mu's name, that was all. But he had spoken as if Jen-mu were an insignificant beetle in his way! She could only think of the man Liang-fan had hit the night before.

Fang-hsin leaned over to Mei-fang's desk. "The Liu party! I can't believe it!" She lowered her voice. "He's fallen in love with you."

Mei-fang grasped both of Fang-hsin's hands. "Why did you give me that article?"

"Because I wanted to show you how lucky you were not to end up with someone like Wu."

"How do you know I haven't?" Mei-fang's feet felt cold and numb, as if she had been standing in a cold rain. "You think Liang-fan might harm Jen-mu, don't you?"

Fang-hsin laughed. "What? He's your way out of this place. That Wu was a gangster, sure, but not in the same league as your Liang-fan. Don't worry about Jen-mu. Worry about having the time of your life."

"I can't . . . Jen-mu . . ."

Fang-hsin's voice narrowed into a hardened hiss. "Listen, Mei-fang. Don't let your imagination destroy you. You love Liang-fan—and he loves you. You can't back out now. Besides, *he* has to be the one to decide to end it all. You know that a man like him won't stand to be shaken free by his girlfriend."

Mei-fang yanked her hands back from her friend. "Go back to work, Fang-hsin. I need to finish my typing." But Mei-fang's hands shook so uncontrollably that she could not reliably finish her work. Her fingers wanted to dance by themselves, to slip between keys, find the places where they could do the most harm. She did not believe that Fang-hsin had given her the article out of innocence. Fang-hsin, hard and resourceful, moved in the same circles as Liang-fan—she had even introduced Mei-fang to him. The article had been a warning that was too dangerous to say aloud. Mei-fang gritted her teeth. She had asked for this position in life, had earned it. Now she had to find a way to protect her daughter from her own stupid choices.

At home, Jen-mu peeked at the dress under the plastic. She had laid it on the bed for her mother, but couldn't resist the temptation. It was a long red gown, cut so precisely in the shape of a woman that Jen-mu could almost see the curves of her mother already inside. With a slit up the side, the dress was elegant but a little too flashy for her mother, she thought. Mei-fang used to wear jeans and sweatshirts when not at work. Jen-mu marveled at the change. Her mother had become a princess, but Jen-mu knew the court in which Mei-fang now presided was not the type that little girls dreamed of. If it had been, Jen-mu would have been at her side, also dressed in finery. For a moment, she let herself dream that she was.

Darkness edged through the streets, and Jen-mu shivered. She hated night—it always seemed so unreliable and forbidding, final, even though, of course, it wasn't. Adults always seemed to like night, she had noticed, though she did not know why. She had some fun imagining that adults turned into great fanged, winged creatures as soon as all the children had fallen asleep. She was only allowed to see snippets of adult life, partial stories and secrets, but they tasted like sweets on her tongue; they made her want more, but they also felt vaguely forbidden. It would be perfectly understandable then if adults were only delightful monsters, ferocious but protective of their young, magical creatures that defied explanation.

When her mother finally arrived home, Jen-mu was bending over her homework at the table, the small light casting large shadows over the words. "Mother! You're late."

Mei-fang's face, when it came into the light, had the pallor of illness. When she spoke, her voice was hoarse. "Listen to me, Jen-mu. Listen carefully." She pulled a chair next to her daughter, knowing that Jen-mu would never know how she had agonized over her decision. How she only wanted to give Jen-mu food to eat, a warm place to sleep, a steady future. "You must take your school books and your prized possessions to your aunt's house tonight. Here." She pressed a thick envelope into Jen-mu's hand.

Jen-mu, her body shaking with a sudden chill, opened the envelope full of money. "Where did you get this? What's it for?"

"I sold much of the jewelry Mr. Lan gave me. You take this to auntie's house. Give her half of it, and hide away the other for yourself. Tell her that she must take you in." *Oh, her baby! How would she ever let her go?*

Jen-mu fought the rising tears in her. *Don't cry, don't cry, don't show her how frightened you are, Jen-mu.* Her aunt would not take her in—her grandfather, whoever that monster was, had forbidden it. But Jen-mu would not argue this with her mother, who danced on the back of a ferocious dragon. She could see the craziness in Mei-fang's swollen eyes. "Don't do this," she said. "Please."

Mei-fang began to cry. If only her imagination had always proved to be too vivid! "I love you, Jen-mu. You know that. I'll keep sending you money. Always save some. For cram classes. So you can go to the best university and make something more of yourself than I have. We'll see each other often, because I'm very good at sneaky visits." When Jen-mu did not react, she held her daughter's face in her hands. "I'm not abandoning you. You must understand that. I'm letting auntie protect you because I can't. She won't turn you away. You're her blood."

Jen-mu pulled her face from her mother's hands. She stood and closed her school books. Deliberately, as her mother watched, she stacked the books, placed them in her knapsack along with a change of clothes, her diary, and the doll she still slept with at night. She slipped into a sweater, for the night was chilly. She wanted to leave without saying good-bye, but as she stood on the threshold, she loved her mother more than anything on earth. Jen-mu ran to Mei-fang, threw her arms about her neck, and for a long time before they parted, they held their hot, wet cheeks against each other, flesh against flesh.

The Liu party, the social event of every year, was held at the opulent Grand Hotel that sat atop a hill overlooking the whole of Taipei. Mei-fang sat numbly next to Liang-fan and watched as he flirted with a woman who owned her own business, an art gallery or a jewelry store— Mei-fang did not pay attention to those details. Mrs. Guo pretended to be a woman of fine background, but Mei-fang recognized at once the coarseness behind the delicate gestures, the forced laugh, the calculations behind her dark eyes. She wanted to shout: *Did you have to give up your child? What did you give up to be invited to this party? Do you have any idea what real suffering is?*

"Are you okay?" Liang-fan asked.

"Yes," she said, but could no longer look at him. The boisterousness of the party felt as orchestrated as the list of guests: politicians, businessmen, old wealthy families who had brought their money from the Mainland, gangsters like Liang-fan who had acquired enough money and power that they could not be snubbed. She wished she could be at home with Jen-mu. Maybe she would talk to Liang-fan and tell him of her fears. He might say, that's nonsense, I would never harm your daughter. Or he might be enraged that she would suspect him of such a character flaw, and send her off alone into the night. He might laugh at her for thinking he intended to marry her. He might simply turn from her and never tell her anything. She could ask him for a public scene in which he made a display of rejecting her, so no one would think *she* had chosen to end their relationship. But she could not give her daughter away, not even to her sister. She would endure poverty for the rest of her life to watch Jen-mu bloom into the woman she would be. Late that night, when she was alone with Liang-fan, she would tell him.

Outside, Jen-mu huddled in the doorway of a small building just below the Grand Hotel. She wanted to catch a glimpse of her mother as a princess, to hold onto the picture so that she would not feel so lonely. As she watched the guests arrive, Jen-mu decided that night must be magic after all, with all the glittering lights, the laughter, the smell of rich food. Stretching her feet out, she wondered if Mrs. Hung would take her in if she gave her all the money. No one in the neighborhood would let her starve, she knew, but only Mrs. Hung would know not to call the police to have Mei-fang arrested. Mrs. Hung did not trust anyone, especially those in uniform, because she remembered when she was a tiny girl and had to flee the Mainland.

A figure suddenly came up the narrow sidewalk, and Jen-mu, surprised, pulled her feet in.

The man jumped back, peered at her through the darkness. "What are you doing here?" he finally asked. His voice was soft, sad, not at all like that of an adult.

Jen-mu looked at the man in the tuxedo, who, unlike the others, arrived on foot and with a backpack not unlike her own. He smelled funny, like the heater where she warmed her hands in the morning. "What's in your knapsack?"

"Firecrackers. And smoke bombs."

Jen-mu scrambled to her feet. Her mother had only allowed such things on the New Year, and even then in very small quantities. "May I have some?"

"No." The man took off his round spectacles and polished them with a bright white handkerchief. "You should go now. This is no place for a little girl."

"Okay," she said. She waved to him as if she were going back down the hill, but when he was out of sight, she jumped back into her hiding spot.

Jen-mu waited for a long time but she did not see anyone leave the party. Her eyes felt heavy and swollen. She sighed, closed her eyes for a minute, let herself fall into a hallucinatory sleep until her head dropped forward and woke her up. A faraway crackle of firecrackers came from the hotel, followed by shouts. Jen-mu thought with excitement: *the fireworks are starting!* She ran up the hill.

Hundreds of guests spilled from the hotel. Jen-mu clapped her hands. They were all coming out on the lawn to watch the show, and she had the best seat of all. She settled into the shadows as the fireworks man stood on the traffic island. But Jen-mu realized that the crowd seemed more agitated than excited, as if something were going wrong. They did not seem to see the fireworks man standing in front of them. Jen-mu did not know whether this was a show, or something else, something to be frightened of, but she felt safe where she sat.

The fireworks man shouted something about small people being ignored in a big place like Taiwan, and Jen-mu, in the shadows, nodded solemnly. His voice was strange, going up and down like a male bird in spring, taking unexpected paths that Jen-mu found funny. A clown, she thought excitedly. A fireworks man *and* a clown. The people in the crowd had fallen silent. Jen-mu wondered whether they were listening or just waiting for the show.

At arm's length, he held a cigarette lighter, which he flicked on with his thumb, a small orange light in the darkness. With a grand sweep of his hand, he lit a stripe of fire on one arm that suddenly ignited him in a burst of blinding fire that cut through the night as if it were the sun itself. A magician! Jen-mu thought. He shrieked like a hawk flying through the air and ran in crazy spirals that streaked the night with tails of fire. But then Jen-mu felt a sweet, swollen sickness in her belly. Was this really a show? The man spun and spun, his screams lasting no more than a minute before he dropped to his knees, his hands, the dark ground, illuminating the faces of the guests with his fire. Jen-mu could not move—her mouth felt dry and raw. The guests themselves made not a sound. No one made a move to put out the burning man. Finally, out of the darkness, a man ran wiggling out of his tuxedo jacket, and her mother flew out of the crowd with a white tablecloth billowing out behind her. Together, too late to save him, the two fell on the fireworks man.

Jen-mu inched her way deeper into the shadows, not sure of what she had seen, or what she should make of it, but knowing that she had witnessed something truly horrible. Until that moment, she had always wanted to grow up, couldn't wait, but now she wished she could remain small and unseen for the rest of her life. She would never understand this mystery world of adults, the way it kinked and folded and spiraled without warning. She turned from her mother, these other strange adults, and ran back into the comfort of the city.

Mei-fang saw a small figure running under the streetlight. Jen-mu! She knew her daughter too well to imagine her in the shape of any other child. What has she seen? Mei-fang thought in horror. She started to run after her daughter, but Liang-fan, not seeing what she did, held her by the arm.

"There was nothing you could do," Liang-fan told her.

Mei-fang looked down at her palms that had blistered in her attempt to smother the fire. Her skin was shriveled and tight, deformed, the way, she thought, they should remain for the rest of her life.

The Dance of a Falling Comet

When Guo Yi-cheng awoke, the sky outside was already gray with the first hints of dawn. He did not want to get up—his legs felt tired, and his wife felt so solidly warm against his back. He rolled over to see Chin-chai, who was still asleep and would be until he and his father returned from their exercises. He watched the soft rise and fall of her breathing, the peach strokes of color high across her cheeks, the gentle way her hair pushed up on one side, askew.

Yi-cheng padded into the next room. "Father," he hissed. The lumpy shape on the bed did not move, so he said a little louder, clearly this time. "Father."

"Yes, yes, yes. I'm coming." His father sat upright as if he had been only pretending to sleep. "Just a moment." He rubbed his eyes with both fists. Although he had always been a smallish man, he had shrunk since Yi-cheng's mother's death to a size not much bigger than a child.

After he dressed, Yi-cheng met his father by the front door. "You look well today," Yi-cheng said, pleased at the luminosity in his father's crinkled brown eyes. "It should be a good day to exercise."

As they stepped out of their building, a thin strip of bright orange stretched along the hilly horizon. Father turned to him, his mouth open and slack, and said, "We're late today! It's already dawn."

"Don't worry. If we walk fast, we'll reach the park in no time." He took Father's arm. Though Taipei was still dark, the first cars snaked their way through the narrow streets. Lights had gone on all over the city as people awoke to do their morning exercises, some already finished and dressing for work, children slipping into their school uniforms exactly the way Yi-cheng used to do—not *too* long ago, he thought. The full smells of breakfast wafted into the streets. Yi-cheng and his father waved to a group of middle-aged men who, also late, headed to the park. "I'm glad to see we're not the only lazy ones!" Yi-cheng called to them.

"We're not late if Mr. Guo is just now going!" one said. "The whole city should be following behind *you*."

Yi-cheng smiled in embarrassment. He was not yet used to such respect.

Then, to Yi-cheng's horror, his father called out, "My son the new assistant deputy to the mayor has been invited to the Liu party tonight!"

"The Liu party! What an honor!" the men shouted variously, appropriately expressing their enthusiasm before hurrying ahead.

Yi-cheng turned to his father to scold him, but when he saw the glow in his father's face, how much younger he seemed right then even on bowed legs, he held back. After all, his father had never thought Yi-cheng worthy or capable or even properly filial. Yi-cheng told himself that for once he should bask in his father's pride, and allow his father to do the same.

As the other men disappeared around the corner, his father's face clouded over with some other thought. Yi-cheng, who always felt most hopeful at dawn, refused to inquire for fear it would ruin his day. He would rather slow his steps to meet his father's brooding ones and enjoy the tingling sensation of his body waking up to another day.

As they neared the park, his father finally spoke. "That wife of yours, Yi-cheng. She doesn't have good friends. You should stop her from seeing them."

Yi-cheng laughed, though he was flattered by his father's concern. "Chin-chai is like a wild bird, Father. If I cage her, she will only try to escape. If I sit quietly under her tree, she will come to me and eat out of my hand."

His father snorted. "You watch out. Love marriages never work out."

"Oh, you're still angry that I didn't marry Hung Shu-tuan. Who, by the way, is fat and ugly at thirty-five."

"At least she doesn't have to work."

"Chin-chai doesn't *have* to work," Yi-cheng began. He stopped himself. His father now walked briskly at his side, looking up expectantly at him, waiting for the fight. Yi-cheng thought: it's not worth it. I can't win.

At the park, Yi-cheng performed the Tai Chi exercises side by side with his father, though he was not comfortable with Tai Chi. He preferred more modern exercises such as swimming and racquetball, but ever since his father had moved in with him and Chin-chai two years before, he had accompanied his father to the park. After he finished his last exercise, Yi-cheng watched his father's steady progress through his movements. His father glowed with the new orange of the risen sun, his limbs seemed supple and strong, his expression peaceful. Yi-cheng smiled.

He and his father walked side by side back towards the apartment. The sidewalks were crowded and more difficult to negotiate. His father walked gingerly, his shoulders hunched a bit, and Yi-cheng wondered if his mother's death had aged his father, or if Yi-cheng had been too busy to notice the gradual progression of old age. As they reached the building, Yi-cheng caught a glimpse of a familiar figure—stiff and square shouldered, wide head, quick but measured gait.

"Peng-yu!" he called after his brother-in-law. But already the city had come alive with the roar of engines and horns, and his voice did not carry. Peng-yu continued down the sidewalk without as much as a hitch in his stride until the teeming crowd swallowed him up.

"That wasn't Peng-yu," Father said as he waited for Yi-cheng to open the heavy door.

"Yes, it was. And I wonder what he was doing here so early."

Inside, Chin-chai had already dressed in one of her European suits, this one a magnificent turquoise. As the two men entered the apartment, she looked up from the table, smiled widely at Father, saved her secret one for Yi-cheng. "Come, come. Eat your breakfast. I have to leave right away for the art gallery. I've too much to do before our big show next week."

Father sat at once at the table and took up his chopsticks. Yi-cheng followed Chin-chai into their room. "What was Peng-yu doing here?"

"Peng-yu?" Her eyebrows rose in delicate arrows over her eyes. Her pearl necklace dangled limply from one hand. "Oh, well. I borrowed some money from him last week to put on the show. He came by to get a check from me. Everything is taken care of."

Yi-cheng took the pearls from her and draped them over her collarbone before fastening them at the back.

Chin-chai tipped her head back after he had fastened her necklace. "I love when you do that."

"You don't have to go in this early, do you?"

She spun to face him. "Yi-cheng! This is my *business*." Her voice was sharp, but she immediately softened. "Yi-cheng, I've so much to think about. You'll see, next week I'll be a better wife."

He kissed her lightly. "That's impossible."

She laughed, gently moved him to one side as she reached for her purse. "Mr. Assistant Deputy has a soft spot for women. Better report that to the KMT."

"Oh, what do they care. The mayor has four 'wives.' You should see me juggle them."

She turned to him with sparkling eyes. "Now there's a feat I would like to see."

By midmorning, Yi-cheng had a headache. One of the radio stations had criticized the government the day before, and Yi-cheng's job required him to tell the reporters swarming over town hall that the producer had been brought in only to be reminded of the law, not to be arrested. *And* an arsonist had torched another building, this time near the stadium, the home of a poor man who had lost both his wife and only son the winter before. *And* the mayor had inadvertently arranged to have lunch with two of his mistresses. The mayor instructed Yi-cheng, who had gone to the university with one of his sons and who thus could be trusted to keep his mistresses a secret, to tactfully cancel one of the liaisons, though he had not specified which one before locking himself in a meeting. Yi-cheng was forced to guess.

At lunchtime, Yi-cheng decided to surprise Chin-chai at the gallery. She had closed it in preparation for the show, and so he could have her all to himself without the awkwardness of customers. He swallowed two aspirins dry, hailed a taxi, and set out. The day was hazy, sticky, with light falling as diffusely as mist on the city. As Yi-cheng stood in front of the gallery, his lungs sputtered a bit in the acrid air—he'd been born in this air pollution and yet his lungs never managed it. Chin-chai, who had grown up in the country, said it only bothered her on the worst days when it lightly burned the back of her throat. Chin-chai always seemed hardier, he thought, though her bones were beautifully thin and long and light.

He let himself in by the back door, calling out, "Chin-chai!"

She appeared at once. Her face glistened with perspiration as if she had been exercising. "Yi-cheng! Is something wrong?"

"I was going to ask that of you." He stepped up to her to wipe over the fine droplets of moisture with the back of his hand. "You're sweating."

"A lot of work." She brushed a wisp of hair from her face. "Lifting the paintings."

He studied her, caught with the memory of her telling him that she never hung the artwork herself for fear that she would damage it. A lover? he thought incredulously. She *had* been anxious to leave home, reluctant to return at night. And what had his father said to him that morning, tried to warn him about? Her friends. His face reddened with the thought that his father knew about a lover before he did. Without another word, he strode out of the back room and into the gallery.

There, instead of a lover, he found only blankness. The walls, supposedly two days away from a show opening, had been stripped of everything, including a phone. White walls, holes, bare lighting fixtures. He stared at this nothingness. "What's going on?" He spun to face his wife. "What happened?"

She faced him with a set jaw, cold eyes. But when she opened her mouth to speak, her mouth shifted unpredictably, her eyes lowered. She burst into loud, shuddering sobs. "Oh, Yi-cheng," she said, "I'm in a lot of trouble."

"Tell me."

"I've written thousands of dollars in checks that I can't cover!" Chin-chai explained that she had borrowed money from family and friends, from Peng-yu, even acquaintances, to fund her show. But when she realized that she had spent more than she could recoup, she began to repay the loans with bad checks. "Soon everyone will know. I've been juggling for too long. They'll come looking for me. I'll go to prison, Yi-cheng, even if I return the money. It's too late. I was going to tell you tonight."

Yi-cheng sat down on a cardboard box. For a moment he hoped that his position as assistant deputy to the mayor might save his wife, but that hope lasted only for a second; he knew he was not important enough to be spared. He held his head in his hands and was amazed at its burdensome weight. "Why, Chin-chai? We were just beginning to have everything."

"Don't worry. I have it planned out." Her voice had taken an edge that he had never heard. He looked up at her, afraid of what he might see, but she was still Chin-chai, no longer crying, her eyes steady, a businesswoman. "I have two tickets to Hong Kong. We leave tomorrow morning. We can't miss the Liu party tonight." She smiled. "Our grand finale." She showed him the tickets, let him hold them, try to decipher what the information printed on them meant.

"Where did you get the money for these?"

She lowered her delicate flower face. "I borrowed more money to finance our escape. It's all safely in an overseas account."

As he held the tickets, his eyes suddenly completed the math. "What about Father? Where's his ticket?"

She sniffed. "You have to choose between us, Yi-cheng. He'd give us away." She started to turn away, but she could not. Her lips began to tremble like newly opened oysters. "Oh, please, Yi-cheng. Please forgive me. I only wanted to succeed."

Yi-cheng nodded, but he could not lift himself from his box.

Yi-cheng sat at his desk, unable to do his work, instead gazing out his polished window to the city below bathed in the dimness of predusk. He loved Chin-chai, thought life without her as barren and parched as a desert—he would die for sure. They had not even started a family yet. But Father! His sense of filial responsibility coursed like blood through him— he could not abandon the man who depended on him for food and shelter, a place to grow old. What should he do? His sisters would care for Father, they would have to, if Chin-chai had not wiped out *their* savings. *Oh, Chin-chai! Why?* She was asking him to leave behind the past as completely as though it never had belonged to him. How could *she* do it? He shuffled the papers in front of him, not seeing the words printed on them.

He thought of the Liu party, how Chin-chai, despite all that brewed beneath her pale, transparent skin, would not leave the country without attending this party. Once Yi-cheng, too, had thought it an honor that he should be invited. Everyone seemed envious of his new success. Now, he saw the invitation as a curse. Every minute he and his wife were visible was another dangerous risk.

And Father. There was always Father. His father would never forgive him for what Yi-cheng was about to do.

Every year, the Liu family held their spectacular banquet at the Grand Hotel. The Lius, perhaps the wealthiest family in Taipei, in all of Taiwan, believed in sharing their wealth in order to bring an even better year ahead. The Grand Hotel, looming like a palace at the edge of Taipei, glowed with yellow lights against the red of its façade. Cars streamed one by one up the hill towards the entrance. Men dressed in tuxedos and women in Western-style gowns stepped out into the night as if each were the most important, closest friend of old Mr. Liu himself.

Yi-cheng glanced at Chin-chai, whose face was beautifully flushed as she stepped into the lobby. He could not believe that her expression did not betray her crimes. She must have guessed his thoughts, for she gave him a steady, stern look. He wondered, as he had for the twentieth time that day, how he could know her so well and yet not at all. And how he could still love her after she had destroyed both their careers and families. Chin-chai smiled at a woman whom she knew from her gallery and left Yi-cheng to himself.

Yi-cheng milled about the guests: some from his office (whom he could not face); members of the presidential staff, though not the President himself, not yet, anyway; generals and their wives; aristocratic families who had established themselves decades ago when their fathers had fled the Mainland; the newly rich who had grasped the future of technology long before it had become a reality; and, of course, the gangsters, who had to be invited because of their legitimate businesses and illegitimate fortunes. With horror, Yi-cheng saw Chin-chai approach several of the gangsters. These criminals and their wives and girlfriends wore well-tailored Western clothing, the men with showy cufflinks, the women with jewelry too big and gaudy for their tiny faces. Chin-chai touched one of the men on the sleeve of his tuxedo and said something. The man laughed easily as though they knew each other.. Yi-cheng felt his heart melt away to nothing, certain that his wife owed money to the man.

Chin-chai had been right—they had no choice but to flee to Hong Kong. Even that was not far enough from the gangsters who lived like deadly parasites in the veins of society. She would tear out his heart for the rest of their days, and he could do nothing but put it back time after time—that was his destiny.

A series of pop, pop, pops sharply stung Yi-cheng's ears. He at once thought that someone had assassinated one of the political figures at the party, or that the gangsters had exposed their true selves at this elegant affair and that someone, surely, had been killed. But as the room filled with smoke, Yi-cheng thought, a fire. The women screamed. The men shouted evacuation orders even as their words were choked with acrid smoke. And where was Chin-chai? She would be crushed by the exodus of all these people. She would be burned alive. Suffocated in the smoke. He shouted her name above the shouts of others. He would forgive her anything as long as he could get her out of the hotel alive.

By the door, he saw the small figure of his wife washed out the exit by a wave of people pushing and shoving. The people who filled the space where she had stood churned and shouted. Where he had once seen elegance, he now saw the savagery of survival. As Yi-cheng stood at the back of the throng, not pushing, not shouting, waiting to die, a man pulled on his jacket sleeve.

"Pranksters!" the man shouted in his ear. "Firecrackers and smoke bombs."

Yi-cheng noticed for the first time that the smoke had thinned. He felt ashamed that he had thought that he would die. Maybe, he realized, he had hoped to die, for then he would not have to follow Chin-chai to Hong Kong.

The air outside the hotel rushed warm and sweet into his lungs. The guests had assembled on the front lawn, choking and sputtering, some laughing with obvious relief. As he started his search for Chin-chai, the crowd hushed. A shrill voice, a man's but as high pitched as a woman's, yelled, "You people think you're too important for little people like me. You can't even stand up and make our country free. You are not rulers! You are despots! When did you ever listen to me? Never! Never!"

Curious, Yi-cheng pushed his way past people until he drew near enough to see, on the traffic island, a small man wearing round glasses that reflected the fire of the cigarette lighter he held. Yi-cheng thought, Who is this man? Should I know him? But then he realized that, of course, the man was crazy. A peculiar scent hung in the air. Kerosene, Yi-cheng thought, just as the man, with a determined sweep of the lighter, set himself on fire.

For an instant, he thought it a publicity stunt, but as a primitive shrieking howl erupted from the man, Yi-cheng knew the truth. A man had set himself on fire in *Taipei*. How could it be? The shock rippled through the crowd in a silent wave. The burning man shrieked in his agony as he ran wildly from himself, spiraling on his own path, faltering, the dance of a falling comet. Images of fire hung in the air seconds after the fire had already passed. Yi-cheng tried to push his way forward. No one seemed able to move. No one seemed to think of saving the burning man from his hell. They stood like stony statues in Yi-cheng's path.

"Move out of the way!" Yi-cheng shouted as he ran towards the hunched heap of fire in the lawn. His nostrils were filled with an odor more sickening than smoke. He wiggled out of his tuxedo jacket, his heart bursting, as he threw himself over the man to try to smother the flames. A woman with a white tablecloth joined him and threw herself on top of the man. Why won't anyone else help us? he wondered desperately as the heat singed his hair, burned blisters into his skin. Finally, the flames went out, though Yi-cheng knew that the man had died long ago.

He looked up into the woman's face, expecting to see Chin-chai, but instead met the sad eyes of a stranger. She was a beautiful woman, obviously well-bred, with a red dress that had split on one side with her efforts. A thin line of tears rested on her lashes, but they did not spill. Yi-cheng wanted to tell her that he, too, would keep his pain inside of him, but instead he forced himself to look away from this woman who had shared with him, after all, no more than another failure. He stood.

Yi-cheng took a few, shaky steps towards the crowd, which had now begun to buzz with the excitement of it all. Chin-chai stepped forward. She came to him with steady eyes that did not wander to the covered figure lying on the ground.

"I was looking for you," Yi-cheng told her.

Chin-chai regarded the burns on his arms. "You'd better go to the hospital," she said flatly. "You will be scarred for life if that gets infected."

But Yi-cheng did not go to the hospital. He found a doctor among the guests who bandaged him using the hotel's first aid kit. The doctor wanted to see Yi-cheng in his office the next day. What next day, Yi-cheng almost said, feeling something shift deep inside him.

Late in the night, while Yi-cheng pretended to sleep, the bed gave ever so slightly as Chin-chai slipped under the covers. She smelled faintly of liquor and smoke, but not of the charred flesh that Yi-cheng could not wash off his own damaged skin. He wondered where she had gone, and with whom, but it barely mattered. He listened to the easy way his wife slipped into sleep. As the night sounds of the city swished in his ear, he thought he would never, ever sleep again, but near dawn, his body finally surrendered.

When he awoke, the day was already bright and fearless. He reached one throbbing arm over to touch his wife, but it fell heavily against the mattress. He sat upright. Chin-chai was gone, and in her place, she had left a note. As if it were porcelain, he gently lifted it and read her words, *You would have given me away, too.* She had not even bothered to sign it. He crumpled the note in his hand with the ferocity of a dragon. The pain roared back up to his shoulders.

The hunched figure of his father appeared in the doorway. "It's late, Yi-cheng. You didn't wake me."

Silent, because he feared his own voice, Yi-cheng looked at him from the bed.

Father drew nearer into the light. His face slowly illuminated with all its familiar folds and creases, the way his mouth turned down just slightly at the corners, something Yi-cheng had always thought a frown of disapproval but which now he saw was nothing more than another feature. "What is it?" Father asked. "Where's Chin-chai?"

Yi-cheng shook his head with the weight of the betrayal he had almost carried out and the one that had been done to him. He smiled weakly. "She's gone, Father. She caged herself, and so had no choice but to try to escape."

Father nodded and turned slowly to leave Yi-cheng alone with his sorrows, for which Yi-cheng was grateful. He did not want Father to see his tears of shame and grief. He did not want Father to see that his love for Chin-chai still burned inside him. He buried his face in his hands and held it there.

After a long while, he swung his legs out of bed and got dressed in his business suit. With burn-stiffened fingers, he secured a knot in his red tie. He looked at his tired reflection in the mirror with surprise. He had thought that he was taller, a little more imposing, younger than the man who stood in front of him. In the living room, he sat down next to his father to eat a cold breakfast before he left for work. Mentally, Yi-cheng plotted out his day. In the town offices, he would arrange lunches for the mayor. He would mollify the press. He would try to explain away the burning memory of the man on the lawn of the Grand Hotel. With his papers then sorted in front of him, outgoing and incoming, he would sit with folded hands to await the consequences of his secret.

At the Lesser House of Pablo Neruda

What makes a poet want a house that looks like a small and dismal fortress? The first time Christina had asked Armando this, she said it with apprehension, for she had not yet stepped out of the garden and into the house. Months later, with a laugh high in her throat, she had asked Armando this same question. But now she stands alone next to the bright blue guardhouse, looking at the vertical block of stone and concrete, the only windows being small portholes like those of a ship, and ponders this issue with a certain desperation. She may never know.

The gardens are bright, still blooming with geraniums, birds-of-paradise, cannas, ornamental grasses, though the ocean wind has the cutting chill of autumn in it. The edges of the leaves have yellowed, just a little, because they are, after all, pampered. Inside the guardhouse, the security men talk, their voices low and rapid, ready to change from easy familiarity to professional should Christina step inside and finger the volumes of Neruda's work. But Christina will not step into the building painted the color of an exceptional summer sky. Instead, she stands in the garden, gazing up at La Sebastiana's gray, grim exterior. With a shiver, she pulls her jacket closer around her body. She's not sure if she has the courage to round the back to the entrance because this may be her last visit, it should be. She wonders if the façade once scared away unwanted guests, people who did not know the real Neruda but thought they did. She wonders how many façades she has run from without bothering to look behind them. She wonders if Armando meant what he told her that morning, or if he intended for her to scratch through his words to discover a different truth. She wonders which truth she wants.

But she is here, at the poet's lesser house in Valparaiso, up in the steep hills overlooking the lower city and beyond that the ocean, massive naval vessels and freighters afloat, dark blemishes. She doesn't know much about Neruda, maybe a little more than the average Chilean, but she knows that the ocean had bewitched him. This explains the portholes and the interior of La Sebastiana, its siting, the wistfulness of this place. If she had to die now, she thinks, she would like it to be here. She will not kill herself, and she doubts that she will be killed at this national shrine, but the idea settles well inside of her, calms her a little. She must go on, she tells herself, she must go in.

The tour guide, in her crisp uniform, stands quickly when Christina enters. Christina knows this woman well by sight, has laughed with her, has asked many questions, and has seen pictures of the woman's children, though she does not know her name. "Hello!" the guide calls out, robustly, too loudly for this quiet place.

Christina smiles politely.

"Where's your husband today?" the guide asks.

"He's not my husband."

They lock gazes, and Christina knows that she has told this woman everything about her and Armando in silence. She is thankful for this wordless communication, because her words always sound either too small or too big, never exactly the way she wants them. How wonderful, she thinks, it would be to know the precise words. What is it about the brain of a person who practices the exactitude of language?

"If you need anything today," the guide says, "you come get me."

Even here, in the entrance, Christina cannot see the hand of Neruda because he had rented this area and the one off to the left to two artists, who, ironically, shared with the poet a love of beauty but evidently not color. The small vestibule is muted. There are hints, though, that lead into the soul of the poet: South American artwork on the walls, the room not rectangular but odd-shaped, asymmetrical, the paned-window doors she had just entered. This vestibule offers the possibility of Neruda but not the poet himself.

The idea of possibilities is what has driven Christina to La Sebastiana today. It was possible, she supposed, that Neruda would not have been awarded a Nobel prize, and then perhaps the Chilean people would have continued to scorn him because of his politics. It was equally possible that the poet's mother would not have died when he was an infant and then he would not have been filled with a lifelong yearning. He might not have become a poet, or at least not a great one, one more like Armando who could be both doctor and published poet without a hitch in his life.

Just before Christina goes up the narrow staircase, she says to the guide, "If anyone asks for me, don't say I'm here."

The guide nods as if this request is natural and without the undertone of fear. Maybe she is thinking of Armando and not his brother-in-law, whom Christina doubts the guide has ever seen.

Upstairs, the poet blooms with the surprise of a midnight flower. Colorful paint and the sparkle of the ocean fill the small rooms with vibrancy. Bottles of all colors catch the sun in pieces of rainbow scattered throughout the rooms. Tall, wide windows not at all like the portholes on the north side of the house illuminate the rooms painted multiple colors, hues of parrot feathers and precious gems. Here, in the heart of La Sebastiana, Christina finds hope. Armando's wife will not have her killed here; her blood would stain the soul of the country. But will his wife really have her killed, or did Armando make up the threat to discourage Christina? Would she want to be murdered instead of dying the slow internal death of old age decades from now? Might she die alone and childless even then? Again, possibilities.

La Sebastiana has the structure of Neruda's *Elemental Odes*: tall, thin, stacked. One room per floor, four stories high. Stairs that wind tightly. The décor has the clarity of language and the boldness of ideas. There are nooks and crannies and alcoves to offer the delights of a second reading. Textures of stucco and wood and burlap and glass promise underlying meanings. Curves and angles in the walls and floors take the circuitous route of a poet's words. Why then the foreboding façade? Is it a warning or a trick?

Christina walks the floors with care though her heels echo sharply against the walls. Today, she has La Sebastiana for herself. She imagines that it will not be for long. A tourist will walk up to the blue and brass gates and pay the admission. Or a bus will block the narrow street while hordes of North Americans spill out into the courtyard. Armando will stroll through the gate with a new, young lover, one who has not been found out, and he will whisper facts about the great poet that smell like cologne. His wife's brother, a *Carabinero* officer, will enter the gates in search of her, Christina, to arrest her on a false charge, to take her into the countryside to shoot her as they used to do. His muddy-colored uniform will be perfectly pressed. She closes her eyes for an instant.

In the bedroom, the top of the house, where a sour and dumpy guardswoman sits on a small chair, Christina thinks of love. She sees the double bed where Neruda lay with his Matilde, entwined, one eye on the ocean that now sparkles a deep blue concealing the cold current brought north from Antarctica. With all this bright light and color, she finds it hard to remember that she is in the middle of a dying season. Lovers can find warmth even in the depths of winter, she thinks, and hugs herself without knowing right away what she has done. She tips her head back to view the orange latticework laid over the blue shredded fabric pasted to the ceiling. Here is the top of the world, the end of the line, the cramped house that gave Neruda Valparaiso at his feet, where he staggered late at night after returning from his Pitcher Club. Matilde would have awaited him with a hungry love. Christina tries not to think of Neruda's second wife Delia who loved Neruda as well, but who languished, twenty years older than he, under the falsehood of their marriage as he romped with Matilde. When Delia learned of the poet's infidelity, she did not threaten to have Matilde killed, she did not try to destroy her husband. Instead—yes, wounded—she stepped aside. Why did this not happen with Armando and his wife? Christina might have been happy to live without marriage, as long as she had love. She wants to lie on the bed, just once, to feel the poet at her back. Filled with this yearning, she glances at the guardswoman, who seems to have read her mind, because she regards Christina with a narrowed, determined stare. Christina has seen this woman who sits like a bag of stones leap into decisive action as soon as a tourist threatens to touch an object, open a window, sit on the bed. The woman is Neruda's protector, his wall, the woman who wants no one to discover the intimacies of the poet's bedroom. Christina imagines that the woman hates intrusions and, by extension, she hates Christina.

The time comes to descend, but Christina cannot safely see the steps because of the unfallen tears washing out her vision. She trips, catches herself, continues, pauses every once in a while to look over her shoulder at the merriment painted onto the walls and ceilings. She can live well without a man. Without love. She can find a vocation that lifts her to heights that no one now can imagine. She is young, full of options; she can face the *Carabineros* with a face blank with bravery. She can be a Neruda in exile who returns a king.

The guide steps forward when Christina rounds the last turn of stairs. "No one else is here," the guide says. "Why don't you join me for tea?"

"Thank you," Christina says. Yesterday, she could not have imagined accepting because then she liked her life in boxes, one apart from the next, food divided on a plate so as not to touch. This guide belongs to a silent world that watched Christina's love for Armando unfold, but perhaps it is this tenuous connection that unexpectedly makes a shared moment desirable.

They sit in the small anteroom at a modest wooden table. Although the guide can see the entrance from her seat, Christina cannot. Her hands perspire with the knowledge that she may not see her enemy until it is too late. Then, she thinks: but he will not be able to see me, either. As the warmth of the tea fills her, Christina begins to relax. The two talk of small things: weather, flowers, traffic.

Christina finally asks, "Tell me how Neruda's women survived him."

"You mean, how they *suffered* him. He openly cheated on them. That's how he left one wife for another, that wife for still another. They put up with him, I suppose, because they loved him."

"It's easy to fall in love with the soul of a poet," Christina says. Would she have met Armando if she had not gone to the reading? She could see herself now with a man her own age who was madly in love with her, willing to do anything to keep her—all if she had not heard Armando read his poetry. "But I say, damn the poets. Full speed ahead."

"Your . . . your friend is a poet then."

"He's a doctor, too. He picks at rashes and looks into cavernous ears."

The guide laughs. "Healthy anger, that's what you have." She sobers a bit, places her cup gently, oh so gently, in its saucer. "He's married, isn't he?"

Christina nods. That's all she can do, she thinks, nod, nod, nod.

The guide sighs. "I used to think ill of women like you, but I've seen how much he means to you. Is it like a death, then?"

Again, she nods.

"My first husband was killed in the aftermath of Allende. If Pinochet says he deserved it, then maybe he did. But I can't think of politics. The gaping hole he left is still in me, even though I have a new, loving husband and two children whom I would not otherwise have had. You see? Things change, but they do go on."

Christina taps her foot; she knows this. This woman is not so wise (not that Christina expected her to be, but she expected *something* to come of this tea). Any life may fly apart in an infinite number of directions, none of them entirely predictable. Armando's wife can go to her brother, who is so enraged that he tracks Christina down. Or the brother may direct his wrath at Armando himself, or may laugh at his sister and say, "Come now, Chile isn't Nicaragua. We don't *do* things like that." Christina knows Armando will never stop cheating on his wife—it will be someone else soon. Perhaps Christina already knows her. Perhaps she will meet her in a restaurant where they both have forgotten their purses. But maybe there would *not* be another because at that very minute Armando might be struck down by a heart attack. "Things change, and they go on," Christina says softly, "but not necessarily with you."

The guide hesitates, the cup halfway to her lips. "You aren't thinking of killing yourself, are you?"

Christina regards her for a long time without saying anything. She enjoys the rising alarm in the other woman; she must seem unpredictable and a little dangerous. Finally, she smiles. "I wouldn't give him the honor."

"You be brave," the guide says as she pours them another cup of tea. "Just remember that he's the garbage."

Christina does not sip any more of her tea. The affair was not only Armando's fault. But she likes the guide's advice. It sounds noble. You be brave. She considers Neruda in hiding because of his condemnation of Videla's government, decrying the lack of human rights. Throughout, undaunted, he remained true to his self: lover, poet, politician. His Communism came into fashion, out of fashion, into fashion again with Allende, but his message and the way he spoke to the hearts and souls of humanity never wavered. He never lost sight of beauty and the vibrancy of life. She stands. "I should be going."

This time, the guide nods.

In the gardens, the light is fading to a golden halo. Outside, the building looks grim once again, the yellowing plants now more inviting than the poet. On the edge of the crushed gravel path, a kitten bats at an overhanging leaf. Christina remembers part of a Neruda poem she had memorized for Armando: "I shall never unriddle the cat./I take note of other things: life's archipelagoes,/the sea, the incalculable city." Armando had chided her for choosing that poem. "A minor poem. You should seek out dense underbrush." What if he had been right? What if she had chosen a more difficult poem? Would he have defended her against his wife? They might be standing in that very spot with fingers interlocked like thriving vines. She bends down to scratch the chin of the kitten, who purrs in her palm.

When she looks up again, she sees the khaki-colored truck parked outside the gates: the *Carabineros*. They could be there for her, or knocking at one of the wooden doors across the street. They could be advance security of an important visitor. Or they could be resting there for lack of anywhere else to go. Christina calms her heart. She can't change anything that will or will not happen. This sanctuary cannot be hers forever, because it belongs to Chile, to the world. With measured steps, she walks towards the gates and the street and whatever fate lies beyond them.

The Nearly Invisible People

The first time it happens, Walter is at the front window watching a pair of teenage girls. He steps back, away from the window, so they don't see him. One girl is big, sturdy. She slings a vibrant blue knapsack over one shoulder and talks with her head cocked to keep her dusky hair from falling into her face. The other has dark hair tied back in a ponytail that reveals tiny, well-shaped ears. Although there is nothing unusual about the girls, they have completely captured Walter's attention. They seem confident, even arrogant, oblivious to all but themselves, as if they have never witnessed or even entertained the idea of mortality. Walter cannot help wondering if one of them will die at an early age; he prays they will never be touched by the raw fear of death, never be betrayed, never be alone. As he thinks this, he sees, out of the corner of his eye, behind him and to one side, a face—a dark shadow the shape of a person, really, because it's barely within his field of vision. His heart lurches as he spins to face the intruder. But there is nothing, no one, not even a potted tree or a coatrack. The shock stays with him for a moment, rippling like ice water splashed on his skin. His fists are clenched and ready to strike.

He attributes this first instance to a glitch in his optical nerves. Not for a moment does he believe that it's Louise. His icy hands sweat a little from the fright, and he wipes them on his pants. When he returns his gaze to the window, he sees that the girls have disappeared behind the dense hedge. Suddenly, everything seems quiet, still, unremarkable. Instead of returning to his column, he turns on the television, the volume up high, and goes into the kitchen to find something to eat.

Throughout the afternoon, his thoughts repeatedly return to that startling moment. He knows how the mind can be fooled; however, despite its vagueness, the face struck him as remarkably solid. He had not seen features, but he had seen a head, one shoulder, he thinks, perhaps an arm. And he had sensed a distinct maleness, though he cannot point to anything to support this idea—the height maybe, or the squareness of the shoulder. A glitch, yes, but a strange one.

In the evening, he picks up the phone to call his sister-in-law, Patty.

When Patty answers, he cannot find his voice until she is about to hang up. "It's Walter," he croaks. He twists the telephone cord around his hand.

"Oh, it's you," she says.

"I'd like to see Lenny tomorrow afternoon."

She pauses. He imagines that she has hiked her buttocks onto the counter as she always does when on the phone, and is now tottering on the edge. "Why not? He's your son, isn't he? Steve won't be home from work till late. Will you be staying for dinner?"

"I think not," he says. "I know you're busy."

Patty does not argue. Instead, she tells him that Lenny gets home from school a little after three now that he's in first grade, and then she hangs up, not rudely but firmly, because they never have much to say to each other.

Walter has modeled several characters in his syndicated column after Patty, although she has yet to accuse him of it. Just last month he called her The Magic Muffin to describe the way that, the more she dieted, the fatter she became. His theory was that diet soda contains a leavening agent that causes her to puff up under the heat of her tanning lamp.

His fans write that he has an uproarious sense of humor, although he thinks he has none. It's the people he writes about who are hilarious. His bewilderment and his attempts to explain the unexplainable fool his readers into believing that his columns are outlandish, but they are drawn from his life. He thinks that his readers cannot be fooled forever and someday his column will be out of fashion. Even now, he is surprised that he is popular. Since Louise's death, he has written with a grim and angry outlook which borders on hysteria, but, to his surprise, his columns only gain in popularity. His only guess is that his readers cannot hear the tone of his voice.

When Walter arrives at his sister-in-law's the next day, Lenny has not come home from school yet even though Walter has timed his arrival to three-fifteen.

"I didn't tell him you were coming," Patty tells him.

She makes a pot of coffee. She is not grossly obese, but she is chubby, especially in the thighs. Walter notices that she wears an elasticized waistband. Although he can see hints of shared blood between her and Louise, especially in the deep-set eyes, Walter feels little for his sister-in-law, maybe a small amount of resentment and a growing jealousy. He feels no affection and no bond; she is a stranger to him. Lately, he has seen her as someone of whom he should be wary.

Patty chatters as she arranges chocolate chip cookies on a plate. She owns a parakeet named Chesterfield who mimics her clipped rhythms, although she does not seem to notice a connection between the bird's sounds and her own speech. She just tells the bird to pipe down, but the louder she gets, the louder the bird gets, until Walter fears that he will go deaf.

He has brought a Super Soaker water gun and a package of miniature peppermint patties. He sits at the table with the bag of chocolates on his lap.

"Well," Patty says, meticulously placing Walter's coffee cup at his right with the handle pointing at three o'clock. She places a spoon just to the left of the saucer, and the cream and sugar in front of him.

He drinks his coffee black, and she is clearly disappointed when he raises his cup to his lips without touching the cream or sugar. She should know by now, but Patty is the type of person who wants everyone to conform to her habits, mostly because, Walter thinks, she cannot comprehend why anyone would do things differently.

"Walt . . .," she begins and then loses her words. "Walter," she tries again, "Steve and I have decided to adopt Lenny. Provided, of course, that you agree."

She catches him off-guard, and the searing coffee spills down his throat. His lungs, his heart, his mind are paralyzed by a javelin of pain. Until this moment, he has thought of Lenny's stay with Louise's sister as temporary, but now he sees how the plan unfolded: his mother-in-law's concern for him, the discussion of what was best for Lenny, his numb agreement. He knew Patty and Steve were childless and desperate to love a child. "Just until you get back on your feet," his mother-in-law said. He had believed her, but he should have known they would fall in love with his child. Isn't it his own fault for not claiming his son this year and a half, for fear that he would upset Lenny's new stability? Part of him wants to agree to the adoption because it might be best for Lenny—having two parents instead of a single inept one. But he cannot give up the child who holds so much of Louise—so much of him. "I don't know," he stammers.

Patty straightens in surprise. "Don't be selfish," she tells him. "Think of Lenny. He has friends, a school, a good solid life."

Walter finds her promise of "a good solid life" uninspiring—he would have laughed under different circumstances. He and Louise used to joke about the middle-class idea of a perfect life: no surprises. Is this what Patty is promising, and is this what Lenny should have? He is saved from the decision by Lenny himself who slams the front door with a bang.

"Hey, Mom!" he cries as he skids into the kitchen.

Mom! Walter nearly chokes.

Lenny freezes when he sees his father. They have not seen each other in a month, a long time for a six-year-old whose summers last nearly forever and whose birthdays seem to fall once every five years. Lenny is getting huskier, looking more like Patty and Steve, and less like Louise and Walter. His true parentage asserts itself in his freckles and small, turned-up nose, remnants of Louise, and his strawberry blond hair and blue eyes, marks of Walter. However, those same features might just as easily be linked to his aunt and uncle—the characteristics were that generic.

Walter is shaking badly. He cannot control his hands and so he places them on the bag in his lap. He notices that Patty will not meet his eyes. "How did school go?" Patty asks, breaking the silence. She holds out her arms for Lenny to come to her.

Lenny eyes Walter suspiciously as he sidesteps into Patty's embrace. "Okay. Miss Robinson is going to put up my picture."

Patty gives him a little squeeze. "I told you it was good."

Walter regrets never asking to see his son's artwork. He holds out the presents. "I brought you some things."

Now Lenny acts interested, and Walter cannot help thinking that he is trying to bribe his son. Lenny takes the crinkled bag of peppermint patties. His lips curl, and he tosses the candy across the table and says, "Yuck. Worm food."

"I thought they were your favorite," Walter says. He remembers how Lenny used to call them "nose whistlers" for the way they cleared his sinuses.

"There's a rumor going around at school that peppermint patties are made of worms," Patty explains. "He hasn't touched them in a couple of months." She smiles at Walter in what he interprets as a smirk of superiority.

Walter wishes for a guide who understands what's at stake, someone who knows what to do with a son. Someone who will stop him from betraying Lenny again.

The next gift scores better. Lenny rips away the wrapping paper and cries, "Oh, wow!" when he sees the water gun. He pretends to spray the adults.

Patty taps her hands irritably on the side of the table. Walter knows that she doesn't approve of war toys, but *he* had guns as a child and loved them and he isn't violent. He doesn't worry that Lenny will grow up to be a killer.

"Can we fill it up?" Lenny asks Patty.

"Ask *him* to do it," she says.

She won't even touch the toy, Walter thinks with satisfaction.

In the backyard, Lenny and Walter romp with the water pistol; they play "squirt tag." Whoever gets hit takes over the gun and tries to tag the other.

"Ice cream?" Walter finally pants.

"Yeah!"

They don't ask Patty; they tell her that they will be back in an hour. Walter knows that he is playing dirty but he doesn't care. He wants to do irreparable damage to Patty's notion of motherhood. The instinct to destroy his son's trust in Patty and Steve is so strong that he must constantly remind himself that such an accomplishment would hurt Lenny as well.

Over hot fudge sundaes, Walter tells Lenny about his mother. He recounts the story of how Louise once bought twenty-five African violets and placed them on every windowsill, and then Lenny, who was four, woke up that night and knocked off every one. "Mommy wanted to stop you," Walter says, "but you were walking in your sleep and she had heard that it was dangerous to wake a sleepwalker. So she watched you go, plop, plop, plop, as you went around the house."

"I don't walk in my sleep," Lenny says sullenly.

Walter shrugs. "Maybe you don't anymore. But I'll tell you, you used to." He doesn't add that the sleepwalking coincided with the onslaught of Louise's cancer. "Your mother—"

"She isn't my mother anymore," he says. He thrusts his chin forward and pouts, just as Louise used to—or did he pick it up from Patty? Chocolate war paint streaks his face.

"She is and was your only mother," Walter says. "No matter what your Aunt Patty says. She loved you very much."

"She did not!" Lenny cries.

"You believe what you want to," Walter tells his son. "But it is better to believe the truth."

"Everyone calls her my mother." Of course, "her" is Patty. "The teachers, the principal, all my friends. You're the only one who doesn't." He pushes the half-finished sundae into the middle of the table.

Walter knows when the battle lines have been drawn. He wants to argue, to cross over to the point where Lenny can no longer argue, but he knows Lenny's next strategy, and Walter cannot bear being confronted with his son disclaiming Walter's role in his creation.

In the car, as Walter reaches across the seat to buckle Lenny in, he thinks he sees someone outside looking in at them, but when he glances up, he sees no one. Lenny also looks up quickly as if he has seen something, but when Walter asks, he shakes his head.

These half-glimpsed images of a face and body continue to haunt Walter throughout the week. He entertains several explanations: that he is going crazy, that he has a brain tumor, that aliens have invaded his home (frivolous speculation but good for three consecutive columns). Through various experiments, he finds that as long as he doesn't turn around, the face will remain hovering on the edge of sight. Walter can even walk around, bend over, read the paper, whatever, and it will follow him like a balloon tied to his back. At first, he fears these illusions, but gradually he grows used to them.

"Okay," he says as he spots one looking over his shoulder as he hunches over his bowl of cereal. He extends his hand backwards, groping for the point at which it disappears. Fascinated, he sees that the figure recedes, just out of reach, but when he draws his hand back to his lap, it is suddenly there, even bigger, practically resting its chin on his shoulder. He takes in a deep breath, and spins his head around as fast as he can, but the figure disappears; it does not remain with him, does not follow the pivot of his head as he would expect.

When the figure reappears later that day, Walter takes care not to turn, to see how long he can keep it with him. For four full hours, the figure hovers behind him. Finally, Walter can take no more. He leaps into the air and twists his body so that he lands like a cat falling from a roof. "Boo!" he shouts. But there is no one there to frighten. He is filled with an inexplicable sadness.

On the following Wednesday, Walter keeps a tennis date with his friend Wild Bill. Wild Bill, whose nickname dates back to his college fraternity days, is a beefy man, hardly wild anymore, though he cheats frequently on his wife.

Walter peels off his racket cover as Bill takes his position in the opposite court. Bill is dressed like a tennis pro—white shorts, white shirt with thin blue stripes on the arm bands, bright tennis shoes—too bad he can't play. Walter tries his best to look as though he belongs on the court, but he always falls short on his sneakers—gray, dingy, tattered things which he can't bear to replace because the soles are still good.

They rally for a few minutes. Walter swings the racket and propels the ball exactly where he wants it; he doesn't play hard, not yet, because Bill tires too easily. His thoughts are not on the game, anyway; he cannot stop thinking of Lenny and how his in-laws have tried to steal him. He sees Lenny becoming just like Patty, the Magic Muffin, fat and starving for affection.

Wild Bill yells, "Serve 'em up, Wally-boy."

Walter brushes aside his thoughts of Lenny. He tosses up the ball and swings through hard, sending the ball into a low, fast spin. Bill grunts as he tries to make contact, but the ball is already past him.

"Jesus Christmas," Wild Bill mumbles as he wipes the sweat off his forehead with the back of his arm.

Walter switches sides. As he throws the ball up, he senses a presence behind him and, with a swoosh, he misses the ball entirely. He stares in disbelief first at his racket and next at the empty space behind him.

Bill holds his stomach as he doubles over in laughter. "Wimbledon is next, kiddo."

After Walter gets over the shock of the nonexistent person, he serves again, this time not as forcefully nor as skillfully. Usually, he can beat Wild Bill with little problem, but today he finds it difficult to maintain concentration, and he loses the first game. As he awaits Bill's first serve, he becomes aware of not one but three presences behind him. Before the next game is over, the faces multiply until there is a whole audience behind him, cheering him on to win or lose, he can't tell which. They stand upright and expectant, waiting to flee the moment he glances over his shoulder. Until now, there has only been one face at a time, and this new turn of events unnerves him. He cannot keep his concentration. Bill wins game after game.

"What's wrong, kiddo?" Bill asks as he scores the final point of the set. "Am I getting too good for you?"

Walter shrugs. "Yeah. Too good."

"Come on. Something on your mind?"

Walter hesitates. As they stand on the baseline, Bill peering down hard at him, Walter tells him about Patty and Steve's desire to adopt Lenny. "It's just so final. It's like saying that I'm dead. But it's probably best for Lenny."

"Is it?" Bill asks as they head for the showers. "Or are you just trying to avoid a fight?"

As he takes a shower, Walter thinks about what Bill has said. He rubs the bar of soap in small, regular circles over his skin. Maybe he is afraid of disturbing the established structure of his and Lenny's separate lives. Louise would have been furious to see him surrender their son to her sister's good, solid life. He lifts his face into the hard spray and closes his eyes against its force.

Bill, already dressed, awaits him on the bench in front of their lockers. "You know, Wally-boy, that you're not competitive enough. You start out great, but your finish . . . Like today, you make a fool out of yourself with one serve, and that's it. You stop trying. It's the same with Lenny. They take him away, and you figure that there's no way for you to win anyway. One lousy serve."

Walter fiddles with his combination lock. "I kept thinking someone was standing behind me."

Wild Bill strokes his chin with both hands. "Hmm. Could be a detached retina, you know."

Relief sweeps over Walter. "Of course. I'll have it checked out." His eyes—just what he suspected from the start.

"You know, buddy-boy," Bill tells him in the parking lot, "what you need is a good woman."

"Yeah," Walter says. He doesn't have the energy to tell Bill that he can't hold a relationship with his son yet, let alone a woman.

He makes an appointment with an ophthalmologist who discovers that nothing is wrong except that he might need reading glasses in a year or two. The ophthalmologist recommends that he see a neurologist. Walter is sure now that he is dying; he calls the neurologist with doom in his voice. What will he tell Lenny? His worst fear seems to be happening: that Lenny comes to love and trust his father again, only to have him die.

After a battery of tests of Walter standing first on this foot, then on the other, eyes closed, under this machine and that one, the neurologist cannot find anything abnormal, not even a tiny hint of a brain tumor. The doctor suggests that Walter see a psychologist, but Walter draws the line at that. Throughout the testing, he has come home crying for Louise. The nearly invisible people swarm about to comfort him until he no longer fears his aloneness. He has begun to realize that these figures are real, not figments of his imagination and not the symptoms of some organic flaw in his body. And he is not dying, at least not yet.

He visits Lenny once a week, much to Patty's growing paranoia. At first he drives down on Saturdays, but he quickly sees how resentful Lenny becomes because he can't play with his friends on "the best day of the week." Walter asks him if he would prefer for him to come on Tuesdays, and Lenny's face lights up. Walter chooses a specific day so that Lenny can count on him.

"I take it that you're against the adoption," Patty hisses angrily at him as he comes through the door one afternoon.

"I haven't decided," Walter tells her, although he has. But he needs the assurance that Lenny will accept him.

"You're messing up his mind," she says. "He won't call Steve anything now. Not Dad, not Steve, nothing. He doesn't know how he fits in with us. And it's your fault." She clearly does not understand the bond between a real father and son.

"Why should he call Steve 'Dad'? It's your fault for encouraging him."

"Hi, Daddy!" Lenny calls from the top of the stairs. He scampers down the stairs so quickly that he loses his footing. Walter quickly grasps his tiny arm and pulls him to safety.

"Whoa, there!" he says, laughing away his initial panic.

Patty crosses her arms, smiling grimly. A sadness fills Walter as he realizes that she, too, loves his son.

Walter takes Lenny to a miniature golf course. His son hops with excitement when he sees the castles and windmills in bold primary hues, and the chutes and alleys and artificial turf that looks like the carpeting in Patty's basement. Grinning, Walter remembers the magic he felt when as a boy he first putted through a clown's mouth.

He teaches Lenny how to hold the club, how to swing smoothly and gently but not too timidly. "It's going to be hard at first," he warns his son. "But we'll take our time. This is a game that nobody wins, so it doesn't matter if you chip the ball out of an alley, or if you miss the ball sixteen swings in a row."

Lenny is hardly listening. He tugs on Walter's arm so that they can begin the first hole. The people crowd up behind them as Lenny chokes up on the putter and tries to send the ball through the door of the blue castle. The ball keeps hitting the walls and rolling back down. Finally, with a shout of triumph, Lenny sends it through.

Walter places his ball down and, in one confident shot, sends the ball through the door. Lenny's face clouds with disappointment. The club hangs limply at his side.

"Luck," Walter tells him. He curses himself. From then on, he makes a great show of almost getting the ball through, of winding up for a powerful swing and then missing the ball entirely, of klutzy shots and clowning. Lenny giggles every time Walter makes a mistake. Walter does a pirouette and sends the ball up a chute. Lenny tries to imitate him and ends up hitting the ball off to the side and into the next putting green. They laugh, their sides touching.

Afterwards, Lenny's voice is high and quick. Walter hikes him onto his back, and they trot back to the car.

Over dinner, Walter asks, "What do you think of adventures?"

Lenny's blue eyes brighten. He expects another game. "Like what?"

"Oh, I don't know," Walter says vaguely. His heart beats frantically. "A trip."

"A trip!" Lenny clutches his hamburger in two hands. "Where?"

"How about to my house?" Walter doesn't dare call it *their* house, although it once was and that is how he still thinks of it. He ventures a little further. "Maybe next Friday."

"For the whole weekend?" Lenny asks eagerly.

"For as long as you like," Walter answers. He accepts the weekend idea, although he had hoped for more. Still, he thinks, a weekend is better than nothing. He shouldn't expect Lenny to leave everything so quickly.

"Aw right!" Lenny cries. In his exuberance, he knocks over his glass of Coke, and, in trying to save it, smashes it against the edge of the table.

He recoils his hand and brings it to his chest, his eyes round and frightened, filling with tears.

"Let me see!" Walter demands as he slides into the booth next to his son. Lenny has locked his elbow, and Walter must pry the arm away from his body. On the tiny palm, a diagonal gash fills with blood.

Lenny shrieks. He tries to jerk out of Walter's grip; he shakes his hand wildly, but Walter holds firm, his heart thumping. Swiftly, Walter wraps the hand tightly in a napkin. His chest feels like it is collapsing on itself; the sight of the bright red soaking through the white napkin terrifies him. Lenny is screaming. Walter thinks, please God, anything, anything, only don't let him cry, don't let him hurt.

The waitress offers a first aid kit.

"Just give me directions to the nearest emergency room," Walter says. His voice sounds loud and harsh.

She tells him that the hospital is less than a mile away. When he struggles to get to his wallet, she stops him with her cool hand.

Afterwards, on the way to Patty's, Walter tells Lenny how brave he was when the doctor stitched him up. "Six stitches!" Walter says. "And I've only had three in my entire life."

Lenny looks over at him, quiet. He closes his eyes and leans toward his father as far as the seat belt will allow him.

Walter is moved by his son's new trust in him. He is also proud that he has handled this alarm without freezing as he did every time Louise needed to be rushed to the hospital. The memory of the last time, when Louise died in their bed, sends shudders throughout him. Louise hadn't slept in days, and he had rested only slightly more. The pain-killers didn't help; she couldn't stop screaming, even when her voice went hoarse. Walter had to send Lenny away to Patty's. When Louise finally lapsed into unconsciousness, he had panicked, had stood at the side of the bed and carried on her screaming, twisting the bed sheets around his hands, not knowing what to do, how to help her as her breath slipped away from her. He could have helped her, he tells himself, if only he hadn't panicked.

"Daddy?" Lenny says suddenly. "Why are you crying?"

"I'm thinking of your mother," he says. Lenny lays his bandaged hand on Walter's lap, and Walter is startled by its solidity.

Patty meets them in the driveway. Lenny holds up his bandaged hand, a little proudly. She turns white, then red. Tears of rage gather in her eyes. "Don't you know to keep an eye on him? What were you thinking?" she yells at Walter, hugging Lenny between her huge breasts.

"Accidents happen," he answers. "Fortunately, I was there."

Lenny nods from his precarious position. Patty glares at Walter before guiding Lenny inside with promises of television all evening. "Poor baby," she says.

Before Lenny arrives for the weekend, the nearly invisible people multiply. They are everywhere, in every room, flirting with Walter, nearly driving him crazy. One haunting face was more than enough, but now there are hordes. They begin to frighten him. He wonders how he will cope with them when Lenny comes. Will he slip and yell out at one, as he has taken to doing, and send Lenny back with ammunition for Patty and Steve? He resigns himself to the possibility that he will ruin everything this weekend.

When Patty comes through the door, her gaze is sharp and critical. Walter hired a cleaning woman so Patty would have nothing to complain about, and she is clearly disappointed that his house seems to be in order, not at all like a bachelor's place. Walter feels as if he has cheated a little by hiring the woman, since he is normally neat, but he tells himself that he should take no chances with Patty.

"Where's Steve?" Walter asks her a little maliciously.

She ignores him and crouches in front of Lenny. "You be good. Remember everything I told you." Her face is pale.

Walter gives Lenny a tour of the house. Lenny is quiet. Although he hasn't been in the house since the day Louise died, he remembers the layout, and soon he leads Walter. He touches walls with puzzlement in his eyes, as if he expects them to give way under his hands. Walter realizes with joy that Lenny has dreamed of the house. His son pauses at the doorway to the master bedroom and stares at the bed where he saw his mother lying for so many months. Walter squeezes the boy's shoulder, but Lenny shakes loose. They stand there for several minutes, staring and searching for the person who should have been there. Finally, Walter kisses the top of Lenny's head. Lenny reluctantly moves away from the door.

The next day, Saturday, Wild Bill brings over his two boys, one younger and one older than Lenny, and they have a "men only" cookout. The boys play horseshoes on the lawn while Bill and Walter cook the steaks.

"This is good," Bill tells him. "Lenny needs to know he can have friends here, too. Hey, Carl! Get your little brother out of the way before you throw those things."

The two men halt their conversation until they see that Jimmy is safe behind the other two. Walter grins as the boys inch closer and closer to the target; they aren't big enough to throw the horseshoes very far, even though the shoes are rubber and not as heavy as real ones.

"That Lenny is growing up to be a fine kid," Wild Bill says.

"He is," Walter agrees.

That night, Walter takes Lenny's pajamas out of his miniature suitcase, watches as he brushes his teeth, and offers to read him a story in bed. They clamber on top of the bed together. Walter reads from a book about a treasure hunt. As the story progresses, the room fills with people; Walter does his best to ignore them. He takes comfort in Lenny's weight against him, the sweet smell of his son's skin, the warmth of his flushed cheeks, the light and regular sound of his breathing. The people move in closer, pressing, taking up all the air.

Suddenly, Lenny squirms loose and says, "It's getting crowded in here." He throws his arms out.

Walter starts in surprise. "What do you mean?"

Lenny says nothing but he snuggles into Walter's chest, hiding his face, and Walter knows that his son has seen them.

"They won't hurt you," he tells Lenny.

Lenny peers up at Walter. "You see them, too? Did they follow me here?"

Walter tries to swallow but cannot. "No," he says, his voice breaking. "They've been here for a while. We must each have our own set. Are you afraid?"

Lenny shakes his head. "What do they want?"

"I don't know, Lenny. Maybe they just want us to play football with them or something."

Lenny laughs, a high, light, child's laugh. "They'll be kinda hard to tackle."

Walter marvels at the quickness of his son's mind. Was it so long ago that Lenny didn't exist? He remembers his awe and disbelief when Lenny fought his way out of the womb, a slippery, squirming, bloody mass that somehow became his son. "You know, your mother didn't die because she didn't love you."

Lenny listens thoughtfully. "I know," he finally says. He stretches his mouth into a huge, toothy yawn.

"It's late."

Lenny slips under the sheets.

"I'll leave the hall light on," Walter says. "Will you be all right?"

Lenny nods. " 'Night, Daddy."

"Good night." But Walter stays perched on the side of the bed until Lenny drifts into sleep. Lenny's peaceful expression contrasts sharply with Walter's anxieties, the wondering if he can raise a son, be counted on, be wanted by someone whom he had once betrayed. He bends over and plants a light kiss on his son's forehead with the hope that Lenny will dream the truth.

As he walks towards the door, he senses the faces reassembling behind him. In the doorway, he feels a light touch at his back, too high to be Lenny. He spins around and sees, for a fleeting moment, a line of people linking hands between him and Lenny, touching both of them with outstretched arms. Their limbs are strong and sure; their foreheads are furrowed in concentration. One glances up and sees Walter staring, slack-mouthed, and he smiles. As their flesh turns transparent, Walter knows that he will not fail.

Maria Angelica

Right now my name is Maria Angelica. The brothers and sisters of my gypsy tribe sometimes call me Chiriklo, Bird, but also Ababina, Sorceress, because of my ability to read minds. This sorcery is not the fortune-telling my people and I peddle in the Firenze neighborhoods, because that is a joke on the gaje—outsiders—who believe what we tell them. No, my gift is knowing the unknowable as it happens, not before. All in all, though, I am an ordinary sixteen-year-old with a gift for fancy words–and not the Queen of the Gypsies, as my Italian classmates call me at school.

At first the girls in school did not know about my gypsy blood because my skin is not much darker than theirs, and I speak perfect Italian. Because we were settled gypsies, I had an address, a television, running water, and a place to store my books. But as soon as they saw me eat lunch with my sisters and brothers, they knew. They also saw how the other gypsy children made way for me. (My generation does not believe much in sorcery, but we are raised with superstitions—my tribal brothers and sisters respect me for fear that they might be wrong.) "What's so special about her?" one towheaded girl asked a sister. "Oh," my sister said, thinking very fast, "she has been anointed the future Queen of the Gypsies. Someday, we will all bow to her."

Oh, we laughed over that one all the way home. Our people are spread all over the world and still the gaje believe that we must have a king and a queen. How can such a person rule so many different types of people? The gaje like the idea, though, and we let them have it.

One day my literature teacher, Signore Leonardi, heard me recite Dante with an Italian so lyrical it broke her heart. She had no way of knowing how well I understood the circles of hell, how the language lifted me out of their grimness, how I prayed for my own Beatrice to guide my heart. In front of the class, with real tears in her eyes, the Signore said, "I get goosebumps when I hear a student so impassioned. Maria Angelica, you just might turn out to be a great actress." She looked at me with her hand clasped to her chest, and a smile meant to flatter.

My classmates were silent. The gaje were humiliated by my gypsy success. The gypsies waited for me to sputter some curse in Romany. I choked back tears. She had just heard a gypsy recite Dante and thought not of a scholar but of an entertainer. I have seen my people run amusement parks, and train bears, and set monkeys on the shoulders of tourists so that they could snap their pictures, and play music at weddings and festivals as my father does. But these people are not powerful. They do not last in the world beyond their ten minutes of gaiety. This is my shame: I want to last. This is not the way of my people; when we move, we leave no trace. Even our history cannot be charted except through the words we borrowed for our language. With stone cold eyes, I said, "I cannot be an actress. I am a sorceress."

She asked me to stay after school.

Signore Leonardi was a thin, powdered and rouged old lady who smelled of artificial roses, but who knew literature as no other I had met. She believed in God, angels, and the power of words. When she was a teenager, an angel had visited her and told her that from her knowledge would spring greatness. Signore Leonardi had not told anyone about this, for people did not believe in angels anymore and if she told, they would stop believing in her. But all these years she had waited for a student to call her his mentor. Instead the children laughed at her. I liked her—she taught me care and determination in my studies, encouraged me to express myself. After school that day she lectured me on the backwardness of the gypsies and how I had to escape superstition.

I stood with a back as straight as a soldier's. "I see no difference between being an actress and a fortune-teller."

For a glimmering second, she understood my point, but something stronger, years of bigotry, pushed it out of her mind. She began to believe that I was not as intelligent as I had seemed. "What is it that you want with your life?"

More strongly than I had intended, I said, "Nothing."

She loathed me right then: an impertinent little gypsy. I didn't want her to hate me. I wanted her to understand, but I didn't have the words for it.

The Signore instinctively glanced over her shoulder to make sure her purse was still on the desk. These gypsies, she thought, will never rise above their squalor. Horse thieves and beggars, the whole lot. How can they be helped if they can't even recognize their own talents? She saw me as a bright flame with a short wick.

I said, "My wick may be short, but my flame burns slowly."

She gasped, leaned back reaching for the support of her desk. I had read her mind! With wild eyes, she crossed herself and fell to her knees on the dusty floor. As I left I thought, someone else genuflecting to the Queen of the Gypsies. Too bad it had to be her.

By that time my brothers and sisters had already scattered, some for home and others to dodge in and out of the narrow alleyways in the city, maybe to visit a parent selling jewelry in the Mercato Nuovo. Alone, sick that I had frightened the only teacher I truly liked, I walked along the railroad tracks. A train rumbled behind me and I stepped back in time to feel hundreds of eyes all at once seeing nothing. My head ached. I stepped away from the rails and instead started across a strip of field that separated the railroad from an olive grove.

A few yards into the field, I noticed a strange bending of the tall, brittle grasses. I crept up to investigate—I was sure I would find an injured animal, but found instead a young gajo lying in the depression. He was a slight boy, eleven or twelve, with skin as fair as linen, hair the color of wet sand. He lay on his back, his limbs splayed about him as if broken. Dried blood streaked his face from a cut above his eye. At first I thought he was dead, but as I bent over him I saw the breath lift his chest.

"Hello?"

His eyelids fluttered open, but his eyes focused only for a moment. He saw me then, knew right away what I was. In his heart, a small fear rose up—all the warnings his family had given him, the stories at school, the dirty children clinging to the hems of the tourists—but his fear quickly gave way to relief. He had been found. He might not die after all. Although he tried to look at me, his eyes would not obey. "Help," he whispered. "I can't walk."

I knew taking a gajo home could have serious consequences, for if the gaje found him with us, the police would storm into our houses, arrest our men for kidnapping, brush aside the women who tried to tell them the truth. My people do not fear famine or disease or fire the way we fear the police. Sometimes they arrive in the middle of the night to yank a few of us out of slumber to interrogate. Or they take our dogs and chickens, saying that they do not belong to us. Most of us accept this as a burden we have to bear, the price of being a gypsy and having the whole world at our disposal. Sometimes when we are forced to move, we call it Fate and leave a patteran or sign to the others who were not home so that they can find us.

I could feel the gajo's homesickness as though it were stuck in my own throat. I thought: this gajo could tear apart our lives. I sat back on my heels. I looked down at the red tiled roofs of the city, the dominance of the Duomo in its center, the glimpse of the river. I could have left him, but I knew the soft, swollen feeling the boy felt in the pit of his stomach. He was a gajo with no tools to rescue himself. His only patteran was me. Already, I saw the tapestry of Fate weaving around me, although I could not yet see the design. I had no choice but to carry him back to the village. If I left him there in the field, it might curse me forever.

I slipped one arm under his head, the other under his knees, and with great difficulty lifted him. We proceeded slowly, for I often had to stop to put him down. I sang in a loud, clear voice to give me strength and to ease the fear in him.

My people saw me coming through the dusk of the fields. At first, they believed that one of our brothers had been injured. The more superstitious believed something closer to the truth: that I carried the body of an angel back from the depths of death. Then, one by one, they saw the glint of the setting sun on the gajo's fair head. The cries went up, "Stop, Chiriklo! Stop!"

My mother came running down the street, her red scarf slipping off her head to fly free on her back. "Chiriklo!" she cried. "It's bad luck." Unlike the others, who had formed a human wall blocking off the road, my mother broke free, ran all the way to me. "What are you doing?"

"He's hurt."

"Put him down. The men will leave him in a gajo neighborhood."

Looking her in the eye, I raised my voice so that the others could hear. "It has been written in the stars that this gajo should enter our camp. We must not fight Fate." My brothers and sisters looked at me with doubt for the first time in many years. I had taken my big toe and pressed it against the invisible line of honor—a gypsy does not tell fortunes to other gypsies, since we all know that it's a fraud, but we believe in omens, signs, Fate that ordinary people cannot see but which I, as an Ababina, must translate. But my words sounded to them like a fake fortune. "Ask Old Ababina, my teacher. See if she agrees." This, I knew, was my only hope. My teacher feared the powers within me. She was not a real sorceress. When she cast her spells, she thought idly of dinner and drink.

The old woman hobbled out to where I had laid the boy in the grass. Her bangled arms jangled. My mother glanced nervously up the road for signs of avenging gaje. Old Ababina did not know what to say because she could not find any reason to admit the gajo into our community. But she saw the resolve in my face and feared crossing me. Because she had no real powers, she had no way of knowing that I would never harm her. For now, it was better that way, because she said, "The girl is right. We must accept whatever he brings."

The clan made way for us as we carried him into my house. We laid him on my blood brother's bed, and the women went to work in cleaning him up with a soft cloth dipped in water.

"Where am I?" the boy asked. He tried to focus his eyes but the room throbbed with his pain.

"Here," I said in Italian.

In Romany I told the women to look at his leg. The ankle had swollen horribly. They placed poultices on his wounds that smelled foul to the boy. He wrinkled his nose in disgust, but his head still spun, and he could not protest. After the women had finished, I told them to leave me alone with the boy. They were all too glad to stop touching his light skin which looked like disease to them.

"What's your name?" I asked.

"Giorgio. What's yours?"

"Maria Angelica. But you must call me Celeste." In France, I had been baptized three Sundays in one month, with three different names, for the feast that the church gave afterwards. Marie Angelique had been my first, Celeste my second, Jeanne Sarah my last. We had not yet settled down, and my mother thought it a blessing to have three different names. Only in Italy, with school papers, had I become Maria Angelica. "Say it. Celeste."

"Why?"

"Trust me. For your own well-being, you must call me Celeste."

None of this made sense, and for a moment the boy imagined that he had fallen into a movie. *Celeste*. An angel from the heavens. No, a newly fallen devil who had touched the majesty of heaven only to be plunged into the depths of darkness. "Celeste." He fell in love with the lines of my face, not as a man would, but as one would with a savior. Part of him liked the fact that he had been carried half-conscious into this gypsy village— it would make a good story when he escaped.

"I don't like that story," I told him. "It'll bring harm. Tell me *your* story."

He closed his eyes, confused about how I had known his thoughts, but he was too drowsy to figure it out. In halting words he told me that he had run away from home. His mother had bought him a new pair of shoes out of the grocery money, and his father had gone crazy when he found out, hitting first Giorgio's mother, then Giorgio. He stopped the story and began to cry. He had no words for his sorrow. After a few minutes, he dried his eyes on the blanket and told me that he had followed the railroad out of Firenze. When he got tired, he built a pile of stones balanced on the rail with the hope that it would derail the engine. When the rocks did nothing, he furiously threw a stone that ricocheted off and hit him in the forehead. The train never even faltered, but blood poured from the wound, blinding him. Panicked, he ran. When he tripped, he was too surprised to catch himself. His head hit the ground with a thud he could still hear. The next thing he remembered was me.

Maybe it *was* Fate, I thought as I counted all the things conspiring against this boy. What were the odds of only one of these things happening to him, let alone all three?

"Do you love your parents?" I asked.

He sighed. "Of course."

"Give me their address."

"You won't hurt them?"

I laughed. "Me? No. I'm going to help you, silly Giorgio. You're going to live, after all. I'll ask one of the men to carve you a nice stick to help you walk. And my mother to give you supper. Until then, you should sleep."

Hidden behind a curtain, I changed into my gypsy costume: red, gold, bright blue gauzy things that I had not worn since my mother last made me tell fortunes. I lined my arms with bangles. As I caught my reflection in the small mirror over the sink, I cringed. Signore Leonardi would turn from me, scornful of what I was about to do, not for the goal but for the means. I pushed her rouged face out of my mind, promising myself that this would be the last time I wore gypsy clothes.

On the stoop outside, my father began to play his violin. When he played, I could hear his soul. Lately, settled in Firenze, he had lost weight, his cheeks had hollowed, his teeth had dropped out. His hand had grown unsteady—except when he played. How is it that standing still gave me freedom but killed it in my father? As I went outside, I kissed his cheek. "I need a ride into the city."

He stopped playing. The shadows of the evening made deep holes in his face. He looked at my gypsy costume with alarm. "But it's night!"

Several of our brothers and sisters had grouped around him in folding chairs to listen to his magic. They took up his cry. "It's too late," and "It's dangerous," and "Whatever it is can wait."

"I want to make sure the gaje stay away," I told them.

They did not believe me, any more than anyone would believe a sixteen-year-old girl who wanted to slip into the night. My status as ababina was failing me; I had pushed too far. But no one would dare tell my father what to do. They watched my scarves slip off my shoulders and thought that I should marry to bring good money to my father's family. But she's almost too old, they thought, for a gypsy bride.

"I'll bring back money, I promise." My hands trembled, but they were hidden in the folds of my clothes.

My father looked me up and down, seeing I had grown too big for the costume. "I'll ask Vittorio to drive you," my father finally said. "He'll stay with you."

Vittorio had bad teeth and was more connected to the old ways than others of my generation, but he could also move a soccer ball up and down the field with the grace of a ballet dancer. When he joked, he had an easy way about him that pleased many of the young girls. He had ready money—at fourteen, he had given up school to work in a factory, claiming to be older than he was, for he looked it. Now, at sixteen, he seemed rich. Our families had tried to arrange a match between us, but I had muttered something about devil children. He was relieved because he could then be betrothed to Clairette, his true love.

We drove in Vittorio's father's truck. The city was aglow with the night, shining yellow and gold and hiding in darkened patches. The Duomo rose above it all like a beacon to the heart of the city, but it pulsed by disappearing behind a row of buildings, appearing again at a corner, disappearing a block or two down. Not too far from Giorgio's address, we found a parking spot large enough for the truck.

We hurried through the alleys of Firenze, those dark and mazelike passages filled with hissing stray cats. The city at night has its mysteries, whether real or imagined, that comfort me with their enfolding. As a gypsy, I know it all, have traveled over nearly every inch of the city's roads. This is not a city for standing still. At every turn, you might run into a marble arm, a bas-relief carved into the stone of an ordinary house, a fountain figure stained at the mouth with lime from so many centuries of dripping water, and just as easily, a criminal or a madman. Paris is exposed, Toulouse suspicious, Monaco intolerant, but Firenze—it is a city of entwinement. This is what I thought as Vittorio and I slipped through the narrow streets: everything is connected.

We reached the address Giorgio had given me. In the shadows across the street, I told Vittorio to stay hidden. "I'm going to tell a fortune. You'll only frighten them."

"I promised your father."

"I'll make a bet with you. If nothing happens, you won't tell my father. But if something bad happens, then I'll let you marry me." I nudged his ribs.

He chuckled in the darkness. "If something bad happens, I won't want you."

Giorgio's building was of the same yellowish-beige stone as the rest of the city, neither rich nor poor, stained, crumbling in spots. I wondered why a boy would run from a place that would have easy meals, durable clothes, a place that would not vanish one day when he came home from school. And why his parents would chase him from it.

His father answered the door, almost closed it on me when he saw the light catch my bangles, but he saw Vittorio move away in the shadows and for an instant believed it might be Giorgio. Giorgio's father was a short man, not much taller than my father, with thick eyebrows.

"Fortune?" I asked quickly. "Please?"

He looked at me. What was a beggar doing here at night? "Go away."

"But I feel great misfortune here. Much discord."

"Who is it?" Giorgio's mother came behind him, not the frail woman I expected, but one putting on the weight of marriage, childbirth, rich food eaten day after day.

"A gypsy girl," he said, starting to close the door.

"Shoes!" I shouted. "Three people and a pair of shoes. And something lost."

"Wait!" the mother said. She pushed her way forward. She saw me, a harmless girl in too much color. "What do you know?"

"I will tell your fortune. Perhaps the world of spirits will help you to find that which you seek." My mother had taught me to speak in regal language so that the gaje would be drawn in. It came as naturally as running across a field in bare feet.

They let me into their simple home, though neither trusted me. Their mutual desperation—and that I was a girl—lowered their guard. Everything about the house was solid and heavy, largely immobile, as if these people planned to stay there forever. I wondered what it would be like to have a sturdy home without fear of being chased from it. This new mystery of another, not-so-distant world thrilled me as it spread out before me in chintz drapery and inherited mahogany chests, hard-cover books with glossy photographs, a faded fresco of an illegible myth above my head. But I forced myself to concentrate on the fortune. I sat on a worn brocade chair while they sat across from me on a sofa, their hands woven together as they waited. I usually pretended to read palms, but these people needed to hang on to each other. Instead, I asked for the shoes, which I held against my chest.

"I see a young boy, sandy-headed, very smart but meek."

"Giorgio!" his mother gasped.

"Quiet." The father knew I could have been speaking of a thousand Northern Italian boys who lived in the city. "What do you know?"

"He has fled of his own accord. These shoes—he is angered and frightened by them. They have caused great pain. He does not understand why his parents care more about the shoes than about him."

"That's nonsense," his father cried out. He feared that I might have something to do with Giorgio's disappearance. He considered calling the police. But the pain of not having his only child safe at home ached in him; if the gypsy could help, he would not chase her away. He *loved* his boy. The phone rang, and he rose to answer it in the next room.

The mother wanted to cry—a strange gypsy understood her son better than she. She already missed the sound of his hurrying footsteps, his voice that grew loud in excitement, the sly way he teased her. "How do you know all this?"

"I am learned in the ways of the spirit."

She leaned forward. "What must we do to get him back?"

I closed my eyes again. "He will return only when you have learned to distinguish between the insignificant and the significant. When you see the soft, white bread under the burned crust. You must accept love and life for what they are."

"Is Giorgio all right?" she whispered. "Is he in danger?"

"I see him in the sun's morning rays seated on steps. Many steps. It is quiet, as in a park. Yes, a park. The birds sing. You find him when you are at peace." I opened my eyes, blinked as though coming out of a trace. "I'm sorry. That is all."

"Thank you," the mother said, feeling hope. She went to the cabinet and removed some lire bills, which she then pressed into my hands. I thanked her with a deep bow without counting it because I knew she had been generous.

Giorgio's father came back into the room just as I was tucking the money into the folds of my costume. "Hey!" he shouted.

The mother hurried to him, pressing him back a little. "It's all right, Marco. I gave it to her."

I slipped towards the door. "Thank you," I murmured.

Giorgio's father lunged towards me. "Stop! You know where Giorgio is. Tell us!"

But I dashed out the door and into the streets. Giorgio's father was slow and breathless from the cigarette smoke clogging his lungs, and his heavy footsteps stopped well behind me. My slippers soft against the pavement, I ducked into the alley where Vittorio awaited me. I did not stop running.

Vittorio sprinted next to me. "What happened?"

"Quick!" I hissed. "Before they call the police." I wished I could toss the false gypsy clothes from my back and sprint naked through the streets until I came to a place where I could rest. Running like that, with my scarves trailing behind us, we said more about ourselves than was true.

At home, in front of everyone, I placed the money in my father's hands. My brothers and sisters watched in amazement as my father peeled back first one bill, then another, and another. Even I could not believe in the generosity of Giorgio's mother. Someone whooped in triumph, and others followed.

My father looked at me with frightened eyes. He believed that I had gone to Giorgio's house and demanded a ransom. He could not bear to accuse me, and yet, if I had done this criminal act, he could no longer call me his daughter.

"I told their fortune," I assured him. "It will bring them back together."

My father nodded. He wanted desperately to believe me.

My mother stroked my hand—her skin felt rough and pitted, as though this life were eroding her. "Your gajo has been asking for Signorina Celeste."

"Oooh, ho, *Celeste*," Vittorio said. By not using my real name, I had shown that I would not betray my clan for the sake of a sickly gajo. My father always told me, "Never give away a gypsy secret, not even a small one. Because then the gaje will fill it with water until it swells so big that we drown."

I went to see Giorgio, who sat up in bed with round eyes. He was happy to see me, for he had begun to fear that I had sold him into slavery. "Go to sleep," I told him. I sang him a lullaby that reminded him of the brilliance of the stars on a dark, country night he had spent with his father. He knew then that I was a friend.

The next morning, I told Giorgio that he had to return home. "The police are looking for gypsies," I said. "They'll arrest us."

"But you did nothing wrong!"

I sighed. How could I tell this boy, who had solid furniture, about the soft ground we gypsies walked on every day? He cried and pleaded with me to allow him to stay one more day. He had such a strong smile, and such a passion for this adventure, that I finally relented. The police knew that our tribe did not get into trouble. Eventually, though, they would get here. "All right," I said, feeling the danger in the air, remembering how Signore Leonardi had once told the class that risks gave rise to either greatness or defeat, never both. "I'll talk to my parents."

But they, with the other adults, were already packing the trucks to go into Firenze. I hopped in the back next to my brothers and sisters, smoothed my school uniform, arranged my books on my lap. My mother gave me a hard look when she did not see Giorgio. She thought that she had a foolish, idealistic girl, but she had never loved me so much as when she looked at me and saw the poise of womanhood on my cheeks.

At lunch recess, I went to Signore Leonardi's room instead of eating. She sat at her desk, her head drooped forward, a half-eaten apple in front of her.

I cleared my throat. "Excuse me, Signore."

She quickly righted herself, her back as straight as an axle. "Maria Angelica! Come in." She no longer feared me, having discounted my mind-reading as mere coincidence. When she saw me, she remembered my voice as I spoke Dante, and was filled with fondness. She had to rein herself in so that she did not reach out to take my hand—she feared that I would misunderstand affection for patronization. "What is it?"

"I'm sorry for being so rude yesterday."

She smiled. "There's a lot between us that we can't understand."

I nodded, still not feeling right. "What do you think is more powerful, stability or mutability? Permanence or a fleeting effect?"

She looked at me, her mouth opened to answer "stability and permanence," but she quickly saw the problem. "That depends on the situation, don't you think? Sometimes a fleeting moment can have a lasting effect."

I slipped into the desk directly in front of her. "Heavy furniture can survive natural disasters."

"But portable belongings can be saved more easily." She rapped the side of her desk; she liked the way I asked questions and gave serious thought to their answers. Most of her students were glib and frivolous.

"But which would you like to be?" I asked. "Permanent or fleeting?"

"Permanent, of course. I don't want to die. But I don't have a choice, do I?"

I realized that the gypsy notion of Fate permeated, at least to a small degree, the entire human race, because no one could escape the inevitability of death. In my mind, I imagined an iridescent orb that contained all of us, except that some lived on the outside and some on the inside.

Signore Leonardi clicked her tongue. "The *effect* of some people can outlive them. Sometimes an act of greatness can take up only a few, brief minutes of a lifetime. And sometimes running away is a heroic act. A single act of greatness can never be separated from the person, or the idea of that person, ever again."

"But what is greater: an actress or a scholar?"

"Ahh." She understood at once her mistake the day before, and could see that my rudeness had come out of a broken heart. "A great actress is a great actress," she said gently. "A great scholar is a great scholar. It's not up to us to judge which is the better person." She peered at me through her glasses. "Do you want to be great, Maria Angelica?"

I looked at her, about to say yes, but all the centuries of gypsies came down on my shoulders. I should fight for my independence, they told me, and the only way to do that was to keep moving, to never stand still or to give anyone my proper name. With permanence, I would lose who I was. Others would capture me in spirit and make me into what they wanted. "I'm sorry," I muttered. I could not stop my legs from running as fast as they could to join my brothers and sisters in the courtyard.

When I got home that evening, I told Giorgio that he was not going to stay with us for another day. "You're a curse," I told him. "You'll destroy us." And I turned from his hurt that trailed after me as I left the room.

The next morning, Giorgio's watch had disappeared off his slender wrist. I swore at my brothers and sisters for not leaving this gajo exactly as I found him, for to take something from him while he slept in our house would surely bring a scourge to the tribe. Oh, how Giorgio cried for his watch—his grandfather had given it to him. He accused me of stealing it.

"You hate me!" he said.

I looked at the tears welling up in his clear eyes. "No, Giorgio," I said softly, feeling how deeply I had wronged him. "I'll get the watch back to you. But now, we have to get you home."

We rode into Firenze with the women who sold wares at the market. Giorgio and I hurried towards the river. As we walked, people did not know I was a gypsy. They saw a young girl in a school uniform talking to a small boy, her younger brother perhaps, who limped while leaning on an intricately carved cane. I told Giorgio that he must never tell anyone where to find me, even if they promised to give me a reward. "Gypsies never get rewards," I told him.

"What should I say, then?" He wanted to tell his friends that he had slept in a gypsy house, one that was clean and smelled of spice and incense and stewed chicken. How the bed was the softest, warmest place in the world. He wanted to tell a story of a gypsy girl who had devoted herself to him and who had at great risk to herself smuggled him into the city. He could imitate the cryptic intonations of their language. He could not see the harm in that. He imagined that he and she would be famous.

I stopped him in the street and took both his hands. "Giorgio, we will not be famous. Please. If you must tell about gypsies, tell them that you disguised yourself as a gypsy and slept in the train station. Tell them how you survived by your wits. How the other gypsies thought you were one of them."

This gajo had the instincts of a gypsy for the art of storytelling; he was already forming details in his head to make the account believable. Then, he thought of me, how he liked me. "I hope we'll see each other again."

"You never know. Now, let's hurry."

We stole into the Boboli Gardens through a space I had heard about. When I last saw Giorgio, he had sprawled himself over the stone steps. A handful of stray cats slunk around in the shadows not at all sure of this strange presence who smelled at once of earth and human. As he watched me leave, he felt a loneliness, for he would have liked us to be friends. He would have liked to live a little longer among the gypsies who were not as fearsome as everyone claimed. He liked our music and our food, the way dogs came in and out of the houses whenever they pleased. With a sad hand, he waved good-bye.

I waved back. Good-bye, gajo, I thought, please keep your word. I wished that I could have stayed with him, even though I saw that his world, too, had its dangers.

I had saved a little money for myself from the fortune-telling, and I used it to take a bus across the city. I thought of Signore Leonardi. I wondered if her house was as solid as Giorgio's. Suddenly I had to see again where Giorgio lived. I hopped off the bus. As I turned the corner of Giorgio's street, I froze. Two policemen stood in front of the house talking with Giorgio's father. One of them held back the arms of a young man. As I drew closer, I saw that the young man was Vittorio. He saw me, and my heart died. I could not turn and run since they would see me for certain and give chase. I could only pray that Vittorio would not betray me. I tried to appear calm as I walked by on the other side of the street. My nerves were too rattled to even try to guess what anyone thought; I could only walk with my eyes focused straight ahead. And pray that Giorgio's father did not recognize me.

"He came with my son's watch," Giorgio's father told the police. "A gypsy girl came here last night. She must have been in on it. My poor wife is out looking for Giorgio when he is being held captive by those savages!"

"We'll get him back," the second policeman said. "I know where this rascal lives."

My knees almost gave way. Walk, Maria Angelica, walk, I commanded myself. Just then, Giorgio's father looked at me, but all he saw was a schoolgirl on her way to class. He did not recognize me without the gypsy clothes.

Vittorio saw the gaje accept me as one of his people and not for the gypsy I was. He smiled to himself. They were stupid, these gaje. He hoped that I could get back to the camp before the police could reach it. He had not asked for ransom, only a reward. He had used the watch to prove that he knew where Giorgio was. He wanted Giorgio safely out of our homes.

I turned the next corner and ran as if on wings. Although we had televisions, water heaters, and small electric ovens, none of us had a telephone. My only hope was to reach the market and the women, so that they could drive back. I ran until the pain in my feet leaped all the way up my legs in a terrible shooting heat.

"Mother," I shouted. "Quick! The police have Vittorio and they think he has kidnapped the gajo! They're headed for our homes!"

She looked at me with her mouth shaped like a gasping fish. She heard my words, but she could not understand them until I said, "Vittorio stole the gajo's watch and tried to get a reward."

My mother shouted words to a sister, and the two hurried off towards the car to try to warn those who had stayed at home. Although my mother knew the police would find nothing, she also knew they would find *something*. My last glimpse of her was a dark head, a worried face turning to make sure that I was safe, a hand flying up as a farewell wave.

I left the marketplace. I sat by a fountain of dancing nymphs and closed my eyes. By nightfall, our homes would be vacant. On the side of the road, someone would have left a patteran for those who had been left behind. The men had been looking north lately, and I guessed that the tribe would follow their gazes, perhaps even as far as Austria, if the border guards would let them through. They did not really have to move. The gajo would be found safe, he would tell his story, it would not implicate my people. But my people would take flight as they were meant to do—

169

it would give them new life. And all the hard work I had done in this city to forge a future for myself would vanish in the dust kicked up by our trucks. There would be another language to learn, and I would not be able to continue my studies. My parents would arrange a marriage within the year.

All day I wandered the city in complete desolation. I had looked through too many eyes to be a pure gypsy, and, having done my duty to protect my tribe, I could not join them. I refused to accept their Fate. Yet, my whole life and the people I loved were there. If only I had been a prophet instead of a mind-reader, I might have averted what happened. But sometimes the sheer force of Fate cannot be stopped because we fall in love with the steps along the way and cannot give them up. This is how it was with me. I would not have left Giorgio alone in the field, no matter what ending I foresaw.

By chance or by subconscious design, I arrived at my school an hour or so after classes had been dismissed. A lone figure hurried out of the building and down the street: Signore Leonardi. With a start, I realized that she was thinking of me. She was mulling over our conversation about permanence, and thought of me in wonderment, a child with eyes that could see to the quick. She wished she knew why I had fled from her room, why I had been absent from school that day. She thought I was lost to her forever, and that once again she had been deprived of a protégée. With all her heart, she prayed to her angel to lift her out of her ordinary existence and deliver the great mind she had been promised. She was tired from trying to prod dull students into action. Her colleagues told her that she took teaching too seriously. After all these years, she should know better. Accept their stupidity, they told her, they want nothing great with their lives. I felt her frustration, her sorrow at not being understood. She was not a bad woman, I thought, as she threw out a crust of bread to the pigeons. She only wanted a student. For that, she would give her entire heart.

I followed her with light footsteps to her apartment. For a long time I sat in a corner of the courtyard feeling the tug of north and south, my parents and my dreams, my gypsy blood and that which had been touched by the gajo. Finally, as the sun set, I knocked on Signore Leonardi's door. When she opened it, her gray hair in disarray from a nap, I said, "I know this sounds crazy, but I—I saw an angel today." I began to cry real tears. "And I'm only a gypsy."

She looked at me, all dirty and disheveled, tears streaking the dusty grit in my face, my uniform twisted and wrinkled. She knew I must have witnessed something extraordinary. She should have known that I was the chosen one—the privileged ones would not have needed her. Here I was, her angel's gift, after all these years of waiting. Maria Angelica. For the first time in a long, long time, she felt that she could *learn*. She crossed herself and fell to her knees on the threshold. This time I knelt with her, for I needed all the grace and strength I could get.

Immigrants

Peter Chu stepped inside the basilica, not having intended to go in at all but ending up there anyway. How many years had he lived in Montréal and never visited La Basilique Notre-Dame? (He could hear his father roaring with laughter over this one—"You, an *architect*, not going to see a famous basilica in your *very own city?*") But Peter had always been frightened of Christian monuments, and this one was no exception. He shivered at the sight of gold leaf dripping from the ceiling and down the neo-Gothic columns and back up the spires of the apse. Surely all this gaudiness could not offer him the comfort he sought. What had he been thinking?

A woman touched him on the sleeve. "Excuse me," she said in French. "Aren't you Peter Chu?"

He sucked in a quiet breath of air. He could lie, he thought, shrug her off, but it seemed too inconsiderate. He smiled thinly, and drifted off towards the right ambulatory.

The woman, a redhead, in her early thirties perhaps, slim in a pampered, wealthy way that Peter was only then getting used to, followed close behind him. On any other day, he realized, he would have found her attractive. Any other place, he might have faced her squarely and listened to her, hoping for a gap in the conversation to ask for her phone number. But her presence at his elbow felt too much like his father, expectant, vigilant, a little like a jack-in-the-box with its unpredictable crank.

The woman switched to English, perhaps thinking that he did not understand French (but how could she believe that, he thought, when you cannot earn a living in the province without having mastered French?). "I admire your work enormously. When I saw the plans for the new Banque de Montréal building, I thought, well, Montréal has another great architect on her hands. It's even more original than your work on the galleria."

He turned to her. His smile, he could tell, was failing—a little more strength, another second, and he could let it go. "Thank you," he said. "But really, if you wouldn't mind, I'd like to be alone."

Her eyes shot to the crucifix above the altar. A pink flush rose on her cheeks. "Oh, I'm sorry. Of course." She rejoined her two friends.

With alarm, he realized that he had just given the impression that he was there to pray. He did not know the protocol. With sweat tickling at his hairline, he followed an old woman down the length of the nave and slipped into a pew behind her. He saw that the woman bowed her head, and that others with hands clasped sat motionless with closed eyes, but he could not bring himself to imitate them. He knew that if he closed his eyes, he would only see an image of his father, not as he had ever seen him but as he imagined him now, dressed in a green smock, under the hood of a diagnostic machine, his face the color of sand.

Where does a man with no religion go for comfort when his father is dying? Peter was not at all sure that this visit would be of any solace. His parents had once marginally followed Buddhism. He remembered with a visceral fondness his native city Taipei and its surprise of tiny colorful shrines amidst all the industrial gray. Only once since his family had emigrated to the United States (when he was eight) had he returned to Taipei—and the city had seemed as big and as confusing as it had when he was a child. He had expected his adulthood to make Taipei manageable, but people had looked at his face and had expected him to speak Mandarin or Taiwanese when he could only remember certain phrases, a word here and there, from a language his parents had forbidden when he was ten. When he discovered a Taoist shrine with incense burning and cool water to wash his hands, a vivid ceramic dragon curled above his head, he admired it solely for its aesthetic virtues and not from any sense of connection.

After a few minutes, he furtively looked around to make sure the woman had left. Oddly, the church's ornateness no longer assaulted him, and he saw the Christians' true love of their God, their faith, painted on the walls and ceiling. Could this be a sign that his father's illness was not as dire as his mother had said? He arose from the pew. As much as he wanted to be superstitious, he could not be. He had lived with too many cultures and in too many cities not to know that symbols were of man's creation and not of a god's.

That night he called his mother in New Jersey. "How's Father?" he asked.

"I told you, he doesn't want you to come until he's ready." He imagined her wrapping her old red cardigan tightly around her thin frame. "Give him time."

He fingered some polished stones that a friend had given him. He had placed them in a simple Japanese bowl he had bought during his year in Tokyo. "Then he's not any better."

His mother sighed. "I know it's hard. Your sisters—they cry all the time. They make him sad."

"Then *they* get to see him? It's just me he doesn't want to see?"

"You live so far away!"

"Wendy lives in California. I'm closer!"

There was a long pause on the other end of the line. Finally, she said, in a whisper, "A man likes to have his dignity in front of his son. It means everything."

Peter understood. His father always acted bossy and self-important around him. If his father could not maintain this façade, Peter thought, then he would be admitting his frailty. With Peter's sisters it was—and always had been—a different face his father presented. His father teased his daughters with a lightness in his voice, but with Peter he was always dry, his tone heavy with other implications that Peter was expected to pick up. As a teenager, Peter had sat in on some of his father's lectures at Princeton (his father wanted him to learn about Asian literature, but Peter had wanted to see his father through a stranger's eyes). It was then Peter first had seen the human side of a man he had given mythological status. His father joked (and the students laughed!), he commanded respect without bullying, he admitted mistakes and gaps in his knowledge. Most surprisingly of all, he seemed perfectly at ease with people. But he never relinquished control. "Okay. But promise me that you'll call before things get too bad. I don't want—I just want him to be able to talk to me."

"Of course, of course." She was crying softly.

"Okay, Mom. I'll let him be."

Peter hung up the phone. He stared out his window over the nightscape of the city's buildings, bold and unique, his heart aching from their golden light. The architecture said modern, old, different, but always, *always*, beautiful. When he had chosen Montréal, he had not realized how much its citizens adored their architects. On some days, he was thankful for this, because he mostly enjoyed the cocktail parties and the recognition, a moderate fame for a moderate man. On others, though, like this one, he wanted to shout out his window, the way his father had yelled at him years before, "What do any of you *really* know about architecture?" He pinched a stone from the bowl. With the strength of his body, he could hurl it through the window and right into the forehead of a passerby. He aimed the stone with one eye shut. He cocked his arm. One quick final decision and—he let the rock fall by his side.

A week later he went to a reception honoring his plan for the bank building. As he rummaged through the hors d'oeuvres trying to find something satisfying, a voice said at his shoulder, in accented English, "So, we meet again."

He looked up into the face of the redhead he had seen at the basilica. Up close, she seemed a little younger, with faint tawny blotches on her skin that could have been, at one time, individual freckles. A blush burned the tips of his ears as he remembered how he had avoided her in the basilica. Had she known of his deceit? He wished he had not been so rude that day. "Hello," he said, nearly choking.

"I thought you were supposed to be the center of attention."

"I bowed out, and no one noticed."

"Well, I did." She smiled. With a sureness that intimidated Peter, she extended her hand. "Claire Favarel."

He shook it. "Peter Chu."

She laughed. "Of course. Now tell me, which should I try? The shrimp, or the pork?"

"Both are pretty bland. Try these Indian things. I have no idea what they are, but they're good." He pointed to a plate of stuffed dumplings, then regretted being so helpful. Now he would have to stay and talk with her. He hoped that she would not bring up their meeting at the basilica and ask him to explain. He edged away from the table, and she followed.

"I love shopping at the galleria," she said. "There's a surprise around every corner—but somehow it still seems coherent. It's the most original part of the whole subterranean system."

"Thank you." He should escape, he thought, before he could not. Her voice was hypnotizing him. He looked over her shoulder to see if he could see anyone he knew.

She followed the thread of his gaze, looked back at him. "Look. I love your work, but that's not really why I'm cornering you." Her eyes, rusty brown and full of rich reflections, seemed to grasp him by the throat. He could not look away. "Ever since that day at the basilica, I've been dreaming about you."

"Me?" His hands grew uncomfortably moist. Her voice had taken on a rasp like rough, warm fur. He told himself that he had been crazy to avoid her in the church, crazy to stand there now so close to her that he could touch the amber hairs on her bare arm. This personal confession dissolved anything that had transpired at the church—the intimacy of it was almost too much to bear. She had been speaking to him half in French and half in English, and suddenly he wanted to switch to French, which he did. "This is a first."

"For me, too. I don't often dream about strangers, even well-known ones. It's either family, friends, or made-up people. But celebrities—they don't impress me."

"I'm really not a celebrity."

"No. I know. But you're well-respected, which is only one step below a celebrity." She leaned towards him; she wore no scent on her skin. She seemed ephemeral, an apparition that would vanish at the first hearty laugh. "So, tell me, why am I dreaming about you?"

He did not dare ask if the dream was sexual, or humorous, or, worse yet, a nightmare. The idea that a stranger (a woman, *this* woman) was dreaming about him felt deliciously smooth, like a custard. "Maybe we'll have to find out," he told her.

"It's a deal." She placed her empty wine glass on a standing tray. "How long do you have to stay?"

"Until the party dies."

"Then I'll see you in the cemetery." She smiled and backed away, just as one of Peter's colleagues took him by the elbow. By the time he had extricated himself, Claire was nowhere in sight. He cursed. What had she meant? Did she expect him to meet her later in a graveyard, and which one? His stomach protested under the weight of too many appetizers.

Throughout the evening, Peter wondered if he should be thinking of a woman when his father lay dying in a neighboring country. But he could not shake the idea of Claire any more than he could that of his father. It had been months since he last slept with a woman. Yes, that was it, he told himself. By the time the party had ended, however, Peter had given up hope that he would see Claire that evening. He comforted himself with the knowledge that she seemed adept at finding him. They would run into each other, he guessed, at another function, or outside his office building, maybe even along the quais where he jogged daily. As he stepped outside, he looked around for her, just in case. Nothing. He hailed a taxi.

His parents had long ago given up asking when he would marry. His mother had told him once that she had dreamed of him marrying a nice, Asian woman ("preferably Chinese") while his father had confided, with a wink that made Peter uncomfortable, that he would be better off with a woman of European descent. The reality was, though, Peter could not succeed with either type of woman. His parents' Americanization of him had been so complete that he felt like a fraud when he dated Asian women. And because he could not change his race with his passport, Caucasian women mostly ignored him. Those like Claire who did not never lasted, though Peter had not determined if it was something about him, or them, that led to failure. Still, he thought, smiling to himself in the back of the taxi, failure never stopped him from trying anew.

As he was about to enter his building, a car door slammed shut. He looked over his shoulder to see Claire coming towards him out of the darkness between streetlights. If he had not heard the click of her heels, he would have believed that she came to him without touching the ground.

"You look surprised to see me," she said. She must have been adequately pleased with his French, because she chose it to begin the conversation.

"How did you know where I live?"

"My father uses your firm."

"Oh, Jean-Claude Favarel." He was not about to tell her that they called her father J.C. because he seemed to think that he was the son of God. ("Son-of-a-bitch is more like it," Henry O'Toole always said.) "You're not on any type of vigilante mission, are you?"

"Should I be?"

"I hope not." He knew she expected to be invited up to his apartment. In the half-light, her hair looked brown, more common—it thrilled him that he knew it was not. "It's a nice night. Want to take a walk?"

"Sure."

As they walked, Peter loosened his tie under his overcoat. "You seem to know a lot about me. But for all I know, you're a lunatic."

"You'll just have to find out." She looked sideways at him: mischievous, smoldering, dangerous. "I'm a graduate student. A late bloomer. Shall we go this way?" They had come to a corner, and she gestured loosely to the right.

"That's fine. A student of what?"

"Business." The streetlight caught a half-smile on her face. "Everyone thinks I'm following in Papa's footsteps. But I don't want anything to do with his business. I want my own. Something risky and not surefire at all."

"But in the end you'll make it surefire."

"Of course. This way?"

"Okay." He hid a growing smile. Although Claire pretended that their heading was casual, even accidental, she was leading them towards Rue Sainte Catherine with all its raucous, often seedy crowds. He wondered if she intended to shock him. Or to test him. Either way, he enjoyed feigning ignorance. He let her talk a little about herself as he watched her expression: intense but modest, not at all self-conscious. As the street noise grew louder, their conversation fell silent.

Claire stopped in front of a particularly noisy club, where college-age men and women spilled out onto the street. "You want to go in?"

"No. Those places are always more interesting from the outside."

She bit her lip, then nodded. "After a while, they *do* get boring."

As they began to walk again, he wordlessly directed them back towards his apartment. Neither of them said anything for a long time. They passed couples kissing in dark corners, stores with darkened interiors, and nightclubs blasting with music that beat in Peter's chest. Finally they reached a quieter part of the city. There, the streets were deserted, as if he and Claire had been plucked out of the mainstream of life and placed, alone, in a private garden of scrawny trees and cement obelisks. Peter felt tempted by the silence to speak, but he held out because he wanted her to weaken first.

As they neared his building, she finally spoke. "Is it difficult being an immigrant here?"

He laughed. "Claire, *everyone* is an immigrant in this city. You're a French-speaker in an English-speaking country. I'm an English-speaker in a French-speaking city. What *kind* of an immigrant you are depends only on how big you want to make the picture."

She looked at him head on, the challenge clear in her eyes. "What were you doing praying in a Catholic church?"

"It's none of your business."

"You *aren't* an immigrant." She pointed her index finger at him. "You're a francophone through and through."

An odd pride swelled inside Peter. Rising up a little on her shoes, she kissed him. When she started to pull away, he drew her closer, surprised at her solidity, drinking up her strength. When he finally released her, she took a step backwards. "I can tell I'll be seeing *you* again." She raised a hand, turned, and hurried to her car.

He should never have loosened his grip on her. As he let himself into the building, he wondered if Claire would be like the other Caucasian women whom he had dated. If they slept together, would she then abandon him, having satisfied her curiosity about Asian men? Or would she never let him get that far? It was just as well, he reasoned. He had too many problems on his mind to worry about Jean-Claude Favarel's daughter.

A few days later at work, as Peter was looking over an associate's design, his mother called. "It's time," she said.

He sat down. "He's dying?"

She clicked her tongue in annoyance. "We're *all* dying. No, no. He wants you to come and visit."

"Okay," he said slowly. His mind scrolled through lists of meetings and jobs, problems to solve, commitments to keep. "Will this weekend be too late?"

"If that's the soonest you can make it."

"It is. Unless it's an emergency."

She paused. "No. It's not. Call me after you make the reservations. Mary and I will pick you up at the airport."

Claire called that night as Peter was trying to read an art magazine. His concentration was off, however, and he had found himself turning pages without knowing what they contained. "You're playing hard to get," she told him.

"No, I'm not."

"I figured you would've called by now."

He closed the magazine. "I knew you'd call me."

"Ah. Then you *are* playing hard to get." Without allowing him to protest again, she continued. "I have tickets for a concert Saturday night. Eight o'clock."

"I'll be out of town." He sensed her disappointment—she probably thought he was trying to brush her off. "I'm visiting my parents in the United States."

"Really?"

He swallowed. He had told no one about his father, and yet he could not rein himself in this time. "My father has cancer."

"Oh, Jesus. I shouldn't have been so flip with you the other night."

"I had a good time."

"May I come over? Right now?"

He considered his magazine, his meager plans for the evening, which had included microwave popcorn and the late night news. "Sure."

Claire arrived wearing a McGill sweatshirt and jeans. Despite the outside cold, her ankles were bare, her feet tucked into simple brown loafers. When Peter answered the door, she gave him a quick kiss on the lips, as though they were old lovers.

"Wow," she said as he took her coat. "Either you did a lot of cleaning while I was on my way over, or this place is always immaculate." She bit her lip. "Immaculate. Listen to me. That's my mother's word."

He smiled at her nervousness. He had expected her to be as brash as that first night, ready to take control, fighting with him over this territory. "Sit down. Beer or orange juice? I don't have anything else."

"Juice, please."

As he left for the kitchen, he watched her wander around the living room, pausing by a collage, or a piece of folk art, his Japanese bowl filled with stones. Her thin figure seemed to ripple like a blade of glass as she was drawn to first one thing, then another.

She took the glass of juice from him. "I expected your place to be less . . ."

"Eclectic?"

She nodded and lowered herself onto the sofa.

"I'm a collector." He sat next to her. "I like to mix cultures. It makes me feel more like a part of the world."

She seemed to relax. One of her feet slipped partway out of its shoe. "What countries have you visited?"

"Besides the U.S. and Canada—Taiwan, Japan, Argentina, Great Britain, France, Germany, Greece. There may be one or two more."

"A true man of the world." She fell silent for a moment and lowered her eyes. Her fingers traced a path along the back of the sofa. "You know, I think I've found out why I was dreaming about you."

"Yes?"

She raised her eyes to meet his. "You seem so familiar. Not boring familiar, but comfortable familiar. As if I'm destined to know you."

"And you make me feel as though I always have to be on my toes."

She laughed softly and drew his hand into her lap.

He knew what she meant; she seemed just foreign enough to him to feel familiar. It was as if they belonged together, and yet could not possibly. He remembered his father once saying to him, "You know you're a real part of a country when the surprises no longer make you pause." Peter leaned over and kissed Claire, this time without so much urgency. This evening, her skin smelled warm and spicy, a little of cinnamon, a little of fresh air. He wrapped his arms around her and felt her body mold to it.

"You haven't shown me your bedroom," Claire whispered into his neck.

He laughed at her cliché, at her forthrightness, at her mix of awkwardness and experience. He took hold of her fingertips and led her to his room.

After they had made love, Peter felt pleasantly drowsy, as he had not in a long time. His schedule had kept him so exhausted that his life had been like electricity, either on or off, never somewhere in-between. He felt Claire slipping out of bed. Alarmed, he sat up. "Where are you going?"

"I brought you something." She picked up her jeans and reached deep into one of the pockets. Clutching something in one hand, she crawled across the mattress towards him. "I don't know if you're really Christian or not, but I don't think it matters." She tucked a small gold crucifix on a chain into his fist.

He held it up to the light in bewilderment. "I don't get it."

"For your visit home." She lay next to him, shoulder to shoulder. "It gives me courage. If you're not Christian, you can call it a talisman. Or a good luck charm. I don't care."

"But it's gold." He tried to hand it back to her, but she firmly moved his hand away.

"Just promise you'll take it with you." She kissed his collarbone.

"You can think of religion when you're naked in a man's bed?"

She grinned. "I admit the timing's off. But once you're a Catholic, you're Catholic through and through. Even if you break the rules."

He studied the crucifix. The soft metal was lightly pitted and scratched, as though it had been worn for a long time. Despite the small scale, he could see the torment in the face of Jesus, and he could not help wondering how such pain could be looked upon with joy. What was he missing? "I'm not a Christian," he said finally.

She shrugged. "I didn't expect you to be. Despite your charade at the basilica." She turned to kiss him, then stopped, grinning. "You never know, though, Peter. After all, you once were an American. That's a sort of heathen."

"I still am an American," he said.

"Bullshit."

He gathered her into his arms. This is what his father wanted, he thought. How strange that, for once, he and his father wanted the same thing. Was it the imminence of his father's death that had made Claire possible, or would he have sought her out even in a less vulnerable time? For once, he was content to let a question rest with the weight of a statement. He fell asleep embracing Claire's warmth, the crucifix still in his hand.

When his mother and youngest sister picked Peter up at the Philadelphia airport, his skin still smelled of Claire. He had problems shaking the French from his mind as he bent to kiss his mother's cool, soft cheek.

"How is he?" he asked.

"The same." His mother looked cheerful as she pushed him towards the car, but his sister cast him a long, soulful look. Peter placed his overnight bag in the truck and climbed into the front seat next to Mary (his mother hated to drive, even pretended that she did not know how, despite her valid driver's license). As they crossed the Delaware River into New Jersey, Peter asked, "Is there anything I should be prepared for?"

Mary sighed. "Just don't talk about hope, okay? It really gets him mad."

"Don't get your father mad," his mother agreed. "I have to live with him."

Her words settled down on Peter like hot ashes. They all fell silent. Peter gazed at the landmarks which had once felt so familiar to him and which now seemed more like a dream revisited, not quite real, not quite right. Would he one day forget this trip as the events of his life continued to pile one on top of another? Or would this trip prove to be some bitter-sweet turning point? He sighed. His sister, her hair short and framing her face, cast a sidelong look at him which said, *I know*.

His father had never been a straight-backed man, but he could intimidate his wife, his children, his students with a glare. When Peter saw the small man with a blanket over his lap, the fire in his eyes put out, his movements clearly painful, he saw the end of a man he had loved his entire life.

"Hi, Father."

"Well, well, Peter. You've finally come to see me. It's about time."

They smiled at each other, sharing the joke that, in other times, might have sparked an argument.

The next morning, Peter and his father went for a slow walk towards the center of town. His father's gait, once fiercely impatient, shuffled so slowly that Peter had to consciously keep himself from taking a step until his father already had.

"Are you a Canadian citizen yet?" his father asked. "You know, we worked hard to make you an American."

"If I decide to become a Canadian, I'll have worked hard for that, too."

His father nodded. "It's never easy in a foreign land." He held onto Peter's arm for support, and Peter was surprised how light his father was. "You know, in Chinese culture, the eldest son must take care of his parents."

"I thought we were Americans."

His father stopped, smiled up at him with nicotine-stained teeth. "You were always the dangerous child." They started walking again. "You understand what I mean, though. I'm worried about what will happen to your mother after I'm gone."

"We'll take care of her. I promise."

His father stopped, looked up the street, back down the way they had come, past the rows of Dutch Colonial houses with manicured lawns and darkened windows. "There's one more thing."

"What?"

"I want a Christian burial."

"Excuse me?" Had it been Claire's crucifix speaking from his pocket, or had his father, always an atheist, requested a religious rite?

His father sighed, began his shuffle again. "Your mother and I started going to a Presbyterian church a year ago. You know me. I wanted to find out more about what made this country tick—and religion kept coming up. So we went. You know, you can't understand a culture until you understand the religion. I'm the first to admit I'm not sure about all the doctrine. But I'll tell you, for the first time in a long time, I feel *significant*. Your sisters won't understand this."

Peter fingered the crucifix at the bottom of his pocket, thinking of talismans and shrines and dragons and Gothic love and faith. "What makes you think I'll understand?"

"Because you're the eldest son. If nothing else, you know that I want my bones to become a part of the soil of this country."

Peter took a deep breath. He understood his father in ways that he could not have mere weeks ago. He was thankful that his father's pride had staved off this visit until now. "I'll do it, Father. But not because I'm the eldest son."

Smiling, his father patted him on the arm. "From the day you were born, I knew I could count on you."

When they returned to the house, the interior was dark and quiet, empty, as though his father were already missing, as though something had been finalized on their walk that made everything else obsolete. The rest of the family seemed to sense it, too, because dinner proceeded quietly and without argument, even from Peter's mother when Mary did not eat her meatloaf. They all retired to the family room to watch an action video. Ten minutes into the film, Peter's father fell asleep. His blanket had fallen to the floor and had gotten twisted around his feet. As Peter passed him on his way to the bathroom, he picked up the blanket and spread it over his father's lap, tucking the edges between his father's bony legs and the arm of the recliner.

On the airplane back to Montréal, Peter stared out the window into the blackness searching for signs of civilization. The flight attendants were coming down the aisles with their plastic garbage bags, and he drained the last of his Coke. He felt light-headed, sick almost. He wished that his feet were on land again, something stable that could hold him up without effort. For the third time since they had begun their descent, he tugged on the strap of his seat belt.

"May I take that, sir?" the flight attendant asked.

He handed her the empty cup and wondered where the seconds had gone between the time when he saw her coming and now, when she stood next to him, already there.

The city appeared out of the sparse countryside first with a sprinkling of lights, then a sudden, huge burst of brilliance as they descended toward the airport. Peter picked out the distinctive shapes and colors of the amusement park, the Biosphere, the casino, the quais outlined with white lights. Along the river lay Vieux Montréal, and then, beyond, the buildings, *his* buildings, with their individuality stamped across the night sky. He knew that Claire would be at the airport to greet him, even though he had told her he would take a taxi. He reached into his pocket and removed the crucifix. He held it tightly, thinking of his father, who wanted to rest his bones under a cross, and Claire, who, until she had given it to Peter, had lived with one around her neck. He wondered what kind of leap it would take for him to accept the religion of his land—death or love? He wound the chain tightly around his fingers and pressed the cross to his cheek. The plane skimmed the air just above the ground, descending gently until the plane landed with a thump and a roar of engines in reverse. Peter sat still in his seat, his eyes closed, waiting for his revelation.

Shinkansen

Shinkansen have tracks of their own. You have to walk all the way across Tokyo Station to connect from an ordinary train to the Shinkansen platforms. Once you've taken a Shinkansen and been propelled through time and space, to, say, Kyoto, you are hooked. You cannot return to an ordinary train. It is an addiction, this highly efficient, late twentieth-century mode of transportation. Anything less than a Shinkansen feels like a waste of time. You gladly part with your money. Hiro knows this too well. His ticket presses against his heart with a stiff discomfort, though he has not been *truly* glad to part with his money. Not this time. He cannot take an ordinary train, but he dreads the Shinkansen. It will take him to a place he does not want to reach.

Hiro stands in line, perfect line, between the yellow, two feet from the person in front, two feet from the person in back. Straight ahead gaze. Before this moment, he has never questioned the orderliness of waiting, but now he wonders what it would take for a man—or a woman—to ignore all the etiquette installed in the soul like a computer program and to step in front of another? What would it take to wait two steps out of bounds? Or, at the moment when the doors to the Shinkansen slide open, to rush forward ahead of everyone else? He concludes that only a grave mental illness would create such a scenario because every seat is assigned. No one cares who enters first because each knows that his seat will await him, now or five minutes from now, as long as he crosses the threshold before the minute of departure. This knowledge saddens Hiro. Like Yoko (or because of her, he thinks with a rush), he craves one small act of anarchy. Nothing to destroy civilization, but significant enough to give all events that follow an edge of unpredictability.

Shinkansen arrive at the precise second they are scheduled. They depart exactly on time, never a minute before, never a minute late. They wait for no one. You can almost believe that they do not rely on passengers for their existence. They live as separate creatures that allow people to ride inside them, but they are not beholden to these parasites. If no one were to board, you can imagine that a Shinkansen would sigh with relief as it slid out of Tokyo Station on its way to, say, Kyoto. They have lives—and agendas—of their own which no one dares question. If a Shinkansen were to fall in love with a different route, a circuitous route, people might find themselves surprised, but they would never demand a return to old ways. No, people respect Shinkansen. They do, because Shinkansen have lives of their own. And because the people are addicted.

The man in front of Hiro stands with a straight blue-suited back, his hard-sided briefcase in one hand, an unopened can of beer and a bento box miraculously in the other. Hiro wants to see this man's life, through the thinning hair in the back right into the skull and the workings of the brain. Does he have a wife? Does he love her, will he forever? Do his children excel at school and cram classes; do they study late into the night with the reward of an excellent score? Why is he headed to Kyoto this Friday night? Is it the lure of the ancient shrines, bright and quiet on a Saturday morning, or does he have a family there who await him with tired eyes? These questions repeat themselves endlessly in Hiro's mind, as if he has lost control of it. His parents tell him that he asks too many questions. Yoko tells him he asks too few. And the Shinkansen that swooshes into place in the station, it does not care.

As Hiro prepares to board the Shinkansen, he stumbles a bit, though he sees nothing in his path, not under him, not behind. Yoko has told him about the powers of the mind, and he now wonders if his mind and his heart cry out to him. He will not bend to the powers of the mountains, he thinks. But he will go to them all the same. (And he can hear Yoko's voice whispering, Be careful, Hiro, for mountains have their way.)

Shinkansen gleam white. Their snouts curve and dip to a dull point like those of airplanes, but they are better maintained. You will not see small circles of rust around a bolt. You cannot see the plates of construction, how the Shinkansen was constructed. It arrives in Tokyo Station whole and intact, almost silent, sweeping across the ground like a lengthy white ghost of an ancestor who no longer cares about small decisions. Someone must polish the train with clean rags the way a good son will care for a shrine in his parents' home. Hiro cannot imagine himself a man patient enough to succeed at that job. His arms would grow tired, his mind lulled by the hypnotic swirls of the rag. But if someone ordered him to clean the Shinkansen, he might try. He might abandon his new degree in mechanical engineering in order to clean the Shinkansen because someone has asked him. Or he might not.

Hiro settles into his clean seat. People find their places in an orderly fashion. One man, perhaps too drunk (but not blatantly so) to read his ticket, has taken the seat of a young lady. They compare tickets, apologize, bow, discuss in calm voices, bow, apologize, bow finally with a gentle laugh, and everyone fits like finely turned pegs into their assigned slots. No one argues. No one pushes. Hiro finds himself wishing he had a mental illness. He wants to make trouble so that someone will escort him off the train and to the police station. He wants them to confiscate his ticket. But this will not happen. He likes his order as much as the next Japanese. Even Yoko, who questions much about life, who challenges everything that Hiro has always taken for granted, would perform an elegant dance of etiquette. She does not accuse people with anger. She likes them to ask their own questions, and so has perfected the art of sowing grains of sands that may one day accumulate into a heavy rock that requires attention. Yoko: with her beautiful white orchid skin, her warm, laughing eyes, the kind of woman with one foot in the future and the other right behind. She can stare into the eyes of a man, and he will fall in love. As far as Hiro knows, she has used this magic only once. Hiro's parents do not believe in magic.

Hiro wears a flawless crewneck sweater from the American company L.L. Bean. He likes khaki pants and Levi jeans, perfectly pressed white cotton oxford shirts. He wears Italian loafers that his aunt and uncle bought for him on their shopping trip to Florence. His father always nods approvingly when they meet. He does not seem to mind the global influence on Hiro's wardrobe, but he says the Western mind slinks through the Japanese body like a tapeworm. It lies still as it sucks up the nutrients needed for life. Hiro and Yoko laugh at this in private. They know that the world can give them feathered wings.

Shinkansen. If you say the word over and over, it can sound like an old-fashioned locomotive rocking back and forth on the tracks. Shinkansen, shinkansen, shinkansen. But Shinkansen do not clack— they hum and whir. They can take a passenger at fantastic ground speeds through the countryside to the city where his parents live. The first-time passenger might not feel the speed until he arrives at his destination sooner than he thought possible. Shinkansen are smooth. They do not strain. They embody the high level of technological competence of this nation, of this world. If you were to look at one, you would swear it was not possible that something so advanced could exist. You would not want to return to an old train. You might say, what's the point? You might even laugh at someone who said he preferred the old way. You would never drag someone off a Shinkansen and force him onto an old train. It would be too cruel. And too ridiculous. Why not let people embrace progress?

Hiro envies the men who sit on either side of him. They flip through comic books full of powerful, half-naked women. The men think they can dominate and be dominated at the same time. Hiro believes in compromise. He also believes that he should not compromise about certain things. He wonders if this will be his downfall. The men look at pictures. They drink beer. They are tired from their week in their Tokyo offices. Hiro wonders if he will be like his father who once confided to him that he never wanted to leave his desk. He wonders if someday he will ache to be home with his wife and children. He wonders who this wife will be. He fears that he will weaken in the knees when his mother cries. If he would sit next to his mother in a temple's gardens after a storm and watch a single raindrop cling to a branch, she would tell him that the raindrop has no choice. It must fall. Hiro would tell her that yes, it must fall, but not necessarily directly down, maybe a little to the left, or to the right, onto a pebble or into a crack in the dirt, onto the hard back of a beetle on its way to somewhere else.

Outside the Shinkansen, the world is gray with dusk. Unless they pass something very close to the Shinkansen, a tree maybe, Hiro cannot tell that he hurtles toward his destiny. In fact, it seems that they will never arrive in Kyoto. He tries to find peace in this idea. He wonders if it is possible to be forever caught between two points so that time ceases to tick off its infinite seconds and possibilities.

Perhaps you might not truly be *addicted* to the Shinkansen once you have experienced one. Perhaps you might find a *logical* reason to choose one over a traditional train. Shinkansen are more efficient. They whip through the countryside like quick-striking snakes. They are the future. You can read more easily on a Shinkansen. You can sleep better because your head does not rock. You can feel as if you are on an airplane flying high and fast and far away from, say, your parents who want to manage your adult life. You knowingly accept the illusion that you are not ordinary. You believe that you have chosen the Shinkansen of your own free will and that no one will question your choice. You believe that you are free and unfettered of the time it takes to travel by ordinary rail. No one will laugh when you mention what an intelligent choice you have made.

Hiro shifts his weight carefully so that he does not touch the men on either side of him. He might, he thinks, do what Yoko has asked and climb to the Kiyomizu Temple to buy her a prayer. When Yoko asked this of him, he said that he thought she did not believe in tradition. With the sun in her short hair, Yoko smiled and told him that people were more complicated than that. She wants a long, happy life. Should he walk backwards there with the schoolgirls, his eyes closed, to see if he will be happy? What if he opens his eyes too soon? What will he do then, to know that he might not be happy? Will it be his own fault because he has not told Yoko the real reason for his trip? She will laugh at him for these questions, but her laugh will be kind. She will tell him that he is to blame for only part of his life. She says that a lot, but it does not comfort him, because he worries about the part for which he must claim responsibility.

His hands begin to perspire. Horrified, he places them palm down on his thighs so that no one will see. He remembers a story that his mother told him when he was a child. A young boy found a treasure chest full of coins alongside a brook. Clutching the box to his chest, the boy started to run home, but the box belonged to some mischievous spirits who wanted it back. So they stopped the boy alongside the path, and said to him, "Here is a chest exactly like the one you have in your arms." They opened an identical box to show him that it was full of coins. "Why don't you take this one instead?" At first, the boy hesitated, because he did not want to let go of his treasure. But the spirits laughed at him. "Silly boy. What difference does it make whether you take this box, or that box? They are the same. The only difference is that if you take this one, we will see you safely home." The boy, who was afraid of the shadows in the forest, agreed to exchange boxes. He ran safely all the way home. But when he opened the box to show his parents, he found that the coins were all tin. Perhaps when Hiro arrives home, he will have the courage to repeat this story to his parents. Perhaps they will listen. Perhaps they will understand.

Shinkansen have their own kind of tracks, and that explains why you must cross Tokyo Station to reach a Shinkansen platform. They do not run on ordinary gauge rails. They maintain segregation because they are different, above the common modes of transportation. You might call the Shinkansen the Emperors of Trains. You might think of them as above the laws of the country. You might think of them as prisoners of their own success. After all, despite their superior design, they must still transport parasites from one city to the next. They must not falter. They must carry drunken businessmen as well as pretty girls. They carry young people away from love matches and to old cities where their parents wait with an arranged match thinking that they can thwart the future. They carry people who agree to everything, and those who refuse.

Hiro closes his eyes because the weight of this trip makes him drowsy. This is not a good kind of sleepy, he knows, not an evening, after a hot bath kind of sleepy, not the kind that makes you stretch your arm lazily over a lover when the birdsong cascades in from an open window. The mountain-gods must feel this kind of fatigue after centuries of rain pouring down their sides and dragging pebbles, little baby-gods, from their embrace. This is the kind of exhaustion you feel when you must pretend to listen to your parents and consider their sage advice. The kind of dev-astation when you must justify your love even though you have sworn never to do this. Hiro does not want to go backwards. He does not want to sacrifice the pebbles of who he wants to be. When he closes his eyes, he feels no rest.

Stop. Shinkansen are tools of humanity. You must not think more of them. They are nuts, bolts, sheet and machined metal, acrylic, synthetic fabric upholstery. When the electricity shuts off, they die. They cannot move about the country by themselves. *People* control them. People must adjust their speeds so that they arrive in the train station exactly on time. People buy tickets and, if they did not, the Shinkansen would perish route by route. Suppose people no longer cared about the passage of time and what they could be accomplishing with those extra hours. Then the Shinkansen would be like any other train, only newer. They are creations, inventions, the palpable dreams of mechanical engineers. Shinkansen are machines that cater to the whims of people, *nothing more*.

Just before the Shinkansen slides into Kyoto Station, Hiro catches a glimpse of the rectangular buildings near the rails, not low-rise but not nearly as towering as those in Tokyo—mundane, postwar blocks. An occasional pachinko parlor lights up the night with gaudy neons that shoot like hot meteorites past the windows. Beyond these things, he knows, is the truly old Kyoto: the few remaining geishas hobbling on their tiny feet, the old shrines and the temples, families who have thrived for generations, the shogun's castle, things that even Japan's one-time enemies had not the courage to destroy. Kyoto is a rock to Tokyo's wind. Here, you can lose yourself to the solidity of history.

Hiro knows now that he is weak. He must not be tempted to betray his future, or he will imprison himself. When he sees his mother and father and the young woman they have arranged to replace Yoko, he will agree. He will accept this tin bride. He cannot refuse his parents when they stand eye to steady eye.

The nice thing about Shinkansen, Hiro thinks as he steps out onto the platform, is that if you arrive in a station twenty minutes before the last Shinkansen departs for Tokyo, you can get a seat. You can change your ticket and hurry back in time to step between the yellow lines and through the door that stays open exactly in place. You will probably be the last one aboard, but it doesn't matter. There will be no pushing or arguing or cries of indignation. You will probably have no one sitting next to you so that you will be able to stretch out your tired legs. At this time, only the truly mad have not yet left for their final destinations. You can ride with them back to the city of your life.

About the Author

Lewis Kassel

DEBBIE LEE WESSELMANN was born in New York City and currently lives in central New Jersey. Her first novel, *Trutor & the Balloonist*, was published earlier this year. Her short fiction has appeared in *The Literary Review*, *Philadelphia Inquirer Magazine*, *North Atlantic Review*, *Ascent*, *Fiction*, and many other publications. End to end, her travel miles would circle the globe more than four times.